The Xonen Archives, Book Three

THE SECOND LIFE OF CYRUS EX

Ande Li

ROOM 808 PRESS

Publishing Imprint for Authors Maximus X, Arvomis & Ande Li

Copyright 2019 Ande Li at Room 808 Press

ISBN-13: 978-0-9834104-5-4 Paperback
ISBN-13: 978-0-9834104-6-1 eBook
Source: Digital copy

Cover image: biletskiyevgeniy.com, Photo ID: 763742035, Nov 27, 2017. Photograph. Shutterstock. Web.

Acknowledgements

To the mothers, the fathers and the children –
For proving that love can transcend time, distance, color and
adversity.

Author's Note

Quotation marks vary depending on the language spoken, so I have distinguished them as follows:

" " **Traditional quotation marks** indicate Xonen languages, either elfyn and common
[ ] **Square brackets** indicate Alliance-speak is used
‹‹ ›› **Angle brackets** (guillemets) indicate Laxuyn language is spoken

Italics usually indicate some form of universal, mental communication, so language is not generally indicated.

A.L.

Prologue

Jaeris of House Thorne, the one-time Emperor of the Realm, was surrounded by his children and his friends from across the Realm, as deeply loved and respected by his subjects and former constituents as any emperor or empress who had ever ruled the Realm since its founding over nine hundred years earlier. It was early in the Year of the Emperors 951, and Jaeris Thorne was celebrating his sixty-first birthday.

It had only been a few short months since he had last shared a drink with Cyrus E'lan, on the night before his friend's fiftieth birthday, pretending to forget the milestone in order to spare Cyrus the unwanted attention. Had Jaeris known that it would be their last hours together, he would've made the most of the time. He would've held the damn party in his friend's honor, anyway, to let Cyrus know how much he appreciated their friendship.

Retiring to his chambers, Jaeris was surprised to find a small box wrapped in colorful paper and ribbon, waiting for him on his bed. Held in place underneath the box was a folded parchment note, which he tugged free and opened.

The note read: *Hello, old friend, from across the stars. Cyrus.*

Jaeris recognized Cyrus's graceful, scholarly script and gently shook the box, startled at first to hear a quiet, tinny "ping" in response, but then he remembered that some of the machines that Jeysen had secreted back during his clandestine journeys with his other-worldly friends, made similarly metallic sounds.

Jaeris opened the package carefully and found, nestled within a cushion of quilted, velvety pocket, a bejeweled cube, crafted of carefully pieced and polished, multicolored woods, encrusted with cabochon stones of various colors on five of its intricately-pieced faces. The box felt heavy for its size but appeared to have no openings or hinges to access the inside.

"A puzzle box for my birthday, Cyrus?" Jaeris chuckled, bemused at his old friend's playfulness. "How did it even get here?"

A tap sounded at his door, and Jaeris dropped the cube back on his bed to answer the knock.

Jeysen greeted him with an expectant smile. "There are still a couple of hours left to your birthday, Father."

"By the Goddess, I've been up since dawn, son," he replied. "I need my rest." Still, he left the door open and returned to his puzzle cube. "Do you know what this is about?"

Jeysen shut the door and took the cube from his father's hand. "Slither sent me a message this morning, asking me to ensure that it didn't get lost with the other birthday packages and gifts from your well-wishers, so I had the stewards bring it up as soon as it arrived." He studied it, admiring its craftsmanship and beauty, and passed it back with a grin.

If Slither was involved, then this was a piece of technology that was technically forbidden and possibly dangerous. "Slither wouldn't have left any instructions about what this is, would he?" Jaeris asked.

Jeysen laughed. "Where would be the fun in that? Did it come with a note?"

"The note is from Cyrus," Jaeris said. He set the cube down on his dresser, plain side down and spun it slowly to analyze each of the faces in more detail. He noticed one of the gemstones had a slight, greenish glow to it, so he pressed it.

Once again, he heard the tinny "ping," but now a couple of the other gems started to glow.

"I'll give you some privacy, Father," Jeysen said softly, giving his shoulder a gentle squeeze before blinking from the room.

Jaeris shook his head at his son's flash of magic, but he grinned with pride at Jeysen's skill, which only seemed effortless through his son's years of practice and disciplined study. He loved all three of his children, but Jeysen was most like him in his pursuit and passion of knowledge, in all of its forms.

"*Hello, Jaeris.*" From the box came Cyrus's voice, clear and strong, as if he were in the room. Before Jaeris could answer, the voice continued: "*I'm not certain when this message will reach you, but I hope it arrives in time for your birthday. I'm sorry to miss it, just as I'm sorry that I was unable to speak with you personally before my departure.*"

Jaeris leaned against the edge of the dresser, with the cube sitting next to him, and he closed his eyes, focusing on his friend's voice. "I'm sorry, too, old friend," he said, during a brief pause.

"*Anyway, I just wanted to say 'thank you' for your friendship and kindness over the years, and I hope we haven't seen the last of each other. You have been as dear to me as a brother, as any man I have ever known.*"

As only sons and only children, they had that in common. Jaeris had many cousins and other distant relatives, such as the ones who had attended his birthday that evening, but he never felt as comfortable speaking openly with them as he did with Cyrus, and with his beloved empress, Karina, before him.

Cyrus's voice continued: *"I was told that there will be a purple jewel on one of the faces. When you have a free, undisturbed moment alone, press that, and let's see what happens,"* he said laughingly.

Jaeris spotted the button-sized gemstone on the side face easily, as it glowed faintly with a slight pulsing rhythm. As he pushed it, it yielded briefly to the slight pressure, stopped pulsing and brightened, and it was a woman's voice that quietly announced: "Transmitting. Please stand by."

Before he entirely understood what he had triggered, Cyrus's voice returned: *"Emperor Jaeris?"*

Jaeris stared at the box. "Yes. Is this another message?"

"No, we are speaking directly," Cyrus's soft baritone laughter resonated from the box, along with some ambient background voices, distant and faint. *"It is good to hear your voice, old friend."*

"This is astonishing!" Jaeris said. "How is this happening? You sound like you're in the room with me."

"I assure you, I am nowhere near Xon, which is for the best. I'm not even sure the nearest star to me is visible to you."

"Are you well, Cyrus? You sound more subdued than usual."

"I haven't slept in about forty hours, so perhaps I am a little bit tired," he replied. *"I am homesick, too, but your voice is comforting. I don't think I'll be able to talk for long, but I'm glad that we are able to speak."*

"The purple button that I pressed; it summoned you?"

"It made a connection to a similar device on my side, and I was here to receive it. If you had reached out a few minutes later, I may have gone out already, and it would've offered to log a message, instead. My colleague and I are smuggling a dissident across borders to save her from execution, so we're just waiting for our contact to let us know when it's clear. The local authorities have orders to kill us on sight."

Jaeris grinned skeptically, wondering how much of Cyrus's account to take at his word; he was always so dry and even-tempered with his delivery. Cyrus's light tone assured him that it really wasn't as dire as it sounded, but it was hard to tell. "That's much more exciting than my life. I was toasted tonight with a brandy that is as old as I am, and I barely managed to finish a slice of well-intended but syrupy-sweet birthday fruit cake."

Cyrus laughed. *"Next time, have more of the brandy, and you won't care about the cake."*

"Easy for you to say, coward," Jaeris berated. "You didn't even want to celebrate your birthday, at all."

3

"I did celebrate, in my own way," Cyrus said. "I was able to spend some time with you at the palace, and that was more than enough. That memory will always be precious to me."

"How the court misses your silver tongue, old friend," Jaeris lamented. "Thank you for the birthday message, and I hope to speak with you again soon.

"That is worthy incentive for me to stay alive," Cyrus said. "Your voice has reminded me of what I'm working to preserve from my little corner of the galaxy. I confess: some days, I am tempted to return home, but as long as doing so endangers our planet, I have to stay far away."

"That is what Sarc and Slither have shared with us," Jaeris nodded. "And I'm saddened but heartened by your decision. If our places were reversed, I'm not sure I would have had the courage to leave, as you did."

"I think you would, my Emperor," Cyrus said. "There is nothing you wouldn't be willing to sacrifice, to save the ones you love." His voice was distant and muffled for a moment, as another voice joined the background chatter. "It's time. I have to go."

"May the stars guide you, Cyrus E'lan."

"May Ajle keep you safe, Jaeris Thorne. Tell Sarc I love him."

"I will. But stay alive, old friend," Jaeris said, "and you can tell him yourself."

Chapter 1: Dione

[Eladryz, there is nowhere to run!]

Oh, how many times I've heard that! My eyes darted around the alleyway: to the crates, the doorways, the dumpsters…anywhere but at the solid cinderblock wall meters ahead of me. There was nothing for me that way.

[You won't be hurt,] my stalker said, her voice closer now. [My patrons want you alive.]

I wasn't fluent enough in Alliance-speak to answer her, and too preoccupied with escape to bother. It was too late to hide amongst the boxes, as I heard the hunter's footsteps splashing in the puddles behind me. My only hope was to face her and find some way to delay my capture. I turned around slowly, and I couldn't help staring at her skin-tight, leather-like armor.

[That's it, nothing to be frightened of,] she smiled, taking a tentative step towards me. She raised her targeting visor to make eye contact with me. Her eyes were a pretty, dark grey, complementing her complexion and cinched hair.

Easy for you to say. She wasn't facing a lifetime of enslavement, but I would, if she managed to capture me for her Ghanisi clients. "You're cutting it really close there," I called out in Xonen elfyn.

The hunter scowled. [What language is *that*?]

Ammo Sulimandri stepped silently into the alleyway and fired a single shot, which struck the hunter directly at the base of her neck. She crumpled into an unconscious heap, splashing into the fetid puddle, and I looked to make sure her nose and mouth were clear for breathing.

[I had to make sure the area was clear,] my tall Laxuyn friend said, nodding towards the main street. [We don't want crowds gathering, trying to figure you out. Get your hood up, Cyrus.]

At Mandri's reminder, I flipped up my dark cowl. Beneath the edge of the hood, I peered at the domed ceiling of the outpost, hundreds of meters above our heads. Through the clear panels, I could see the darkness of space. I looked down at my feet in time to avoid a small trickle of leaked water from the pipes, which the sewage system would inevitably recapture and recycle to support its occupants and its industries. Nothing could be wasted at an outpost located so far from the nearest worlds and stations.

After the past several months of traveling with Mandri, I was enthralled by the technology and ingenuity of the Alliance and other galactic collectives. It was true that many of them were hunting me and my kind, but it didn't make their achievements any less significant or impressive. Just more dangerous.

"That makes the second hunter this week," I said quietly to Mandri. "Fifth for the month?"

Mandri nodded, understanding my Xonen language easily. [Arkanist commission this time?]

I shook my head. "She said her clients were Ghanisi."

[Them, again,] he muttered, rolling his eyes. [Let's get out of here, before more show up.]

"Cyrus E'lan, time to wake up, sunshine."

I cracked my eyes open and peeked at the cool, sterile environment of my bunk. It was dark outside, but we were in the middle of deep space, traveling between systems, so the outside was always dark. If not for the on-board clocks, it would've been impossible for me to track the passage of time on board Mandri's skiff, the *Oelivan*.

Mandri had a slew of nicknames for me, depending on his mood, and my state. "Sunshine" was usually his cue to me that I was glowing, literally.

Sure enough, I was my own nightlight in my darkened bunk, glimmering with a dark amber glow. I was working on keeping it under control during my waking hours, but it was harder to suppress when I was unconscious.

I had been dreaming of my homely, cozy pillbox of a house in Mione, located on a coastline in the northern hemisphere of Xon, that tiny, shining marble of a planet that I had called home. It didn't help my homesickness that I was awoken in Xonen elfyn, my native second language.

I sat up in my upper bunk. "How long before you stop dreaming of home, Mandri?"

"It's been less than four months since you left Xon," Ammo Sulimandri reminded gently, his citrine-yellow eyes reflecting my dimming glow in the dim light. "And you only spoke to your friend Jaeris last month, so your memories are still very fresh. I still dream of

Xon from time to time, and it hasn't been my home in over a century."

My friend and mentor was leaning against the doorway, with a cup of coffee in hand, the tantalizing, aromatic scent of the brew wafting to me. "How long was I sleeping?"

"Not long," Mandri said, taking a torturously prolonged sip from his cup. "But there's a lot to do before we arrive at *Dione*, my young apprentice." His yellow eyes captured and reflected the scant light like a cat's eyes, while his rangy build and long limbs reminded me more of a large wolf.

"Agreed," I said, tossing aside the thin thermal blanket before I could be tempted to slip back into the warm pocket. I accepted Mandri's teasing nickname in stride, as sometimes, I did feel like I was just starting my life journey under the guidance of my older Laxuyn friend. Over the past several weeks, I had learned from Mandri how to sleep lightly, eat quickly and redefine my perception of personal space, so that the snug, cramped spaces of the skiff didn't feel as claustrophobic anymore.

I swept my overgrown hair back from my forehead and eyed Mandri's cup covetously. "You got one of those for me?"

"Nope, I just poured the one cup," he said, smacking his lips. "But there's a fresh pot, so help yourself."

"Thank you." I followed the smell of fresh-brewed coffee to the efficiency galley, and I briefly entertained the idea of drinking straight out of the pot, but opted instead to serve myself the largest cup I could manage. After living most of my life drinking tea and wine, I had acquired a habit over the past several months for the bracing, tannic flavor of coffee, requiring nothing to adulterate or temper its toasted, bittersweet taste. I had Mandri to thank for that questionable vice, too.

"How are you feeling this morning?" he called, following me into the galley.

I took a long, near-scalding first drink from my mug before I answered. "Better now, thank you. Anything happen overnight?"

Mandri shook his head and finished his coffee. "The comm feed is quiet. This isn't a very high-traffic area, to start."

"When are you scheduled to meet with your new clients?"

"The rendezvous is a few parsecs out, so maybe three or four hours," he said.

Parsecs. Kiloparsecs. Distance standards based on a "light year," defined as the distance traveled by light to Xon from its sun, multiplied three-fold, approximately. Those concepts had all taken me some time to internalize, but I was getting used to them. I had logged several kiloparsecs already, during my brief stint with Mandri, but the distance still felt unfathomably vast.

"Enough time for a training session and a shower before we meet them," he said. "Some target practice may not be a bad idea, in case our negotiation goes sideways, and depending on where this next job takes us."

I finished my coffee and craved more, but decided to wait until the effects from my first cup hit, to determine if I needed a refill. "Sounds good. What do you know about the commission?"

"Medical supply run to a prison settlement on one of the Arkanis-controlled worlds," he said. "Contraband items like pain-killers, antibiotics, syringes…that sort of thing."

"Those are contraband items?"

"They are for a civilization that considers a thirty-percent prison survival rate a waste of rations and water," he said cynically. "And 'contraband' means the supplies need to get inside through unofficial channels."

Mandri held out his empty cup, and I refilled it from the pot. "Who's paying the bill, then?"

"We'll find out in a few hours," he said, finishing his coffee. "All right, my young Eladryz friend, let's hook you up to the simulator, and you can practice mindless shooting and blowing things up for a little while. You kids usually enjoy that kind of thing, right?"

Space is boring. No one ever warns you about that, but it really is.

Not the concept of actually travelling through space, which is as unforgettable and life-altering as one could imagine, but the actual logistics of going from one location to another, is mind-numbingly dull. The vastness of empty space can be disquieting and lonely, feelings that are exacerbated when your traveling companion is used to spending long stretches of time by himself.

I appreciated the opportunity to travel off-world, of course, and for Mandri's begrudging hospitality. While he had allowed my son, Sarc, and his friend, Jeysen, aboard the *Oelivan*, he hadn't planned to subsequently play host to another Xonen, certainly not me. He had only known me previously and briefly as Sarc's middle-aged father, and probably the least likely of candidates for off-world hijinks.

But Mandri and his siblings saw something else in me that made them reconsider. They knew, probably before I did, that I wasn't like the other Xonen natives; I was an outlier, an outcast remnant from a dead world, not too different from them and the remainder of the Laxuyn people. Their ancestors had left their homeworld, Nafre'Numolotal, centuries earlier, but the descendants continued to look over their shoulders, always fearful of being hunted. It was for that reason, perhaps, that Mandri took pity on me and offered to keep me safe, until I could find a way to return home without endangering it.

In retrospect, "safe" is not the first word that came to mind when considering my time spent with Mandri, but I trusted him. I often accompanied him into dangerous areas and met with suspicious characters, but Mandri was careful, and he felt better having me nearby than hiding on the *Oelivan* alone.

Besides, Ammo Sulimandri was nearing his two hundred and sixtieth birthday by the time I met him, so he was well-set in his habits, and knew far better how to survive out in Alliance space than I would ever presume to. He treated his birthdays like any other day, not even really thinking about the years anymore. He had spent his birthday—as he spent much of his free time—relaxing in his prized seat at the helm of the *Oelivan*, alone.

As if he realized that I sought more interaction than he felt comfortable providing, he allowed me free use of the on-board trainers and simulators to pass the long stretches of idle time. Looking back, it's possible that he was giving me unlimited access of the learning devices just to see how much I could tolerate at a sitting; my record was eighteen uninterrupted hours on historical archives about the planet of my origin, EladryzZurylan.

I was in the middle of one of the training modules, when I opened my eyes during a break and noticed Mandri staring at me from his pilot's seat. I disconnected from the simulator and set aside the headpiece. "What is it?"

Mandri didn't answer right away and just studied me for a moment. We saw each other for most of our waking hours, day after day, so I had no idea what Mandri was noticing. Even when we looked at the same thing, sometimes, it was difficult to decipher his object of focus.

"When was the last time you looked at yourself in a mirror?" he finally asked.

"This morning, when I washed my face and brushed my teeth."

"No, I mean, *really* looked at yourself?" he said pointedly.

"I don't know," I said, confused by the question. "Maybe a month ago? A little while after we left Xon. Why?"

"I think you should take another look at yourself," Mandri said. "Full lights on."

I went to the basin and switched on the cool white lights. "What am I supposed to see?" My glow was hardly noticeable anymore, thank *Ajle*. My features looked the same, and I hadn't trimmed my hair in weeks, so I needed a haircut. My skin had a pallor, since I hadn't been exposed to real sunlight in weeks, but I still had... *No, I don't.*

I stepped back from the mirror, shaking my head. "*Hilafra*, what's happened to me?"

"You still recognize yourself, don't you?" Mandri took position outside the washroom.

It was like an awful dream, in which I saw my reflection but didn't recognize myself in it. The strands of silver that had streaked my hair were blending back with the brown, which in itself was lightening to a dark amber. The creases by my brows, my eyes and mouth had softened to faint lines. "This is almost how I looked twenty years ago. What's happening to me?"

"It's like we told you back on Xon, your fiftieth-year transformation is like a second growth cycle," Mandri said mildly. "All your stem cells, hormones...everything gets reset, and your whole body gets a refresh. What's the matter? Most people would love the opportunity to be young again."

"Well, I don't," I snipped. "I earned every scar, every wrinkle, every white hair on my head." I had shared some of my best years with Sariah and with my children, and it felt as though those years had been erased. "Half my life has been voided. I shouldn't look the same age as my own son!"

"To be fair, your son doesn't look his own age, either," Mandri said. Despite his dryness, his concerned eyes showed that he did sympathize with my dismay, at least a little. "For many people, self-identity is tied to appearance. For you, as you're still learning who you are, this disconnect between how you look and how you feel must feel jarring."

"This is a nightmare." I shut off the light and left the washroom without a last look back.

"You shouldn't consider this an undoing of your life experiences," Mandri said, "just an extension of them. Your memories are evidence of your time well-spent, as is your son; you will always be his father, no matter how you look. Think of this as a new opportunity, a second life, to do what your instincts are telling you."

"My instincts are telling me that I need to protect my son," I said. "Sarc won't remain on Xon forever, will he? Sooner or later, he'll be called away from home again, and I have to keep him safe from danger."

"Always the concerned father," Mandri smiled. "It is a big universe, so you can't possibly protect him from every possible peril out here." He added jokingly: "Maybe you can leave some notes for him where he can find them, so that he won't bump his head or scrape his knee."

"You make it sound like I'm the father of a toddler," I frowned.

"That's how you sound!" Mandri snickered, tossing his hands up helplessly. "You and your son are both grown men, destined to have your own separate lives, with different experiences and specialties. You've already spent more time off-world than he has, and you'll be out a good deal longer, so what do you want to do with this time?"

What do I want to do? "I can't keep dodging poachers and collectors the rest of my life, so I'd like to stop running at some point. You've been able to keep me out of trouble these past few months, but eventually, I should learn how to protect myself, hopefully beyond the use of weapons and ships."

Mandri nodded, heartened by my goal of independence. "That's good to know. Honestly, it's been interesting to have you along; I'd forgotten how determined the poachers can be, when they see a chance to capture an Eladryz."

Mandri sounded amused, like I was a special lure that he was using for fishing, which I suppose I was, in a way. "I'm not sure I'll ever get to your level of proficiency for dispatching them. I haven't even seen some of the poachers hunting me, before they're gone."

"That's by design," Mandri said. "I'm used to killing, but you're not, and I think it's better that you not witness too much bloodshed, lest you become inured to it. I'd rather you become more comfortable with your Eladryz nature and develop your own network of allies to support you, once you've outgrown me."

That milestone seemed improbably far off. "I don't think I'll outgrow my dependence on you for a while," I said.

"I didn't say it would be soon, but the day will come. And when it does," Mandri grinned, "the galaxy will be your playground."

As Mandri pulled the *Oelivan* into the assigned berth at the Alliance outpost *Dione*, he placed a call to his client contacts to notify them of our arrival and reconfirm their upcoming meeting in the Acropol within the hour.

In the meantime, I checked my weapons and holstered them with barely a thought, something I had only managed to do within the last few weeks. Growing up with swords and bows, I was still getting used to energy and projectile weapons, but with Mandri's patient instruction and training, I liked to think that I was making quick progress.

My current weapon of choice was a medium-caliber Alliance guard energy pistol, which was commonplace wherever Mandri's business dealings took us, both inside and out of the Alliance territories. The Alliance standard-grade weapons were designed for easy care and use, rather than power output or efficiency of design, but their ubiquitous presence allowed me to move among the Alliance denizens largely unnoticed.

It was essential that I not attract unnecessary attention, as the Eladryz were rare enough that even someone like me would've commanded a high price in the grey markets, if I was somehow flagged; at fifty, I apparently still fell into the "young and viable" category. Mandri was an excellent chaperon-guardian-mentor, but I made an effort to stay inconspicuous and self-reliant, in case I ever had to manage on my own for a while.

Mandri pulled on his heavy, fur-trimmed coat and waited for me at the hatch of the *Oelivan* and made sure our comms were properly functioning before we stepped off.

"Keep your hood up when you can," Mandri said, gesturing to my dark cloak and cowl. "Stay close, but come straight back if we get separated. Don't worry about me. You got that?"

I nodded. I rarely saw Mandri with a weapon of his own, but somehow he was never caught defenseless, so if he did somehow get into a difficult spot, I was more likely to worsen the situation with my distracting presence than help it.

The walk from the ports to the central square was too brief, as I would've liked to explore more of the massive outpost before entering *Dione*'s Acropol. It was like walking through a city, complete with streets, buildings and a teeming, diverse population, and it took a passing glance out a window at the inky darkness to remind me that we were in the expanse of space, with nothing nearby, not even a planet or star. Everything that *Dione* needed to function was created there, or imported from parsecs away.

"We're looking for a wiry young man in an Alliance uniform, and a woman in black, both with red hair," Mandri said, using elfyn on purpose to keep others from eavesdropping on our conversation.

I scanned the throngs amassed in the open-space marketplace and spotted a couple that matched the description, seated at a table at one of the drinking establishments. "To your left, seated by the bar entrance," I said, without pointing to draw attention to them.

"Good eye," Mandri said, as he continued to scan the area before he started towards the bar. "Get a drink, and cover my back from the bar. You have some credits on you?"

"A couple," I said, consciously fighting the urge to check my pockets to be sure.

"One will be enough to cover a growler of Draesian beer and tip.

It's watered-down swill, but if you drink it slowly, it'll look less suspicious than if you just sit there with nothing. Go."

Mandri slowed his pace and let me go ahead, to minimize the likelihood of us being observed together, and I took position at the bar, within sight of the table where Mandri had joined the couple.

[What can I get you?]

I turned around and lost myself momentarily in a pair of vivid orange eyes, the color of a setting sun, contrasted against a dusky, smoky lavender backdrop. The bartender blinked, breaking our eye contact with a flash of her purple lids and lashes. At least, I thought the barkeep was female, judging by the softness of the voice and features.

[Ah... Draesian beer, growler...please,] I managed, consciously switching the words in my head to Alliance-speak. Over the past months, I had practiced my Alliance-speak with Mandri diligently, and I hoped I was fluent enough to not sound like an ingenuous tourist. I forced myself to relax by lowering my cowl, but just a little.

[Here you go,] the bartender said, setting the large mug of frothy green ale in front of me.

I was abashed that I had momentarily forgotten which pocket held my currency, but the bartender flashed a friendly smile, a couple of white teeth peeking between full, darker purple lips.

[It's okay, honey,] the bartender said. [This one's on me.]

I bowed my head slightly in gratitude as I returned the smile. I took a tentative drink of the beer; Mandri was right, it was almost flavorless, with about as much alcohol as watered-down wine, but it was inoffensive and potable. I swept my eyes over the counter areas and tables, including Mandri and his clients, to catch sight of anyone else who was could also be watching them.

[Are you staying long at *Dione*?]

[Unfortunately, no,] I answered, hearing the bartender pass behind me, and the muffled clink of glasses. [Just passing through.]

[I hope you stop by again, the next time you're 'just passing through,'] the bartender said, leaning against the counter. [Maybe I'll know my gender by then.]

I was in the middle of sipping ny beer and nearly coughed. [You don't have a gender, yet?]

The bartender smiled teasingly. [I haven't decided. Now, you're a...male?]

I nodded. [I've been male my entire life.]

[And in your species, do you prefer the company of other males, or females, or something else?]

What a personal conversation to have with a complete stranger. I deliberated on the question, as I scanned the bar again and saw Mandri and the couple standing from the table. [I never really thought about it. I socialize with everyone.]

[But for pleasure,] the bartender pressed, [what is your preference? If you have one?]

The tone of the question seemed more analytical than flirtatious, and the bartender's expression had turned serious and searching.

[Me, personally? Females,] I said. [Sorry, I have a very binary mind.]

The bartender shrugged amiably. [At least you're honest. Some people and species are more fluid in their preferences than they are willing to admit.] The bartender's eyes focused over my shoulder. [Ammo Sulimandri, welcome back to *Dione*.]

Mandri leaned against the bar with a wink and a smile for the bartender, and I realized that the bartender had been keeping me occupied, by prior arrangement.

"If you wanted to keep me out of your way, I could've just stayed on the skiff," I said automatically in elfyn, without thinking.

[I didn't want you out of the way, I wanted you out in public, to give you a chance to interact with others,] he replied in Alliance-speak. [Well, Nevis, how did he do?]

The bartender grinned, the orange fire-opal eyes bright with an inner glow. [I must admit, I was a little distracted because he is very cute, but I think he did all right. I would've liked to hear him speak a little more, but that's just for my personal curiosity. For blending in, it's better that he stay as quiet as he was and keep his hood up, at least partially, when he's in dimly-lit spaces.]

[And your language, Cyrus,] Mandri reminded. [Try to stick to Alliance-speak when we're in the company of people you don't know well. Your native tongues sound too close to Laxuyn, and believe me, you don't want to be mistaken for one of us.]

['Us,'] I echoed, looking back and forth between Mandri and Nevis. [So you're both Laxuyn?]

Nevis nodded. [All my life.]

[Are you really genderless?] I asked.

[I am, for a couple more years. When I reach maturity, I'll pick how I want to live the rest of my life. Right now, I'm leaning towards becoming female,] Nevis said with a flirtatious simper and flicker of dark, spiky lashes at me.

This is a first. I had never had someone from another species flirt with me, and I may have blushed. [I think you'll be beautiful, regardless of your choice.]

Mandri coughed softly. [We should get going. I have the details on the job, but there are some calls I have to make before we start.]

[Thank you for the drink,] I smiled, leaving a credit chip on the counter for a tip.

[Come back soon,] Nevis smiled, collecting the half-empty growler and the tip. [Next time, I'll get you something better than Draesian beer, on the house.]

Walking back to their berth, Mandri muttered, [Your pheromones and energy surges may be a problem if we can't dampen them. Your goal should be to blend in, not to be unforgettable.]

I pulled his dark cloak closer around myself and had to quicken my step to keep pace with Mandri's long stride and stay close enough to keep my voice at a whisper. [I didn't realize I was still giving off signals.]

['Still'? It's only been a few months since you started transitioning,] Mandri reminded, keeping his voice low, too. [You wouldn't notice, it's not something that young Eladryz can consciously control or suppress. Luckily, it has a subliminal effect on most species, so not many others will notice, either, but Nevis and I happen to have more experience with Eladryz than average.]

[How did your meeting with your contacts go?] I asked. [Are we proceeding with the job?]

[We are, but we'll need a few more hands,] Mandri said. "Turn right at the next corner," he said quietly.

I raised his brow at Mandri's sudden switch to elfyn, but followed him into the tight, empty alleyway. "Did you see something?"

Mandri slowed and let me pass him. "Yes. Go to the end of the alley but stay where I can see you. Keep your hood up."

I was halfway down the alley when I glanced over my shoulder and saw Mandri crouched behind a short stack of crates, which should've been absurd, given his long, lanky build, but somehow he managed to compact himself. I took a steps back when a trio of dark-armored figures entered the alleyway, drawing their weapons.

My mind flashed back to my last day on Xon, when I had seen my house littered with the dead, mangled bodies of similarly-clad off-world hunters who had tracked me to Mione, and who had suffered Sarc's retaliatory wrath. I recalled Mandri's cold indifference when he had seen the awful scene of carnage, and I knew that these people were doomed.

[You need to walk away and forget you ever saw me,] I warned.

Before the dark figures could consider my advice, Mandri popped up behind them and killed them as effortlessly as snapping his fingers: the first two he killed by twisting their necks, the third he dispatched with the plunge of a carbide dagger into the throat, through layers of protective fabric. Before I could shout a warning about a last armored figure approaching from behind, Mandri turned and shot the new arrival in the head with one of the fallen hunters' silent-shot weapons.

Everything happened so suddenly that I could only stare, dumbfounded. Four lives, extinguished in an instant...

"Hey!" Mandri said sharply, snapping me out of my daze with a shake of my shoulder. "We need to go before security arrives."

"We just leave them here?" I asked, stealing a last glance at the bodies. We had encountered poachers before, but usually in the anonymity of space, not in such a public, populated area.

"You want to stay around and let more people guess that you're Eladryz?" Mandri reminded, tucking two of the dropped weapons into his belt loop, underneath his fur-trimmed coat and a couple of other small devices into one of his several pockets.

"It's better that we get off *Dione* now," Mandri said, continuing down the alley, tapping my elbow to spur me to follow. "For everyone's sake."

Back on the *Oelivan*, once we were some distance from *Dione*, Mandri sent a message back to the outpost, to Nevis's attention, with the details that he was able to glean from the stalkers he had put down in the alley. "It was a well-funded outfit, based on their gear and arsenal. After your contacts dispose of the crew, they're welcome to strip and salvage the ship. If you find out who sent them, let me know."

Mandri seemed to have little sympathy for those who followed the poacher way of life, and he felt that he was providing the Alliance a valuable service by exterminating the ones he encountered. While poachers were essentially just mercenaries seeking rare, high-value targets, Mandri had had too many encounters with them over the years to grant them any patience or mercy.

Mandri set out the souvenirs from this last encounter on *Dione*, emptying his pockets and belt holsters onto the floor as he turned sideways in his pilot's chair to face me. I was feeling queasy, watching him take inventory of what he had confiscated.

"Looks like pillaging or grave-robbing, doesn't it?" Mandri said grimly.

I shook my head with a shudder but didn't answer.

Mandri sighed, "I forget how unused to this kind of thing you really are. I've done you a disservice by not sharing the statistics with you, so that you can understand our unique position in this galaxy." He checked one of the silent-shot weapons and handed it to me. "Take it; it's better than your energy pistol."

As I took the gun in hand to examine it, Mandri continued. "In all of Alliance space, with an official population of over thirty billion, there are perhaps one hundred thousand pure and part-strain Laxuyn still alive—that's less than three ten-thousandths of a percent, or one in three hundred thousand who are like me. Can you grasp how rare that makes me and my family?"

I nodded. "I have some idea, yes," I said. "That would certainly qualify your people as endangered."

"We are," Mandri said. "Even so, our numbers are very high, compared to yours. By the best, most optimistic estimates, there are fewer than five thousand Eladryz remaining in the galaxy. That's counting the non-Alliance pockets and uncharted worlds like Xon. You, my friend, are outnumbered over six million to one."

I looked up from my new weapon. "You make it sound like I'm in a war against the rest of the six million."

"Maybe not against all six million, but a good portion of it," Mandri countered. "You left your world and your son because you suspected the kind of chaos and destruction that would converge on you, if you were to stay. You didn't start a war, but you're in one, nonetheless."

"If you knew it was so dangerous to be around me, why did you agree to stay with me?"

"Because I owe your son a debt for saving my brother from the Praimos," Mandri said solemnly. "And because I know what it's like to be stalked and have my people decimated to near-extinction, and I see that happening all over again with the people of EladryzZurylan.

"Plus, I despise the Praimos, so I welcome any opportunity to thwart his genocidal ambitions, even if it means saving a single Eladryz."

Chapter 2: Team of Misfits

A day after we left the space station *Dione*, Mandri and I arrived in orbit around a barren ice planet, on the edges of an uninhabited star system. Viewing one of the displays, I marveled at the red star looming at the center of the system; it was dim for a sun and looked bloated and lethargic.

"It looks like it's dying," I said, its scarlet glow reminding me of cooling embers.

"It's been dying for a long time," Mandri said. "The last inhabitants of this system abandoned it centuries ago, and there's nothing left to mine or salvage here, so this is one of the places I come when I need some privacy."

The *Oelivan* was joined shortly by a larger cruiser, several times the size of Mandri's skiff and large enough to swallow it whole. [Impressive, isn't it? That was my mother's ship, years ago; she used it to move heavy equipment and cargo.] Mandri switched on the comm to hail the other ship: [Greetings, *Shakti*. Are we missing anyone?]

A woman's voice replied: [Good to hear your voice, Captain. All present and accounted for. Shall we bring you in?]

[No, thank you, Sistine. I'll bring the *Oelivan* in, as long as the bay is clear.]

[Ready and waiting for you, Sir.]

I took care of shutting down non-essential systems, to let Mandri focus on guiding us into the *Shakti*'s bay. Mandri didn't like auto-pilot systems, so he performed the docking procedure manually, staying unflappable even as the ship complained that it was less than a meter from the *Shakti*'s bulkhead. Once we were docked, I shut down the rest of the systems and power and joined Mandri by the hatch.

A colorful quartet awaited us in the bay, near our hatch. Jovial shouts of welcome dwindled into confused silence as the four figures noticed that Mandri wasn't alone. I glanced at them quickly in turn, observing what distinguished each of them from the others: one was a coffee-skinned woman with dark hair and oversized, owlish sea-blue eyes that were stunning against her dark complexion; one was a brick-red brute wearing a shell-like mask, whose armor-plated arms seemed longer than its trunk-like legs; the third and fourth looked like brother and sister, judging by their similar willowy figures, milky complexion and blue-grey hair.

[Team,] Mandri greeted the group, with his arms open. [It's good to see you all. This is Cyrus. He'll be joining us for a while.]

The group was wary and nodded their greetings, but I noticed some reined hostility from the dark-brown woman with the blue eyes.

[Who is he, and why is he here?] she asked bluntly, her chin raised. [Do we need him?] I recognized her from her voice as the woman who had greeted us on the comm.

[It's not a matter of need, Sistine,] Mandri said amicably. [I say he comes with us, so he comes with us.]

She scoffed at my unsullied appearance. [He doesn't look like he's ever spent more than a year off-world, anywhere, so what can he do? We're not running a charity here.]

[Sistine,] the female half of the pale twins broke in, [Mandri found all of us floundering in one corner of the galaxy or another. We should give him a chance.] Her male counterpart nodded in agreement.

[In which corner did you even find him?] Sistine challenged Mandri. [In a Ghanisi sky palace?]

[Where I found him is irrelevant,] Mandri said coolly. [I promised some important people that I would help keep him safe.]

[Ah, Mandri,] said the brick-red figure, disappointed, with as booming a voice as I had expected, [then you shouldn't have brought him here. I'm with Sistine. We're no good at babysitting or keeping things safe.]

[I'm not asking any of you to babysit, Rosie,] Mandri said, calm and resolute. [Cyrus will remain my responsibility.]

The crew balked collectively, and Mandri raised his hand to command their silence. [I'm not leaving him behind or partnering him with any of you, so he stays with me. End of story. Now, do you want to hear about the job, or not?]

After briefing the team on the details of the aid mission for their Arkanist clients, Mandri asked me to return with him to the *Oelivan*, under the pretense of finishing our preparations, but it was really to spare me the awkwardness of being snubbed by his erstwhile team of associates. Mandri knew the histories of his team members well enough to understand their prickly and suspicious nature, and decided it was better to keep our initial group introduction short.

"They don't like me," I said, as soon as the hatch to the *Oelivan* closed behind me.

"I wouldn't worry," Mandri said, strolling to the cockpit to activate the passive security protocols and set the on-board systems for regeneration and maintenance during its prolonged downtime. "My associates don't like anyone, at first, but they'll get used to you."

"They don't like me, or just Eladryz, in general?" I asked, picking up our satchels of supplies and spare clothes. "I noticed that they became very quiet when you mentioned my background during the briefing. Are they more concerned for me, or for the team's security."

"A little bit of both," Mandri said, swinging around in his seat. "Eladryz are unusual and scary to certain species—on the level of fairy tale monsters—especially to some of the younger generations that have been indoctrinated by the Praimos's propaganda campaigns."

"Why? What's scary about the Eladryz?"

Mandri got to his feet, towering over me. "When Eladryz reach full maturity, they're able to influence others to do their will, through the power of their voice, or just their minds, in some rare cases. You're not quite there and have some growing to do, yet, but the potential exists, so that's what intimidates them."

"But you're not scared of me. Neither was Nevis, back on *Dione*."

"No," Mandri said. "The Laxuyn and Eladryz ran in the same circles for eons, we even partnered for a period, so your species doesn't intimidate us. You may be able to influence by your nature, but we're able to repel and block by similar instincts."

"I recall that your brother Slither seemed to wield more influence than one would expect from a Guardsman," I recalled. "I always thought he was just very persuasive and well-connected."

"He is that, too," Mandri said, opening the hatch again. "Out of our entire clutch, he is perhaps the most adept at communication and networking, in all its forms, with everything from people to machines. But even he had to hone his skills for years before they became like second nature to him."

Mandri bounded down the ramp, with me close behind, to where Sistine and the Twins waited.

[Frey and Grey,] Mandri called, taking the satchels from me, [perhaps you can show me what you're thinking for charting our courses in and out of the drop-off site. And Sistine, please show Cyrus where we're stowing the package once we pick up. We'll regroup in the galley to go over the plan.]

Sistine watched Mandri and the Twins leave the bay before she whirled on me. She gave me a quick head-to-toe glance, and seemed irked by my general impassivity. She had already determined that I wouldn't fit in with the rest of the *Shakti* crew, and she was outspoken about her stance. [I don't know what your game is, Eladryz, but if you mess with Mandri, that'll be the last mistake you ever make.]

[I have no game, Sistine,] I said. [I assure you, I'm not that crafty.]

[Why are you even out here?] she asked, turning on her bootheel to lead the way out of the docking area. [What's your dark secret? Ammo Sulimandri doesn't let just anyone tag along for a ride in the *Oelivan*.]

[We already told you. He's sheltering me, until I figure out how to keep my planet safe.]

Sistine scoffed. [You're not fooling me. Eladryz the Vanquished has been a dead world for ages. There's nothing to preserve there, anymore.]

[My adopted world,] I clarified. [If I can't keep it safe, then I'll have to find another home.]

She shrugged. [It's never a good idea to get too attached to a world, even if you think of it as your home. I haven't been back to my homeworld in years, ever since I joined Mandri's team.]

[If you have a team that feels like a family, that may be enough.]

She narrowed her eyes, shooting a look over her shoulder at me, but I was purposefully avoiding her direct gaze. I was looking at the bulkheads, display panels... anywhere but at Sistine. Testing whether I was still paying attention, she stopped short, and I didn't crash into her. [I never said that,] she said, [but I know and care more about this team than I do about you.]

I had struck a nerve, so I backed off and kept my reply neutral. [I can respect that. Thank you for your honesty, Sistine. I will keep my presumptions to myself.]

[See that you do,] she said, as she resumed the march to the fore cargo hold.

Rosie was finishing up with the cargo area when Sistine and I arrived. It was difficult to tell what Rosie's dark-red skin actually was; it seemed flexible and pebbled like thick hide but was also shiny and hard like polished stone. Rosie seemed machine-like, moving the last metal crates to the side without showing any kind of strain or effort. It was only once I had a close-up look at Rosie that I realized that the blank, shell-like mask was part of Rosie's actual face.

[Cyrus,] Rosie greeted with a welcoming nod and a slow blink of its glassy, pupil-less black eyes. [Everything is cleared away that can be, Sistine.] I couldn't tell exactly where on the face Rosie's voice originated, but the voice was very clear and precise.

[Thank you,] Sistine said. [So, will this be enough room for the package?] she asked me, not entirely expecting a concise answer.

21

I didn't answer right away, taking a moment to measure my steps from one end of the hold to the other. [There's plenty of room,] I said, [but some of the cargo is fragile, so the crates will need to be stowed where they can be immobilized. There, and there.] I pointed to the rings on the floor where the chains and straps were normally fastened. [Also, three of the boxes will need to remain temperature-controlled until we reach the drop-off.]

[There is an empty compartment in the back for that,] Rosie said. [Please tell me the temperature before we arrive.] It looked at me, then at Sistine. [Will there be anything else?]

[May I see the back compartment?] I asked. [I'm sure it's ample, but better to confirm now.]

I did not miss the quick glance at Sistine, or her terse nod. [Meet us in the galley when you're done.] She left without waiting for our acknowledgement.

[Don't mind her,] Rosie said, leading the way to the rear cargo area. [She did not speak to me for a week after she arrived. She had never met an asexual drone before and did not trust me.]

I had never met a drone before, either, at least not one who could or wanted to converse. [What pronoun do you prefer when others speak about you?]

[I am fine with being called 'it,'] Rosie said. [In my hive, I was only ever called Rosanthus.]

[Mandri gave you your nickname, I take it.]

[He did. He renamed me when he saved me from my depleted hive.] Rosie set its segmented fingertips—the only part of its hand that would fit—onto the touchpad of the insulated cargo chamber to open the door.

[How do you mean, depleted?] I asked.

[When our Queen died, the royals abandoned the caverns to establish hives of their own, while the workers like me received the death signal and began to die off. Many of them destroyed themselves within the first day, and others starved themselves to death.] Rosie's voice was neutral, but I imagined that the experience had been a difficult one to endure. It entered the cargo chamber and waved for me to follow.

[You didn't receive the same signal from your dying Queen?] I paced the length of the space, looking at the interior from all angles and noting where the vents were placed.

[No, I did not. My fellow drones had been told that they had outlived their life purpose, but I did not receive the message, so I did not share their instinctive imperative. In time, I was the last remaining drone of my hive.] Rosie watched me pace. [Will this space suffice?]

[This will be fine, thank you,] I said. [Are there hot and cold spots in here? The serums need to be stored below ten standard degrees for maximum efficacy.]

It nodded. [The systems were maintained recently and will remain at whatever temperature you require. That vent is the main air feed,] it said, gesturing to s small grate near the floor. [The air there averages two degrees colder than the rest of the chamber.]

[That's perfect, Rosie,] I said. [That will help preserve some of the more sensitive liquids.]

As I mentally mapped the expected placement of our cargo, Rosie watched me silently.

[How long have you been with Mandri?] I asked, just to fill the awkward silence.

[He took me from my hive almost fifteen years ago,] Rosie answered. [He found me in the pit caverns and used his water and mineral rations to restore me. He told me that I was the last of my hive. All the others had died or had fled the planet, so he offered to help me find another hive, if I wished it.]

Mandri had been compelled to save Rosie, out of respect for its tenacity and instinct for self-preservation. [You chose to stay with him, even though you weren't obligated?]

[I had been born and lived as part of a collective, so the isolation was painful and confusing,] Rosie admitted. [But my purpose had died with my Queen, so even if I had been able to locate another hive, I would have been an outsider, and most likely killed for not being spawned by the new hive's Queen.]

[So, you transferred your allegiance to Mandri, instead.]

[He had not wanted me to perish alone, in a dead pit, so he offered me a place on his ship, to travel with him until I found my new path and purpose.] Rosie paused thoughtfully. [Is that what he has offered to you, as well?]

[It is, of a sort.] I smiled, feeling as though I had found a kindred spirit, at least for the moment.

By the time Rosie and I joined the others at the galley table, the team had already discussed the meeting and pickup details.

[Just in time,] Mandri said to us. [How is our cargo capacity?]

Rosie and I both nodded, waiting for the other to speak, then Rosie answered for both of us: [It is suitable.]

[Good,] Mandri said, leaning back in his seat, like a lord holding court.

[We haven't discussed the split,] Sistine said, giving me a furtive glance.

[I take my usual cut, twenty percent up front,] Mandri said. [The rest is divided equally amongst the four of you, minus costs and expenses. Cyrus is just an observer, until I say otherwise,] he said, assuring the team that my presence would not affect their paychecks.

[That is fair,] Rosie said. [It is still close to a hundred thousand credits for each of us.]

Sistine nodded, satisfied with Mandri's answer. Out of the team, she was the most like a royal drone: independent and self-confident enough to stand on her own, but fiercely loyal. She was unlikely to ever refuse Mandri's order, but her expressive saucer eyes would've conveyed any dissenting stance clearly enough. Presently, the deep sapphire flecks that accompanied her initial sullen defiance was fading into the more peaceful, paler blue of her irises.

With Sistine appeased for the moment, the rest of the team was more visibly relaxed. Rosie even seemed to go into a resting state, closing its black eyes and becoming perfectly still. With the business discussion concluded, the conversation turned to more personal, lighter topics, with Sistine and the Twins sharing anecdotes of the team's recent exploits during Mandri's absence.

Mandri's citrine eyes softened, and his general demeanor eased, as he enjoyed his team's lively tales and reenactments. He looked like a weary but bemused father, surrounded by his rambunctious offspring vying for his approval and attention. It wasn't far from the truth; despite their obvious differences, he had assembled them into something like a family. By his small smile, it was apparently a family of which he couldn't be prouder.

I couldn't sleep in my assigned bunk, with the ambient noise of the *Shakti* a higher, shriller pitch and the smell of the air a little more metallic and machine-like than I had gotten used to on the *Oelivan*. I managed to slip from my upper bunk without disturbing Rosie in the bed below mine and crept to the galley. I hadn't spotted any tea or other sedative draughts in the common area, but I had noticed a small, well-stocked bookshelf tucked away in a corner, so maybe I could find something to help me drift off to sleep.

By the dim safety lights, I browsed the shelves for books written in a language that I could actually read, and I found several works written in Alliance-speak. I fought the temptation to let myself glow to provide more light, after having finally mastered the ability to dim and brighten at will. I picked a few books from the shelves and rifled through the pages before putting them back, just for the simple pleasures of feeling paper between my fingers and the smells of ink and lignin. I paused in my bibliosmia to uncover an anthology of poetry, filled with sonnets and narrative works.

I straightened at the sound of approaching voices, and I recognized the melodic, whistling tones of the Twins' native tongue, that they only spoke when they were alone, out of courtesy to the rest of the crew. The voices quieted before the Twins entered the galley, and they nodded their heads to me in unison.

[Cyrus,] greeted Frey. Her long hair was plaited into a single braid.

[E'lan,] finished Grey. He kept his long hair pulled back from his face but loose. [You have a curious surname, an abbreviation.]

[Shortened from 'EladryzZurylan,'] Frey said.

[Yes, that's right,] I said, impressed with her effortless, inflected pronunciation of the name. [Where I grew up, it didn't carry any significance or attract as much attention as it does out here in the rest of the galaxy.]

Grey nodded. [If it does not work for you, you should give yourself a better name.]

[A less conspicuous name,] Frey added. [Just as we did.]

[You changed your names?] My book and all thoughts of sleep forgotten, I slipped into one of the seats around the galley table. [Why?]

[Alliance-speakers cannot manage them,] Frey said haughtily, but her smile was too sweet and guileless for me to take offense. [In our native tongue, my name is,] she began, then launched into a melodic, five-octave, eight-second bird song.

Grey grinned at my stunned expression and rejoined, [And mine is,] before answering his sister's bird song with his own, equally complex melody. [Thus, we call ourselves 'Frey' and 'Grey,' for short.]

[The first syllables of your names,] I noted. [It does make communicating with your teammates much easier, doesn't it?]

[Sistine and Rosie, perhaps,] Frey said. [Mandri has never had problems pronouncing our names. And we've been with this crew for...]

[Five years,] Grey finished.

[Have you always finished each other's sentences like that?] I asked, looking back and forth between the two of them. [I know you're not really twins, but it is a very twin-like behavior.]

[Twins are the norm in our species,] Frey explained. [In a regular year, we would've been born the same day, but in the year that we were conceived, conditions and weather were challenging, so my brother's embryo was carried in suspension and allowed to develop the following year, when conditions were more hospitable.]

Grey shared a smile with his sister. [It was fortunate that

circumstances were not worse when you was developing, Frey.] He looked at me. [In very lean and famine years, the second twin is miscarried and reabsorbed to feed the viable offspring.]

[It pays to be first in line sometimes,] Frey simpered. [What is your world like, Cyrus?]

[I've never been to EladryzZurylan,] I said. [But my adopted home, Xon, is a jewel of a world. It's lush and teeming with life. I've never experienced a famine year in all my time there,] I said, feeling almost guilty for the abundance I had taken for granted. [Life is very balanced there.]

[That is indeed a blessing,] Frey said. [I wonder whether, given your personal association with Mandri…]

[Your planet was one of their engineered ones?] Grey finished.

[Engineered.] I considered the implications of that. [You mean, it was modified or manipulated by the Laxuyn?]

Frey and Grey nodded in tandem. [It is a question best left for Mandri to answer,] Grey said. [We can only confuse with our conjecture here, but it is rare to encounter worlds so well-suited to supporting life without some intervention.]

[Or subsequent exposure and exploitation,] Frey said. [Returning to the matter of Cyrus's name, brother, isn't it customary for individuals to take the name of their worlds, in place of surnames?]

[Xon and Eladryz,] Grey mused aloud. [Eladryz and Xon…]

[Perhaps just 'Ex',] Frey proposed. [It is simple.]

[But also suspicious,] Grey said. [No one would naturally have a name like that.]

[No one would typically have a name like 'E'lan,' either,] Frey returned.

I considered it. In various languages, it meant: former, excluded, removed… *Ex*. Removed from my past life and identity, at least for the foreseeable future: *Cyrus Ex*. [That'll work for now, thank you. Until something easier comes along.]

[Rotation locked,] Sistine announced. [We're aligned with the planetoid. *Shakti* will be landing at the pickup site in twenty minutes.]

Sistine's voice was even and even casual, but the navigation of our approach to the rendezvous point had been nerve-wracking to witness. The planetoid with our cargo raced around its sun in a seventy-day orbit, while maintaining a dizzying, six-hour rotation. Landing in the right spot was like threading a needle on a spinning pin-cushion as it whirled around on a carousel.

But Sistine did it, without even a stain of indigo in her ice-blue eyes to show any break in her composure. [Remember, we'll have two hours left before daybreak.]

[We won't linger, don't worry,] Frey said.

[None of us want to get roasted by the sunlight,] Grey added.

[Keep the *Shakti* warm, in case we need to take off in a hurry,] Mandri said, clasping his hand on Sistine's shoulder for a job well-done. [Cyrus.]

[Ready.] I had checked the gear for pressure, temperature, air feeds and lights, as Rosie and the Twins finished donning their suits. I had spent some of our transit time studying the home planets and species of my crewmates for a better sense of what they needed most. The Twins performed better with more nitrogen-rich air and lower air pressure, while Rosie liked a warmer environment, so I had adjusted their equipment for their preferences. The equipment for Mandri had the same settings as mine: Alliance factory defaults, roughly equivalent to the averages on Xon.

Given the weight and bulk of our suits, I was glad that the gravity of the planetoid was low, easing our hike to the pick-up. With his superior, light-sensitive vision, Mandri led us at a brisk pace, and thankfully, the terrain was flat enough for us to follow easily. Given its inhospitable daily extremes of heat and cold, the surface was dead and featureless.

Our contacts were waiting for us, including one of the individuals who had met with Mandri back on *Dione*; hidden within the padded environment suit, it was hard to tell which one. We skipped the pleasantries and checked the cargo to make sure that everything was present, and that there was nothing extra. Frey and Grey even scanned the crates to ensure that there were no trackers hidden within them.

[We want the supplies to get to Tartarus Arkanis safely,] the contact reminded, surprised at our caution. [We wouldn't do anything to jeopardize the effort.]

[I'm sure you wouldn't,] Mandri said easily, as the Twins and Rosie unhitched the loaded pallet from the transport and took off some of the crates to lighten the load on the pallet, dividing them amongst us. [But unless you've sourced and packed each of the boxes yourselves, there's no way to be certain that someone else hasn't tampered with them.]

Frey passed me the smallest, insulated boxes with a wink and a nod. [These would be the serums, and need to be handled with a gentle hand.]

I looked at the crates stacked and fastened together behind her, almost as tall as she was. [Are you going to be all right carrying those?]

The Twins and Rosie laughed at my naïveté and returned to their allotments.

[You don't need the transport to get this back to your ship?] the contact asked, gesturing to the emptied carrier.

Mandri shook his head, slinging one of the strapped crates over his shoulder like a satchel. [We have our own.] He returned to his lead position, patting Rosie on the arm. [You have the bulk of it, Rosanthus. Can you manage?]

[Easily, Sir,] Rosie said, hitching the pallet to a harness it wore, and crouching slightly for a more balanced stance, almost like a sprinter waiting for the signal.

Mandri looked at the Twins and me, and we nodded our readiness.

I thought I was ready, anyway. Mandri turned and broke into an all-out run, which was impressive to watch, given his exceptionally long stride. It took all my effort to keep him in view. The Twins were close behind me, flanking Rosie to keep our heading.

[Mandri's scouting to make sure the way is clear,] Frey called to me.

[You can slow down,] Grey advised. [He won't lose us.]

[Now you tell me,] I said, gasping for air as quickly as my suit could feed it to me. I kept up my jog, despite my struggle, if for no other reason than to not let the Twins overtake me. Despite the heft of their haulage, they seemed unencumbered and had adjusted their pace to stay in line with Rosie.

Sistine's voice joined our comm. [I think we may have some company. A couple of Alliance ships just came out of jump... Arkanist call signs. *Merde.*]

[It's all right. We're close,] Mandri joined in, his voice calm. [Stall, if you can.]

[I'll try,] she said, but she didn't sound hopeful.

[We will hurry,] Rosie said gamely, but I was sure it was already exerting considerable effort to carry its share of the cargo, which had to be several times its weight, by conservative estimates.

[Cyrus, stay with Rosie. Twins, get back to Sistine,] Mandri ordered. [Help her chart our exit route and get on weapons, if we need them.]

[I call weapons!] Frey chirped immediately.

Grey whistled his annoyance. [Not if I get back first!]

The Twins raced past me, laughing, and with their melodic, avian voices, and I could almost imagine for a moment that I was hearing care-free woodland songbirds.

I trotted back towards Rosie, careful not interrupt its gait, and glanced at the gauges on its suit. [Pressure's holding. How do the temperature and air feel?]

[I will manage,] Rosie said. [We will be back to *Shakti* soon.]

[Two Arkanist drones deployed and headed your way!] Sistine warned. [Moving fast.]

We still had the darkness on our side, and as we disabled our suit lights, we were visually harder for the drones to detect. Rosie and I froze for a moment as we heard and saw the silhouette of one of the drones zip over the horizon towards us and pass overhead. As it continued on its trajectory past us, Rosie and I redoubled our efforts forward.

Mandri had directed me to prepare and supply the suits for a three-hour excursion, and I had stashed a little extra something in each for emergencies. *This could qualify as an emergency*, I considered.

As the ground shook under us, I looked back at the way we had come and saw the distant cargo transport in ruin. Without enough air to sustain any flames, the blackened wreckage had stopped smoldering by the time we could make out its mangled parts. The drone was still circling overhead, but it was only a matter of time before it located us.

Yes, this would be an emergency.

I reached over to Rosie's suit and cranked up its suit temperature by five degrees, and adjusted the airflow for the extra boost. I added an extra trickle of oxygen into my own feed, too.

Rosie noticed a change immediately and seemed invigorated. [What did you add to my air feed?] it asked, quickening its pace to stay astride with me.

[Selenium gas, fifteen hundred parts per million,] I said. [Just like on your planet. It doesn't help me any, but it should do something for you.]

We instinctively ducked our heads and froze as we heard the drone circle back overhead. We were in darkness, but our suits were still powered, and our conspicuous shapes on the otherwise flat terrain gave away our presence. The drone turned on a light, nearly blinding us and spotlighting us for targeting.

With nothing to lose, we charged ahead with renewed determination. [We keep moving, until we can't,] Rosie said.

One of the Twin's slender silhouettes appeared at the edge of the low horizon, with a cannon-like object in hand. [Cover your eyes,] Grey's voice intoned in our comms.

Rosie and I dropped our heads but still heard the whistling shriek of some kind of projectile streaking over our heads, striking the drone above us. Had it not targeted us with its light, it might have remained unseen against the night sky, but Grey had used its glow to his own advantage. We didn't have a chance to rest, as the second arrived, drawn by the destruction of the first.

Grey adjusted the settings on his weapon, as he said: [Stand still, Rosie.]

Rosie braced itself, and a web of energy struck it squarely in its center, spreading outward until it encircled me and our cargo, as well. [We keep moving now,] Rosie said, resuming its advance, undeterred by the drone stalking us.

An ordnance of some sort dropped over us but detonated in mid-air, and I realized that Grey had erected some kind of mobile shielding over us, particularly over Rosie, the tallest and most central point to be protected.

At last, the *Shakti* loomed into view, and Grey continued to provide cover against the pursuing drone as we sprinted the final length, with our shield weakening under our pursuer's dogged, intermittent bombardment.

[Pick up the pace, guys,] Sistine scolded. [Mandri's keeping the ships distracted up in orbit, but the *Oelivan* only has so many missiles.]

Once we were within range, one of the *Shakti*'s turrets swung towards the drone and blew it apart with a single shot. I was relieved that it was destroyed but still tried to follow the trajectory of its falling shrapnel, at least the larger chunks, once our shield wore through.

[Rosie, on your left!] I warned, seeing the hunk of metal hurtling towards us.

Rosie avoided the larger mass but missed a smaller wedge that tore down its shoulder, ripping a hole in its suit. I tried to see if there was some way to seal it shut, but Rosie waved me off. [Get the cargo on board.]

As I removed one of the crates from Rosie's load, Grey joined me and removed two more, and it seemed to help alleviate the strain.

[What's happening?] Sistine called. [*Shakti*'s showing something wrong with Rosie's suit?]

Rosie turned off its comm and charged the rest of the way with a single-minded focus, pulling the remainder of the pallet up the cargo ramp, into the belly of the *Shakti*, before slowing to a stop.

Grey retracted the ramp and sealed the hatch, as I helped Rosie off with its harness in order to get a better look at the suit's damage. [We're all aboard,] Grey reported to Sistine and Mandri, then gestured to me. [Get the serums in cold storage first. I'll take care of Rosie.]

By the time I stowed and secured the serums and medicines in the cold cargo area, Frey had joined Grey to help Rosie out of its suit and unload the pallet. The Twins chirped quietly to each other, examining Rosie's back and shoulder with concern. Sistine announced on the ship comm that the *Oelivan* was returning, and that the Arkanist ships were no longer in orbit or in pursuit.

[How bad does it feel?] I asked Rosie, ignoring the Twins' dire expressions for the moment.

[Rosie's gone dormant,] Grey said, as Frey opened a medical kit in front of me. [Drones do that when injured, to conserve energy.]

I had learned that recently, just as I had read about selenium and temperature effects on Rosie's species, but I was concerned that the dormancy had already started so soon. [The last rush must've taken everything Rosie had left.]

Frey and Grey both darted away to see to the cargo. [We must secure the crates before the *Shakti* launches, but we're listening. Tell us what you need.]

Rosie's tough, armored hide was blistered and open where the suit had been torn. I inspected it more closely to try to see the extent of the damage, but I couldn't distinguish anything like muscle tissue or bone within the oozing, spongy blue matter. I took a wad of gauze from the medical kit and wiped away the blood that had seeped and already coagulating, then held the wadding in place, even though there was no fresh bleeding.

Come on, I scolded myself, *why isn't Rosie bleeding anymore? What do you remember about its anatomy? Semi-open vascular system, with circulation facilitated by muscle movement.* Rosie had gone dormant to keep from bleeding out. I peeled back some of the bandaging to look at the ragged edges of Rosie's injury and could see where some of the tissue was already dead from exposure to the extreme cold outside.

[We should debride the necrotic tissue, then restore fluids and minerals to help with regeneration,] I suggested. It was my best guess, based on what I had read about Rosie's species and my own rudimentary healing knowledge from watching my father-in-law at work. *Nahe, what I wouldn't give for your wisdom right now!*

A muffled clamor sounded from the *Shakti*'s docking bay, signaling that Mandri and the *Oelivan* had returned. The floor and hull trembled as the *Shakti*'s systems prepared for launch, as the Twins moved the last crates into place and fastened them to the floor.

[Everything is stowed,] Frey reported to Sistine and Mandri.

[Except for Rosie,] Grey added. [Perhaps we should move Rosanthus to a more sterile environment for treatment?]

I taped a bandage securely to Rosie's wound; it wasn't bleeding, but it was still an open sore. I wasn't sure where Rosie's center of gravity was, to figure out how best to hoist its weight, but the Twins seemed familiar with it. Frey lifted Rosie under the arms, while Grey carried its legs, and they marched towards the exit.

[Where do you want to work on it, Cyrus?] Frey asked.

Me? I fought the instinct to shake my head. I had no qualifications! Sarc was a healer, and Nahe and Clyara before him. I had no business treating anyone, certainly not an entirely different species that I had only met a few days earlier.

Frey and Grey were waiting for an answer, so I blurted out the closest private room with a large enough bed. [Mandri's quarters.]

[Fine,] came Mandri's clipped affirmation through the comm.

Mandri was waiting at his open door when we arrived. His bedding lay on the floor next to the mattress, but knowing Mandri, the bed had been that way since he awoke that morning.

[Put Rosie down on its side,] Mandri said, following us to the bed. [Let me take a look.] Peeling back the taped dressing to take a peek, he said, [I heard your assessment over the comm, Cyrus, and I agree. But Rosie needs to be awake to speed regeneration, otherwise, it remains in stasis. Last time Rosie was hurt, it stayed dormant for three months.

[Grey, get the box of mineral supplements from the galley. Frey, we'll need more bandages; there should be some in storage.] I was ready to step aside, to let Mandri assume Rosie's care, but he wasn't done with me. [Cyrus, I'm needed on the bridge, so you'll need to stay with Rosie.]

[You'll do fine,] he smiled at my consternation. [You're a natural.]

Chapter 3: Accidental Healer

Cyrus, a voice stirred from my dreams. I was standing at the top of the *Ajlekuun*, waiting for the morning clouds to part and reveal the jewel-hued autumn foliage of the Moonteyre valley. The air was cool and sweet, and I didn't want to move from my perfect vantage.

[Cyrus.] The low, husky female voice was closer now. [You would sleep better in your bunk.]

I lifted my head and felt the stiffness in my hunched shoulders and curved back. I looked around at the empty galley, and my half-empty cup of coffee on the table in front of me. Staring at the neglected cup with me was Sistine, shaking her head.

[Uh, oh. Mandri hates wasting his coffee,] she said.

[Me, too,] I said, and emptied the rest of the cup. Cold or not, it revived me a little. [Pathetic, isn't it? I couldn't even stay awake for one drink.]

Sistine slipped into the seat across the table from me. [Not pathetic. You spent a long time working on Rosie,] she said. [Thank you.]

From the set of her jaw and her brow, I knew it wasn't easy for Sistine to get the words out. I tossed aside the clichéd responses like "It was nothing" and "It was the least I could do" and just replied, [You're welcome.]

[I know I was a little harsh with you. It's just that you were a stranger,] she said. [You're the first Eladryz I've ever met. Most of the people I know have never met one, for their entire lives.] I nodded silently, and she felt comfortable enough to continue. [I thought you were inside Mandri's head somehow, using him for his connections and resources. After spending so many years with him, you'd think I learn to trust his judgment a little more.]

Sistine stopped and was silent for a moment before she looked at me. [You're not going to say anything?]

I shook my head with a patient smile. I had learned earlier in my life not to interrupt women when they spoke, and to only offer my opinion or guidance at their express request.

[Why not?] Sistine asked.

I shrugged. [My daughter and wife taught me that listening is usually more helpful and welcome than speaking.] Janin had been ten years old when she burst into tears because I tried to offer some unsolicited advice about how to deal with her little brother's disrespect of her property. As I recalled the aftermath, Sariah had refused to speak to me until after I had put the children to bed and apologized to Janin.

[You're married, with a child?] Sistine asked, surprised.

[I was. My wife died nearly twelve years ago, and my daughter, the prior year,] I said, the dates still indelible in my memory. [My son's still alive, and he's the only family I have left. He's still figuring out how to talk to girls,] I said jokingly.

Sistine snorted. [It's just like talking to boys, or drones, or anyone else.]

Kind of, I wanted to reply. [He overthinks, sometimes. He'll figure it out.]

[Is he back on this adopted world of yours, that you mentioned on your first day?] she asked.

I nodded, impressed that Sistine had remembered the small detail. [What about you? I know you had mentioned that you haven't been back to your homeworld since you joined Mandri's team, but do you have family?]

[No.] A few flecks of sapphire began to creep into the irises of her pale blue eyes, as she swept back a stray, dark brown curl from her face. I thought for a moment that it would be the end of our conversation, but she took a deep breath. [I was born and raised in a feedlot.]

Surely, I misheard what she said. [Did you say...]

[Feedlot. Stockyard,] she said plainly. [I was taken from my mother when I was born, hand-weaned for docility, then moved into a pen with countless others like me. When I was old enough, I was moved to a carrier bound for the abattoir, and when the train stopped at a switch-point, I found my chance to escape.]

I felt ill, imagining a pen crowded with others like Sistine, waiting helplessly for their turn to be slaughtered as livestock. [I'm sorry, I'm still trying to understand how it is that your species is used for food. You're sentient, intelligent and articulate.]

Sistine smiled grimly. [Thank you, but so are many food species in the galaxy. I had the dubious advantage of becoming imprinted on the rancher's son who raised me, and I learned from watching and listening to him. Ultimately, I was still intended to become meat, not anyone's pet. The rest of my herd was happier and less traumatized

34

by remaining ignorant.]

[Did you try to speak, to appeal for your life?] I asked.

[No!] she shook her head vehemently. [That would've gotten me culled immediately, to be dissected for possible pathology. At least in the feedlot, I could survive for a few years, and keep listening and learning without detection.]

[So, you learned enough to plan an escape when you saw the chance. How did you find Mandri, or how did he find you?]

Sistine grabbed my empty cup to satisfy her need to fidget. [After I escaped the train, I wandered through the woods for several days, foraging on what I recognized as edible, and found a gigantic barn to hide in, until the ranchers gave up their search for me. At some point, the cost of their time and effort to find me outweighed any profit that I would have netted them. After the ranchers left, Mandri found me in the barn; I found out later that it was his property, and he had paid the ranchers to get off his land before they could discover his hangar of ships.]

[Which he kept in the barn, I presume?]

[Which he kept inside the barn,] Sistine nodded. [I thought he was going to kill me, especially when he realized that I could speak and give away his secret, but he let me stay. He just couldn't let me stay *there*, of course.]

[So he brought you onto the *Shakti*,] I said. Mandri had a habit of rescuing strays of all sorts, it seemed.

[Eventually. First, I had to unlearn some of the behaviors that I had acquired on the farm, like shying away from machines and following the rest of my herd without thinking. Mandri taught me to stop acting like cattle. You're less likely to be treated like meat, if you stop behaving like meat.]

['Only food tries to run,'] I said. [It's a saying we have on Xon.]

[Mandri told me that one, too,] Sistine said. [He said that, in the wild, most predators instinctively chase prey that tries to elude them. So, if I learned to be assertive and self-reliant, I could stand with confidence, and not be victimized as easily.]

[What about the predators that are too stupid to follow those rules of engagement?] I wondered.

[They adapt or die,] she said. [Same as prey, except that Mandri refused to let me live as prey. He had me choose my own name.]

[How did you come to pick 'Sistine'?] She didn't strike me as the sort to be interested in ancient religions.

[It's a play on the word 'sixteen,'] she said, passing me back my cup. [In the feedlot, we were assigned numbers for the inventory.]

[You were Number 16?]

[I was Number 2816,] she corrected. [One out of a requisition for three thousand head, for that day. It was a holy feast week, and there needed to be enough food to serve all the worshippers.]

We paused our conversation when we heard the rhythm of Mandri's footsteps approaching the galley.

[You should both be resting,] he chided us. [*You* need to be up in three hours to get us to Tartarus Arkanis without being fired upon,] he reminded Sistine. [And *you*,] he gestured to me, [just spent the last eight hours patching up an armored-skin drone, and you look like you're about to drop. Go take a nap; I'm sure the Twins will give a chirp if Rosie's condition changes.]

[You should be asleep, too, Captain,] Sistine said.

[I would, but my quarters are too crowded for my comfort, at present,] Mandri quipped. [I guess Rosie and I will have to swap bunks until it's up on its feet again.]

Mandri noticed my peculiar, wide-eyed stillness after Sistine left us. "Is everything all right?" he cued in Xonen elfyn.

"Sistine shared her story with me," I said in kind, now that we were alone. "She's lived through some harrowing experiences."

"She has, but she's only thirteen and resilient," Mandri said, tugging at my sleeve. "Unlike us old codgers, who need our beauty sleep. Come on, up you go."

"Do you do this sort of thing often?" I asked, getting to my feet. "Rescue foundlings from early and certain death?"

"Not as often as I used to," he said. "I slowed down after I finished my two-hundredth year."

"Two hundred by Xonen measurements, or by Alliance standards?" I asked. "It's the same, isn't it?"

Mandri walked backwards to face me as we headed back to the bunkrooms. "Figured that out, did you?"

"I know that time on Xon follows the Alliance standards exactly: days, months and years... I'm guessing that it's not a coincidence. The Twins had suggested that Xon may have been engineered?"

"There was some manipulation going on," Mandri confessed. "You are aware that Xon's population was carefully curated for the benefit and convenience of our *Char'she*, yes?"

I recognized the Laxuyn name for the augments. On Xon, we had called them magestones. "Your Treasured Ones. Slither had mentioned that you had allowed them to try out different host species, and they bonded best with the humyn ones. You're saying that there was more to the process than just letting the *Char'she* test-drive potential host candidates."

Mandri stopped in front of the open door to the bunkroom I had shared with Rosie. "My ancestors needed to provide a controlled environment, so that the trials wouldn't be affected by variations of time, temperature and so forth. They found an uninhabited, still-developing system and modified the conditions of Xon to match the Alliance standard."

The vast scope of such an undertaking was beyond my limited scientific grasp. "So, the Laxuyn didn't just pick out host species to populate the planet; your ancestors actually changed Xon to fit the Alliance norms, too. In everything?"

"It took some work, but yes, Xon is synchronized with the Nexus, to the second. You are fifty years old, anywhere we go in the galaxy. When a month passes on Xon, it is the same month for everyone."

"You would've had to change Xon's mass, its orbits…" Who knew what else?

"*I* didn't do it," he said smartly. "My Laxuyn ancestors did, millennia ago. They had created sentient life, so they felt that the least they could do was provide their creations a safe home and conditions where they could grow and thrive." Mandri watched me ascend the ladder to the upper bunk, just in case I was more tired than I seemed and lost my grip, before he dropped into Rosie's oversized bed.

"Personally, I'm torn on the idea of world-building," Mandri said. "While it's worked out well overall for Xon and for the evolution of your darling humyn race, I'm also aware of several native species that became extinct as a result of Laxuyn meddling."

I closed my eyes and felt my limbs growing heavy almost instantly. "That's not something within your power to fix or undo."

"No, I suppose not," he said, his voice growing softer with his tiredness. "Species spring into existence and die off every day, and most of their fates are beyond our control, but I feel like we should act to save the ones we can. You never know when one of them will come in handy."

I felt a tap on my shoulder, which prompted me to pause the simulation trainer, and the image of the half-stitched wound froze in front of me. I was in the galley, but I was in the middle of a holographic tutorial, so it was easy to get lost in my study. I eased my eyes half-open and squinted at Rosie, who held out a flask to me. I noticed the mouth pincers twitching under Rosie's faceplate, which meant that it was speaking.

I whipped off my headpiece and took the flask from its hand. With the trainer detached, the images cleared from my mind, as well. [Thanks, Rosie. I'm sorry, I missed what you said.]

[Mandri wants to confirm that Sistine has received all her thirteenth-year inoculations before they leave the *Shakti*. They're meeting the contact in an hour.]

Hilafra. I grabbed the comm earpiece that I had set aside prior to starting my training module and reinstalled it in my year. [Sorry, Mandri,] I called, [I didn't realize I was disconnected for so long. Yes, her bloodwork came back clean, and she's been vaccinated for everything you requested.]

[Thank you,] Mandri replied. [Since she's leaving the ship more, I feel better knowing she's protected. How many inoculations did she receive?]

[Thirty-two in total,] I said. [Some of them were combined, so five treatments in all.] I could still remember which ones I had given her, as easily as I could recall any of the medications and procedures that I had administered to the rest of the crew recently. I had become the team's medic, by default.

As Rosie turned to leave, I glanced at the regrown skin on its shoulder. In the three months since Rosie's injury, the blistered gash had healed so fully, that I could only discern the welt-like scar because I had been the one to staple it closed.

[Are you still taking the sclerotin supplements?] I asked.

Rosie nodded. [Until the end of the week, as you prescribed. The thermostat in the bunks can be reset, too. The higher temperature has not been comfortable for you.]

We had raised the ambient temperature in the bunkroom to speed Rosie's recovery, and I tolerated it for short periods, but it was true that I didn't sleep as long or as deeply in the heated space. [I'm fine, Rosie. If I'm unable to sleep, I can study, instead.] I took a drink from the flask and savored the coolness of the water. [Proper medics and healers spend years honing their craft, and start at a younger age, so I feel at a disadvantage.]

[You are learning to treat multiple species, for a variety of conditions, in a very shortened timeframe,] Rosie said. [You are very useful and capable, for someone who is not very strong or fast. And older.]

I laughed in humble agreement. I was second oldest on the *Shakti*, behind Mandri, with a fraction of the experience and agility of any of the others. I was perhaps not the most skilled or knowledgeable — that would still be Mandri — but I was the most patient and nurturing of the crew, so I was the best suited for the role of medic.

After ten missions, over three months, I had managed to gain some credibility and trust with the others, but nothing had proven my value to the team as much as taking care of Rosie after our first outing together. Mandri had counted on that—not on Rosie getting injured, but on my effort to help, and the team's easier acceptance of me as a result of it.

Rosie tilted its head at the tinny, rhythmic sound still coming from my headpiece on the table . [I recognize that sound. It is usually played more loudly.]

I had been playing an assortment of music from the crew's pooled collection, and the piece in question was a discordant, angry-sounding vocal screeching over a noisy, mechanical melody. I picked up the headpiece to hear it more clearly. [Something from Sistine's collection, I think.]

Rosie nodded its head in time to the grinding, machine-like rhythm. [Not from your own world?]

[Xon has barely discovered electricity,] I said. [We're probably centuries away from producing anything like this.]

[That is perhaps for the best,] Rosie remarked. [I recognize it now. There is little harmony in this song, and the lyrics are almost nonsensical. I hope your planet produces more competent artists than the Atomic Plague Mites,] it said primly.

[It's from a compilation of popular works, so I thought I would try it,] I shrugged. [Music helps me maintain my focus while studying.]

Rosie shook its head, returning to the door. [It is odd what some of your species call 'music.']

By the end of my eighth month with the team, we had completed twenty missions together, and Sistine and Mandri trusted me enough to let me take some of the off-line shifts alone, while the rest of the crew slept. The quiet stints were welcome and peaceful respites from the hectic and dangerous encounters that seemed to come more and more frequently as the weeks wore on.

During one of the shifts, I sat in the *Shakti's* navigator's seat and contemplated the digital clock display. There was no day or night to consider for most of the trips we took, as there were no regular sunrises or sunsets to mark our time, but we always had a point of reference by following the Alliance Nexus. Back on Xon, in the Realm, it was nearing the end of 951.

Eight months with the team, nearly four months with Mandri before then. I had been away from Xon for almost a year already? I looked down at my skin and noticed the subtle sheen that still showed from time to time, and hoped that I would somehow finish my transition on the shorter side of five-to-ten year range. I was impatient to return home.

At a quiet shuffle by the door, I leaned back in the navigator's seat and saw Frey's slender, pale figure looming in the doorway. She wasn't looking at me, but rather out at the stars and distant nebula, stretched thin like a tuft of candy floss. From the loose fall of her long, blue-grey hair and the unstructured shirt she wore, plus the comm device missing from her ear, it was apparent that she had come directly from her bunk.

[Unable to sleep?] I asked.

[I sense danger.] She continued to stare into the blackness, as if she expected something to emerge from it.

[What kind of danger? A presence, a ship?] I watched the sensor screens, but nothing appeared out of the ordinary.

[A danger from within,] she said, narrowing her eyes. [But not here.] She turned and slipped back into the hallway. I watched her wander back towards the bunks, wondering if Frey was sleepwalking. I had never witnessed her doing that before, but then again, I also rarely saw her without her brother close by.

I had only returned my attention to the sensors when Frey's panicked shriek sounded from the bunkroom that the Twins shared with Sistine. I fought the impulse to run to the back and instead activated everyone's comms. [What happened?]

I heard the commotion and footsteps, as everyone went to Frey's aid. A few endless seconds later, Mandri rushed into the cockpit and clutched the back of my seat. [Sistine's unresponsive. I can't figure out why, but maybe you can. I'll stay here. Go!]

I snatched the medical kit from the wall and waved Rosie and the Twins out of my way, as I crouched next to Sistine's sallow, unconscious figure. Frey looked especially distraught, as Grey held her to comfort her. I checked Sistine's pulse and breath, both much weaker than they should have been. Her skin was also much warmer than normal, but she showed no signs of injury. *An infection?* Without Sistine awake to tell me how she was feeling, it was hard to diagnose.

[Well?] Mandri's voice demanded.

[I can't tell yet,] I said, trying to revive her. Not even a dose of adrenaline managed to stir her from her unresponsive state, so I tried something new, out of desperation.

I set my hands on her face and closed my eyes, envisioning Sistine's internal systems as a natural landscape, full of activity and energy. Except that when I scanned the environment for something amiss, there was too much going on, globes of bright light darting in and out of my range of vision in a rush.

I followed the flow of light and activity to a darkened area in

Sistine's landscape, a web of tangled membranes and rapid-fire sparks. *Nervous system. Why is it dark?* As I approached, I noticed a pulsing, grub-like mass wrapped around a cluster of membranes, as though feeding off it. *It's a parasite—*

Cyrus is glowing, Rosie noticed. I heard its voice in my head as much as in my comm.

[Cyrus, whatever you're doing, stop it!] Mandri snapped. [Three ships just appeared out of jump to engage us.]

I struggled to stay in the vision, to identify what was attacking Sistine. [I just need another minute.]

[You have twenty seconds,] he said sharply.

In my frustration, I envisioned reaching out to the parasitic mass, and sinuous tendrils shot out of my hands, entwining themselves around the squishy, slippery foreign tissue. The tendrils constricted, choking the parasite and ripping it apart in the process, and my actual, physical form was aware of Sistine's sudden, jerking spasms under my hands. With my eyes still closed, I fought to maintain contact...

All became still. The mass attacking Sistine's body was gone, the tendrils receded back into my imaginary body, and I felt Sistine's steady breath on my hands. But there was no time to enjoy our success. [I'm done!] I shouted, emerging fully from my vision.

My ears popped, as they sometimes did when I was aboard a vessel traveling through a jump-gate. To distract myself from the discomfort, I checked Sistine's vital signs again to make sure that she was stable, while Frey watched her with concern. The commotion over, Rosie ambled back to bed, and Grey went to get his sister something from the galley.

[How did you know that she was in danger?] I asked.

[I sensed a foreign presence,] she said, taking a seat on the edge of Sistine's bunk. [I couldn't tell where it was, just that it wasn't welcome. What was it?]

[A neural parasite of some sort,] I guessed. [I'm still not exactly sure what it was, or where she had picked it up—maybe during one of the last missions—but it looked like it was harming her, so I removed it.]

[You didn't have to cut into her, so how did you do it?] Frey said. [We just saw you start glowing, then the light enveloped both of you, and then the light and the illness were gone.]

[I don't know,] I said in earnest. [I just did what I felt was natural.] I thought back to what Mandri had said. [Mandri said that we were under attack?]

Grey returned, with a snack for Frey and a flask of water for me. [Almost as soon as you started glowing, multiple ships began to

41

appear, like vultures near a carcass, and just like carrion birds, they turned on each other for first rights. Mandri thought you were attracting them, like a beacon.]

[We think you acted properly,] Frey assured. [You did what was needed to save Sistine.]

So, why did I feel so bad? [I was endangering the rest of you.]

[We accept risks for one another, and Sistine would have done the same for us,] said Frey.

Grey nodded. [It is what we do for family.]

Given that we were between missions anyway, Mandri scheduled a break for the team to relax and recuperate, and to provide Sistine extra time to recover from her recent illness. He landed the *Shakti* at an isolated outpost away from the usual flow of Alliance traffic, at a small settlement called Harbor. The planet itself was so sparsely populated that Harbor was the considered its largest enclave, so the planet shared its name.

The crew was glad to have the time to rest, and the locals in Harbor welcomed us all with generosity and warmth. It had been at least five years since the crew's visit, judging by Rosie and Sistine's knowledge of the town and the Twins' lack of it. Mandri, of course, was greeted as an old and dear friend by all.

It was a sweet luxury to rest in a soft bed, complete with thick quilts and pillows. Sistine took advantage of the abundance of water provided by the nearby lake to take a long soak in the local bathhouse. Rosie helped Mandri with unloading and restocking the *Shakti*, and the Twins took some time to acquaint themselves with the town and enjoy the balmy, verdant year-round climate of Harbor.

I had started to doze when I was awoken by a knock on the door. Even that—a simple wooden door with a mechanical latch—was a welcome return to the familiar. I was met at the door by a slightly shorter, slightly younger, more scholarly-looking version of Ammo Sulimandri: clean-shaven but with the same yellow-blond hair and citrine eyes, and shirtsleeves and tweed waistcoat in place of Mandri's fur-trimmed coat.

"I am Ammo Fenrir," he greeted in Xonen elfyn. "Sulimandri's brother."

"You're the second eldest," I recalled from Mandri's passing mentions.

"That's right," he smiled, with the same broad, close-lipped grin that Mandri and Slither shared. "And you are Cyrus?"

"I am." I looked over my shoulder at my spare room. "I would invite you in, but…"

"Our rooms are small, I understand," he said. "We generally spend most of our time out of doors. May I offer you some refreshment, or a tour of our house and the area?" He stepped aside, and gestured for me to follow him.

"This is your house?" I asked. "When Mandri told us to make ourselves at home here, I just thought…" My voice trailed. It didn't really matter.

"It belongs to the family," Fenrir explained. "I live here year-round, but there are more than enough rooms when one of us visits and brings along guests." He turned aside. "Can I get you something? Tea or wine, perhaps?"

"Some tea would be very nice, thank you." I followed Fenrir to the kitchen area, with its multiple burners, expansive pantry and polished stone counters. Herb planters crowded the sills of the tall windows that let in the full sunlight. "I haven't seen a kitchen like this since the Imperial palace."

Fenrir filled a cup from a tea kettle sitting on one of the burners. "Thank you. As the caretaker of this place, I try to keep it livable for myself." He offered the cup to me but did not prepare any tea for himself. "How are you adjusting to life away from Xon? Has it been ten months since you left?"

"Closer to a year," I said, taking a sip of the green-tinged brew flecked with tiny white flower petals. It was herbal but not grassy, and faintly sweet but more in its scent than on my tongue. "This place reminds me a little of home, actually."

Fenrir's grin broadened further, which I hadn't been sure was possible. "This was one of the Laxuyn haven worlds for a time, also. Our ancestors honed some of their world-forming skills here, and applied their lessons when modifying Xon and other subsequent planets."

So, this was one of their engineered planets, too. I looked through the windows at the inviting, sunny field outside and couldn't see anything amiss. "This place seems perfect. Why did your ancestors bother to move elsewhere?"

"It was too exposed, in time," Fenrir said. "The Alliance grew and developed around us, and this planet became too closely-situated to some of the gate hubs and routes, so it was no longer suitable for hiding the *Char'she* as our ancestors had planned." He refilled my teacup absently and set out a plate of thin biscuits. "There was also too much abundance here, and the universe seeks a balance, always."

A large black cat, the size of a fox, appeared seemingly from nowhere, leapt onto the counter and gave the biscuit plate a dismissive sniff. It stroked its proudly erect tail against my arm and returned to the floor soundlessly, departing from the kitchen as quickly and uneventfully as it had arrived.

"What kind of abundance?" I asked, staring after the cat.

"Too much water, too much sunlight, and too much space," Fenrir said. "Sounds like that kind of bounty should be wonderful, shouldn't it?"

I thought of the consequences of imbalance. "Too much water and sunlight can lead to too much rainfall and flooding. Too much space?"

"When the Alliance came across this large uninhabited world teeming with resources, some genius decided to try to settle it, but they also inadvertently brought their pests and not enough predators to contain them. The vermin flourished and overran the wild spaces, too, with all the bounty of this world to sustain them, including the Alliance's staple crops."

I could figure out the rest. "Without predators to keep them in check, the vermin exhausted the bounty and began to die off, bringing disease after the famine."

"Other things came, too, that eventually convinced the Alliance to abandon their plans for this world," Fenrir said. "Magic came."

After gradually weaning myself off the belief in magic in favor of science and technology, Fenrir's mention of it was surprising. "What do you mean, 'magic'?"

"You know, *magic*," Fenrir said, wriggling his fingers mockingly. "Phenomena and creatures that can't be explained by science or logic. We Laxuyn aren't too proud to admit that we don't understand all the workings of *Nafre*—the universe—and that there are still mysteries left to challenge, enthrall and humble us."

As I considered Fenrir's remark, the black cat returned, through a different doorway. Again, it jumped onto the counter, but this time it nuzzled my hand against the teacup, inviting me to pet it. I obliged, scratching it gently behind the ears, and it purred with satisfaction before it left us again.

"Like that cat. I call her 'Carbon,' but I don't know whose cat she is," Fenrir said, "if she in fact belongs to anyone. All I know is that I have fewer rodents and other pests in the barn, and I feel happier when she comes to visit. Maybe she stowed away on one of the Alliance ships, or maybe she stumbled through a spatial rift and ended up here. It's a mystery."

Mandri joined us in the kitchen for the tail-end of his brother's comment. ‹‹Are you filling his head with nonsense about magic?››

I kept my eyes focused on my teacup. I understood Mandri's

remark in Laxuyn-speak as clearly as I had heard the elfyn words spoken by Fenrir. Which was particularly odd for the fact that I had never studied a Laxuyn language module.

‹‹Not nonsense, eldest,›› Fenrir replied. ‹‹Your mind has grown too rigid over the years, too buried in logic and technology…››

‹‹It's called survival, Fen,›› Mandri remarked.

‹‹…to entertain the idea that not everything can be dissected and analyzed!›› he finished.

‹‹That's the only purpose such an idea would serve: to entertain. And you're right, I don't have the patience to puzzle out the greater meaning of why people continue to hunt us,›› he said bitterly. ‹‹And want to exterminate *him!*›› he added, nodding his head subtly towards me.

‹‹While I have all the time in the universe to contemplate such trifles, here in our little safe Harbor,›› Fenrir said quietly.

‹‹That is not what I said,›› Mandri growled. ‹‹I know we all have our roles to play.››

‹‹Yes, we do,›› Fenrir said, ‹‹so loosen your grip on what is not yours to handle or beyond your control. Our new friend here knows something about that. Don't you?››

Before Mandri could interject that I didn't understand their language, and before I realized that Fenrir hadn't turned to direct his question to me, I nodded mutely. I didn't know how to reply, but I had followed their conversation with no problem.

‹‹Surrender to the fact that there's only so much you can teach Cyrus,›› Fenrir said gently. ‹‹Yes, you have prior experience with others of his species, as we all do, and whatever knowledge our ancestors were able collect about them, but you yourself are not Eladryz. The best mentor for him right now, especially for the fifty-year transition, is another of his kind.››

‹‹There is no one else,›› Mandri said. Fenrir seemed about to disagree, so he amended: ‹‹No one else with whom I would entrust his company.››

‹‹Then let him stay here in Harbor, until someone can be found for him,›› Fenrir suggested. ‹‹This is a safe haven for all types of refugees, so he will fit in easily. Here, he won't be hunted.››

Carbon returned to the kitchen again, circled Mandri with a caress of her serpentine tail and returned to the counter to sit next to me, regarding the three of us with her blue-green eyes before she tired of our inattention to her.

‹‹You've always preferred dogs, while I'm more tolerant of cats,›› Fenrir said. ‹‹You prefer order and fealty, whereas I like companions who are more independent. Which are you, young man?›› Again, he did not avert his eyes, but I knew the question was for me.

"Are you asking which one I am, or which one I prefer?" I asked, tickling the cat's twitching ear. "I am a bit of both, but I think most sentient creatures are. I am adaptable."

Fenrir grinned. ‹‹Spoken like a true son of EladryzZurylan.››

At the evening festivities at Fenrir's house, where most of Harbor turned out for the free-flowing wine and ever-full platters of free food, I was advised by several locals to visit the lakeside after dark for an unforgettable sight. Not wishing to ruin the surprise for me, they provided few details about what to expect, but recommended that I take a lantern with me, in case I stayed out longer than planned and needed help finding my way back.

As the sun dipped below the tree line, I followed the winding, sloping path and the quiet lapping sounds of the water down to the lake, but I saw its shimmering edge well before I reached the shore.

The algae that flourished and clustered in the shallows during the day, glowed with a brilliant blue-green light at night, as bright as the moonlight overhead and intense enough to cast a shadow behind me. As I swirled my fingers through a patch of algae, I noticed the small, glowing, bioluminescent specks that caused the plants to glow. Knowing that the algae's light resulted from a chemical reaction made the vision no less breathtaking. In fact, I was moved by the extraordinary beauty that was everywhere around me, reminding me that something could be commonplace and ubiquitous, yet still be magical and miraculous.

I perched on a dry boulder and kept my lantern extinguished, preferring an unadulterated view of the phosphorescent, blue-green shoreline and the last crimson embers of the sunset fading behind the forest. Nocturnal creatures moved through the water, leaving ripples in their wake, some displacing far more water than I would've expected of fish.

Fenrir's feral black cat, Carbon, or a relative, approached the shoreline and pawed at the algae, the glow captured and reflected in her blue-green eyes as she glanced in my direction, before returning her attention to the creatures of the lake. After a moment, a mammoth, serpent-like shape rose from the water, the displaced glowing algae coating its skin and hinting at how massive the creature actually was.

I scrambled to my feet, ready to run to the cat's aid if it was threatened, but Carbon merely looked at the giant serpent with simple curiosity, even familiarity. The snake-like head and neck of the behemoth craned down slowly, and it seemed to grumble a quiet greeting to the cat. Carbon meowed her reply, and the serpent sank back into the depths.

Carbon skirted the edge of the shore and sat next to me on a smaller lip of my boulder seat. She meowed at me and seemed to be awaiting a response.

"I'm sorry, I don't speak 'cat,' but you are very sweet," I said, presenting my empty hand. She rubbed her head against my hand, then leaned more heavily against it, inviting me to pet her again. "Sure, why not."

[I thought I heard your voice,] called Sistine from further up the path. [Some view, isn't it?]

[It's spectacular,] I agreed, gazing out at the shimmering blue-speckled shore. [I'm glad I came down to see it.] As if realizing that my attention was now elsewhere, the cat shook her head and bolted silently from my side, deeper into the woods. [Well, that was fun! Hope we can chat again soon!] I called after her jokingly.

Sistine stared after the cat uncertainly, then at me.

[It was a joke,] I clarified, finally lighting my lantern. [She just uses me for my hand.]

Sistine's blue eyes widened and darkened with her dismay, and I regretted my phrasing. [I guess it's not really my business,] she murmured.

[I pet her between her ears with my fingers,] I said painstakingly. [Why does everything have to be an innuendo with you teenagers?]

Sistine shared my boulder seat, once I nudged over to make room and raised the lantern to light her way to me. Her eyes were pale and calm again. [I'm assuming that you mean late adolescents. I may be thirteen in years, but I'm at the end of the average lifespan for my species.]

The average lifespan for Sistine's species was inordinately short since most of them were slaughtered as livestock before reaching adulthood, but it wasn't my place to remind her of that. She was an adult, by all measures, and knew exactly what she was talking about.

[I thought my life was just about done a year ago,] I said, [but the universe seems to have other plans for me. I wonder what it has waiting for you.]

She leaned into me, a self-soothing gesture that I usually saw her do with Mandri. [Were you afraid, when you left your home? Your home planet, I mean, with Mandri.]

I had to think about that, honestly. [I was flooded with hormones at the time, so all my emotions were heightened. I was terrified, but also excited and exhilarated by the opportunity to explore and do something more with my life.]

47

[That's how I felt when Mandri found me, too,] she said. [I was frightened of the unknown, but I always knew that he would protect me. He's always been good to me.]

Her tone was soft, in a way that I hadn't heard her voice before. She loved Mandri, beyond devotion or familial bonds. I would almost say that she was *in* love with Mandri and was trying to sort out her feelings, but I didn't dare to presume beyond that. Sistine had rebuffed me sternly in the past for reading too much into her words, so I refrained from comment.

[I don't think I ever thanked you for saving my life,] she said, straightening. [I know we watch out for each other when we're doing our jobs, but what you did... I don't even know what you did, except that you destroyed a parasite in my head with your touch. A mind grub usually means death for those of my species who are infected.]

[I'm glad I was able to help, but I'm not sure what I did, either,] I said. [I just followed my instincts and hoped for the best.]

[Instincts, really?] she scoffed. [If all Eladryz share such instincts, I can understand why people are scared of your kind. You can perform miracles, without even trying.]

[Yet, our population has dwindled, to becoming outnumbered six million to one,] I recalled grimly from Mandri's statistics. [Fenrir has offered to let me stay here, in Harbor. I think it would be safer for the team, if I did.]

Sistine's eyes darkened again, this time in earnest. [Is that what you want?]

It was a different reaction than I would've gotten months earlier, when Sistine would've gladly ejected me from the *Shakti* at the first opportunity, either literally or figuratively. [The team would be better off without poachers stalking you, just for a chance to grab me.]

The familiar melodic twittering of the Twins interrupted our conversation, and the light of the lantern guided them to our location. They stopped at the edge of the trees, the glow of their own lantern illuminating their way.

[Are we interrupting something?] Grey asked with a mischievous smile.

[No!] Sistine yelped, rising to her feet. [I was just heading back.]

[Are you coming, also, Cyrus?] Frey invited.

[No, I think I'll stay a little longer. I'll see you back at the house.]

I extinguished the lantern to watch the glowing algae and emerging stars, and for a moment, I was reminded of the Red Lake back on Xon. When Janin and Sarc were small, we would spend hours by the maroon shore, shaping figures with the red clay soil, but in the years before the children were born, Sariah and I had spent many evenings watching the stars, listening to the quiet lapping of the gentle Red Lake waves, and dreaming of our future together.

"Would you stay here with me, if I asked you to?" Sariah had asked me once.

"You don't have to ask," I had replied. *"My home is wherever you are."*

She had giggled at my romantic pledge. *"Where wouldn't you follow me, mi aelore?"*

"I would follow you anywhere, my love."

In the end, that was a lie. When Sariah died, I had held onto life, rather than follow her in death. Sarc still needed a parent, and Sariah wanted me to continue living, except that now, I would live for both of us. As long as I was alive, some part of Sariah survived, too.

Time to rejoin the living. I relit my lantern for the return to Fenrir's house, where the festivities were ongoing and now illuminated by strings of electric lightbulbs. Fenrir was right; the settlement was populated by all manners, colors and shapes, and Sistine, Rosie and the Twins were as happy as I had ever seen them. Sistine and the Twins had managed to get Mandri up to join their circle of dancers, and Rosie was carrying a cluster of laughing children on its back for a ride through the party grounds: a raucous parade unto itself.

"Have you decided, Cyrus?" Fenrir asked.

"Almost," I said, observing the interactions amongst the settlers, especially the children. "It seems so peaceful and harmonious here."

"I'd like to think so," he said. "We had established Harbor as a shelter for our fellow Laxuyn, but others are always welcome. Over the years, it's become a bit of a nature preserve, actually. We have some unique specimens here, so we try to keep everyone protected from hunters and poachers."

Rosie joined the rest of the team in the dance, and they did seem happy and complete by themselves. They had accepted me, finally, but they didn't really need me. "Could you use a novice healer here?"

Fenrir smiled. "We could always use another set of hands, if they're guided by an open mind. You'll stay, then?"

"I think I will," I said, lulled by Harbor's simple charms. "For just a little while."

Chapter 4: No Place Like Xon

‹‹Papa! Where are you? Papa Fen!››

I refrained from answering the question, as it was not intended for me, but I did clear my throat to avoid startling the new arrival. I looked up from the kitchen counter where I had been preparing the morning tea, with a smile readied for whomever would appear in the doorway.

"Nevis?" It had been a couple of years since I had seen the *Dione*'s bartender, but the fire opal eyes and the dusky lavender complexion were unmistakable. In the morning light, Nevis looked like the embodiment of a sunrise, a mesmerizing combination of purples, reds and gold. The angles on the delicate features had become softer and more feminine since last time.

[Cyrus the Eladryz!] Nevis ran to me and threw her slender lilac-hued arms around my neck. She even smelled a little like lilacs: heady, sweet and floral.

[It's good to see you again,] I smiled, returning her embrace briefly. [You look beautiful.]

[Do you like?] she asked flirtatiously, twirling for me. [I told you I was leaning towards becoming female.] Her scarlet-orange eyes widened. [Papa hasn't even seen me yet!]

[Fenrir's collecting herbs in the garden.]

Nevis set her long-fingered hand on my chest. [Don't go anywhere. I'll be right back.]

I heard Fenrir and Nevis's joyful reunion through the open kitchen window, then their shared laughter as they returned inside together, their arms entwined. Nevis was almost Fenrir's height, perhaps a centimeter shorter, and shared his slender build but none of his colors.

Fenrir noticed my confusion. ‹‹She's adopted, but she's every bit my daughter,›› he said proudly, giving her cheek a gentle peck. ‹‹With plenty of uncles and aunts to keep an eye on her, too, wherever she is in the galaxy.››

‹‹Oh, I just saw Uncle Mandri on *Dione* last month!›› Nevis exclaimed. ‹‹He didn't say anything about Cyrus being here?››

‹‹Really? It's been well over a year,›› Fenrir said, laughing at her insulted grimace. ‹‹I think the idea is to keep this place and Cyrus secret. Speaking of which, how did you even get here? Did you pilot yourself?›› he asked, noting her fitted clothes.

‹‹I won an Alliance adder on a friendly wager,›› Nevis smiled. ‹‹Milton Sunsprite is down one ship, but he has dozens more, so he's not too broken up over it. It could use some upgrades, but she flies well, and she's in good shape.›› She noted her father's unsure frown. ‹‹I parked it in the designated clearing, don't worry,›› she assured. ‹‹None of the crops or animals were disturbed.››

‹‹Adder-class, eh,›› Fenrir said. ‹‹Did you check to make sure the weapons work?››

‹‹Of course, Papa,›› she said. ‹‹I took possession before he could off-load the missiles and rest of the artillery, too.››

Our barn cat, Carbon, strutted into the kitchen carrying something with large, sheer iridescent wings in her mouth. At first, it looked to be a dragonfly, but then I remembered where I was, and I tried to be gracious when Carbon lay the dead fairy at my feet and purred contentedly.

During my time in Harbor, I had become accustomed to shooing pesky fairies away from Fenrir's prized garden and grain stores, but it was still jarring to see the tiny winged, humyn-like beings dead, usually as gifts from Carbon or one of the other cats. Mercifully, they were quick and efficient killers, and the slaughtered fairies usually bore clean mortal wounds, like broken necks or punctures from a well-placed fang.

‹‹Oh, is it fairy season again?›› Nevis remarked, watching me dispose of the fairy in the composting crock, out of Carbon's view.

‹‹Not as many this spring,›› Fenrir said. ‹‹The cats keep the numbers under control.››

‹‹Uh, huh. And what's keeping the cat numbers under control?›› she challenged playfully.

‹‹Smart ass. We're still spaying and neutering,›› Fenrir said readily. ‹‹Except for Carbon; she seems to know when it's time and avoids us, so I don't even try to catch her anymore.››

‹‹That's our girl,›› Nevis smiled, flashing her pearly white teeth. ‹‹Survival of the fittest, isn't that the norm? And she certainly is that.››

I was just finishing my communication with Sarc when I heard a meow outside my closed door. It was late in the evening already, but I had needed to speak to my son. It was almost the end of the year 953 back on Xon, and Sarc's twenty-third birthday, and I was kiloparsecs away from home; the least I could do was wish him well and inquire about his current affairs. In turn, the sound of his voice and laughter was his gift to me, as always.

"*Harbor sounds like a nice, peaceful place,*" Sarc said.

"It is, but it's not home." I missed the ruggedness and wilderness of Xon, especially the soaring *Ajlekyrn* mountains of the Dark Lands and the soft pink sands of Mione. I missed being able to embrace my son.

"*Are you happy there?*"

"As much as I can be," I said. "It's best not to be entirely content, otherwise, complacency starts to set in, and I need to keep my focus on self-development. Fenrir helps, however he can, but it would be so much easier," I said irritably, "to just have a guidebook that teaches Eladryz how to be Eladryz."

Sarc laughed. "*You could write one.*"

"If I ever figure it out, myself," I said, thinking my vocabulary and skills were probably better suited for children's stories, for foul-mouthed children. "I'll get there, but it may take some time."

"*It would be nice for you to meet Glory before she's full-grown,*" he joked.

"That would be wonderful," I smiled, thinking of my granddaughter whom I had never met. "She's seven, now?"

"*Yes. She's precocious and impertinent, but her mother is devoted to her,*" he said, less begrudgingly than I had expected. There would never be a true reconciliation between Sarc and the woman who bore and raised his daughter, given the awful circumstances of Glory's conception, but Sarc remained a steadfast part of Glory's life. "*Glory asks about you.*"

"And what do you tell her?"

"*I tell her that you're thinking of her, as you travel amongst the stars.*"

"I think about both of you, always, my *aelore* boy," I said.

The meow sounded again, more stridently, and Sarc chuckled. "*Your lady friend beckons you,*" he teased, having heard Carbon's summons during prior calls. "*Let me not keep you. The Empress has insisted on hosting a dinner for me tonight, so I should look presentable.*"

I pictured Sarc in my head, the way he had looked the last time I saw him, almost three years earlier. With his dark golden colors, his strong, athletic form and his clever, charming half-grin, he didn't need much to look presentable. "Brush your hair and teeth, and make sure your clothes are neat and clean."

"*Yes, Dad, thank you for that reminder,*" Sarc laughed. "*I love you.*"

"I love you, too, son."

I disconnected from the comm and opened the door, expecting to see Carbon alone, but Nevis was with there, too, carrying the cat aloft in her arms. Carbon looked absurdly oversized in Nevis's slender arms, like a giant black pillow, but neither seemed to be uncomfortable with the arrangement.

[Sorry, I was just about to take her downstairs,] Nevis said. [I didn't want her to disturb your call with your son.]

[We were almost done,] I said. [She's just used to visiting me in the evening before she retires to the barn.]

Nevis loosened her hold, and the cat dropped soundlessly, purring as she circled me. Once done with her evening ritual, Carbon bounced away from me and raced down the hall and down the stairs.

Even days after her return to Harbor, I was still unused to seeing Nevis in a sundress. After remembering her in a plain shirt and apron behind the bar on *Dione*, I thought the feminine, flowing dress was far more flattering and well-suited to her personality. I was aware of her curiosity about me, but I also thought of Fenrir whenever I looked at her, and as a father myself, I understood the importance of setting firm boundaries.

[I'll see you in the morning,] I said, planting myself in the doorway. I just had to keep her at a distance for two more weeks, before her return to *Dione*.

[You know I'm older than you,] she said, her bright orange eyes riveted on me. [I'm not a child.]

[It's not the years,] I said, shaking my head. [I'm a father, and Fenrir is my friend. That makes you my child, too, by proxy.]

[I'm pretty sure that's not how that works,] she snickered. [But I respect your parental code of honor.] She sighed. [You are one of the most particular, challenging men I've ever met.]

I smiled. [I'll take that as a compliment,] I said, hoping that it meant the end of the matter.

[It is,] she said, backing away from the door finally. She twirled her way down the hall towards the stairs. [It makes the pursuit that much more interesting, and the eventual victory all the sweeter.]

Fenrir was no fool. He was nearly two hundred sixty when I met him, and he was as canny and observant as any of the Ammo siblings, so he noticed Nevis's interest in me easily. He also recognized the one-sided nature of the interest, for which I was extremely grateful, but he still cautioned me to be wary.

[Are you used to being pursued, romantically?] he asked me one morning, as he watched my target practice session in the pasture, a safe distance away from everyone else.

While I was no longer traveling with Mandri, I had continued to hone my weaponry skills. I had kept the energy pistol that we had looted from the poachers on *Dione* years earlier, and Fenrir allowed me use of his generator and workshop to keep it powered and well-maintained. When I wasn't training, I enjoyed the farm and house chores, feeling more relaxed when I didn't have to think about self-preservation.

[No, Fen, I can't say I am,] I said cagily, hitting the wooden bulls-eye easily from a hundred meters. [I've only been with a few women, and the last one was my wife.] I added, for clarity: [And I'm only attracted to women.]

[To each their own. That was fourteen years ago, nevertheless, and before your transition started,] Fenrir said. [I think you will find that prospective partners in Alliance space are more assertive with their overtures than they were on Xon. Laxuyn women, in particular, are not raised with the same gender constraints and norms as in male-dominated cultures and species, so they tend to be more expressive and outspoken.]

I aimed more carefully for the second target, ten meters further, and struck the center. [I just need to be firmer in my resolve, then.]

[I know and trust your character, Cyrus,] he said. [And Nevis is an adult, capable of making her own decisions, so if you wish to—]

[I *really* don't,] I said resolutely, pausing before attempting the third target. [Nevis is incredibly beautiful and intelligent, so my choice is not a slight against her. I'm just not looking to get involved, with anyone.]

The third target was two hundred meters away. It wasn't my best shot, but I hit the innermost circle. As I lowered the pistol, Carbon appeared. She was one of several black cats in Harbor, but she seemed to be the matriarch. She was the largest, and most accustomed to people. Carbon circled around us in a figure-eight, ending with her tail swishing around my legs.

Fenrir smiled. [With all the changes that you're undergoing, your transition gives you an extra allure, even across species.]

[Carbon's not even eligible,] I scowled. [I'm not *that* open-minded about female company.]

[I see your concern, now,] Fenrir said, rolling his eyes. [Finding you companionable doesn't mean she wants kittens with you,] he said patiently. [It just means that she likes being around you. It's not just about sex; there may be a hint of physical attraction in some cases, but probably not in this one.]

[So, if I'm clear about my boundaries, there shouldn't be any issues.]

[Not with Nevis, no,] he said amicably, then laughed as Carbon walked between my legs and stretched out between my feet. [You may need to take stronger measures with other species, who aren't as respectful of boundaries. Come to the barn when you're done,] he said, walking away. [I can use your help with preparing the tillers.]

[I'm almost finished here,] I nodded, then peered down at Carbon. [Wouldn't you rather go with Fen? I'm sure there's a nice, juicy fairy for you to dispatch there.]

Carbon swished her tail disinterestedly, then perked her ears and raised her head to stare off into the tall grasses. Before I could focus on what she had sensed, a large puff of black appeared in front of me and hissed. Carbon was on her feet instantly, but it was too late. I felt a rough shove against my leg, then my eyes went dark.

It only took me a second to realize that I wasn't in Harbor anymore, as the acrid, sulfur-stench air tightened my throat and stung my eyes. My knees buckled as a weight slammed into the back of my legs, and I fell painfully on my side, and I could just make out the black feline shape next to me.

"Carbon, what the…"

Nope, wrong, not Carbon, I realized, as the glowing yellow-green eyes glared at me. Carbon's eyes were blue-green, and she usually didn't grimace at me like this cat was doing, with teeth bared.

A muffled "pop" sounded next to me, and Carbon's sleek black shape appeared suddenly and tackled the other cat into the dusty, dead grass. The cats hissed and swiped at each other briefly, before Carbon got back on her feet and stepped back to guard me, with her back arched and her tail waving with agitation. The other cat gave a low yowl, almost indignantly, and I understood.

"Oh, for *Ajle's* sake!" I snapped. "I'm not after your girl, you stupid tomcat!"

Carbon also growled a low rebuke, stepping purposefully towards the other cat, challenging his dominance. He lowered himself and stepped aside in a show of submission, and she seemed to accept his apology. She meowed a command, and came back towards me, and he followed close behind. Together, they brushed against me.

And we were in Harbor again, back in the same spot in the pasture; my pistol was still on the ground where I had dropped it. I took a couple of deep, clarifying breaths between my last coughs, and the labored hacking noise drew Fenrir out to see what the matter was. He watched Carbon and the other cat run off into the grass and laughed.

[You finally met Nero, I see,] he said. [I should've warned you: he gets jealous easily.]

[That's an understatement.] I picked up my pistol and half-stumbled to the barn, to the water pump to wash the burning grit from my eyes. [He took me somewhere I've never seen.]

[Oh, he really didn't like you, then,] Fenrir winced. [Sorry, he usually doesn't go *that* far, otherwise I would've warned you.]

[What the hell was that place?] I asked, gulping some water to wash the acrid taste out of my mouth and throat.

[I don't know, I've never been there. I've just smelled what lingers on their fur afterwards, sometimes,] Fenrir said, without much concern. [I call it their special catch-and-release place. From time to time, I'll see one of the cats literally vanish with something, then come back a second later without it.]

[Well, that's terrifying,] I said. [If Carbon hadn't followed us, I'd be dead, or stuck there.]

[She wouldn't let anyone hurt you. You're like one of her kittens, as far as she's concerned,] he said, strolling back to the barn. [She doesn't catch fairies for just anyone.]

The evening before Nevis was scheduled to return to *Dione*, she and I took a stroll down to the lakeside to watch the sunset, as we did on most nights when the weather allowed. She was still flirtatious, but in the manner of a young woman who was testing the limitations of her charms. She knew me as a safe practice target, and Fenrir knew that I could be trusted around his daughter.

[*Monsieur du Lac*,] Nevis called out to the lake, as the first algae shimmers heralded the approach of dusk. [Jacques!]

Jacques du Lac. I had thought Fenrir was joking when he first told me our lake serpent's name, but he explained that the children of Harbor had given him that name decades ago. As the children grew up, they taught the name to their offspring, so it was permanent now.

[Does he always come when you call?] I asked, perching on my usual boulder. I hadn't seen him miss any of her calls, on every occasion that I had accompanied her to the lake.

[If he's awake,] she said. [And he's usually awake at this hour.]

Nevis and I didn't have long to wait, as the waves parted for the emerging serpent's head, followed by his long, graceful neck. She walked down into the lakebed, until the water reached almost to the hem of her knee-length dress. [I'm leaving in the morning, *Monsieur*. I've come to say farewell.]

Jacques the water serpent exhaled with a mournful sigh, bowing his head down to gently tap Nevis's crown with his chin.

She reached up and stroked the side of his jaw. [I'll miss you, too. Watch Papa for me, won't you?]

The serpent nodded glumly, with an inquiring warble.

[Next year, around this same time. Don't forget me, *Monsieur*.]

A chorus of yowling caterwauls erupted, startling Nevis and Jacques. Without the convenience of a comm, we couldn't tell what had happened, but Carbon bolted from the forest towards us, her fur spiked with agitation. The other large cat, Nero, was with her.

Facing the way that the cats had come, Nevis and I saw the looming glow of ships over the settlement. We had only started to fathom their significance and shapes when a sudden light filled the sky, followed by a quake and a deafening boom that shook the ground and air around us.

Nevis screamed and turned back towards Fenrir's house out of instinct, but she only got as far as the tree line when I grabbed her, also instinctively.

‹‹Let me go! We have to help!›› she shrieked, struggling against me.

[I know, but listen to me!] I shouted over her. [We won't be of any use, if we're dead.] I turned her to face the burning forest between us and the settlement. [We can't go back that way.]

Jacques growled, his head lifted to the sky briefly, before he plunged into the inky water. I tugged Nevis back from the shore, as one of the ships approached overhead, stopping over the lake where the serpent had dived. It dropped a couple of explosive charges into the lake, seemingly trying to spook or anger Jacques into revealing himself.

[No, they can't,] Nevis sobbed, shaking her head. [He's the last of his kind.]

The ship seemed to be waiting for some sign of movement, for something to target. Even Carbon and Nero were perfectly still, watching the ship with their wide and wary reflective eyes, but Carbon was pointed with her paw raised expectantly, ready to bolt.

[Don't leave unless you see a clear way back,] I said to Nevis, then met Carbon's eyes. [Lead the way.]

As Nero stayed to guard Nevis, Carbon was off like a shot, weaving between boulders and the old-growth trees that were more resistant to the inferno consuming the younger trees. After my months of missions keeping up with Mandri and his team, the habit had been ingrained in me to keep my head low, as I followed closely through the tight spaces. As I had hoped, the ship had redirected its attention towards Carbon and me, the main moving targets within range, and began to follow us.

Carbon led me away from the lake, which I hoped would keep our lake serpent and Nevis out of danger, but I stopped when I realized that the ship was turning back. Then, I saw the Jacques's shadowy form emerge from the lake again, and head towards the opposite shore, luring the ship away from Nevis, who was screaming to him to save himself.

In my frustration, I hurled a rock at the ship. It didn't even come close to it before falling into the lake with a sad "plop," but my motion and subsequent yell drew the ship's attention, just momentarily.

It was enough. Jacques disappeared into the water again, and another ship came to join our gathering. It fired on our attacker, only damaging its wing, but the attacking ship began to fly erratically, anyway, and plummeted into the lake to its ruin. Our savior circled back towards the settlement.

‹‹That's my *Persephone*! Who's flying my ship?›› Nevis demanded, watching it fly away.

I looked around Nevis. [Where's Nero?]

A quiet "pop" signaled Nero's return, and he shook his sopping black coat, with a shredded scrap from a flight suit still stuck in his teeth, as he yowled indignantly about his involuntary plunge in the lake. He had blinked into the attacking ship and was ultimately the reason for the pilot losing control. Carbon stepped to his side and began to groom him as a way of expressing her affection and approval, and he quieted to a surly purr.

In the meantime, I tried to focus on the smoldering debris of the ship slowly sinking, noticing some movement amongst the wreckage, and I realized that someone had survived and was sputtering and struggling to stay afloat. [Look, over there. Maybe we can get some answers—]

Jacques arced gently out of the water, clamped his jaws onto the screeching man, and dove back under with barely a ripple.

[Never mind,] I murmured.

[We don't need answers,] Nevis said, her voice hard. [I know *exactly* who ordered this.]

Nevis and I followed Carbon and Nero back to the settlement, where the fires were stifled and smothered by the settlers, or had started to burn out on their own, without enough flammable material in the stone structures or the new spring growth to fuel them. Nevis and the cats returned to the house to check on Fenrir, while I helped to extinguish the remaining fires and treat some of the injured, depending on where the help was most needed.

[Cyrus.] Hearing Fenrir's voice, I scanned the crowd and spotted him coming from the clearing where Nevis had left her ship.

[You flew *Persephone*,] I realized. [Nevis is up at the house, looking for you.]

[She'll figure it out and come back down,] he said. [Is Jacques all right?]

[*Monsieur du Lac*? He's fine. The lake is a little cluttered with wreckage, though.]

‹‹Papa!›› came Nevis's relieved cry, as she came running into Fenrir's waiting arms. ‹‹Thank Nafre that you're all right!›› She pulled away and wrinkled her nose with a pout. ‹‹You smell like the pine air freshener in *Persephone*'s cockpit.››

[If you bring a ship to Harbor, I claim the right to test-fly it,] he said smartly. [You want to explain why Ghanisi ships came all the way out here to Harbor?] he asked mildly, but his expression was much sterner.

Ghanisi. The name set off alarms in my head immediately, from my personal experience during my early days traveling with Mandri.

[I hadn't told anyone where I was going, just that I would be out of contact for a couple of weeks. I haven't done anything against Ghanis, I swear,] she said. [Uncle Mandri just sent me a message telling me to stay out of sight for a while.]

Fenrir frowned. [When he and I last spoke, he had mentioned that he had left Ghanis in a hurry, but he didn't tell me that you might be in danger because of it. You should've told us when you arrived, whether or not you expected to be followed.]

Nevis twisted her dark purple lips worriedly. [I'm sorry. The damage to the buildings looked bad, even from the lake.]

Fenrir sighed. [Everyone will be fine, and our homes have survived worse. That's not the point.] He grasped her shoulders. [If there was a chance that we would be visited, it's better to over-prepare. Jacques and Cyrus shouldn't have to put themselves at risk, if they don't have to.]

Nevis looked at me abashedly. [I didn't mean to cause trouble.]

[I know. Forget about it,] I said, trying to deflect the blame from Nevis. It wasn't her fault that Harbor had been attacked. [Do you know where Mandri is, now?]

Fenrir answered, [Not the specifics, but he's not far from Ghanis. The *Shakti* was captured in neutral space and impounded, and the crew detained, so he's trying to figure out how to get them out without getting himself caught.]

I worried about the welfare of the team. [How far is Ghanis from here?]

[Ghanis has its own jump gate,] Nevis said, [so distance is not an issue, and *Persephone* has her own short-range jump engine to get closer, if necessary.] She looked at my warily. [I won't take you to Ghanis.]

[Then let me take *Persephone*,] I said. [Is it still registered under Milton Sunsprite?]

[No!] she shot back.

[Yes,] Fenrir corrected. [He hasn't transferred the ownership to you yet. The displays on *Persephone* are still showing his name, which is probably how the Ghanisi found you. They probably paid him for the locations of all his ships and saw that his adder was here.]

[Well...] she started, then sulked. [She's still my ship.]

[Of course,] I said. [But we can *pretend* she's Milton's a little longer. You can drop me off on Ghanis and jump away before anyone notices.]

[What's your offer?] Fenrir asked. [Everything on Ghanis revolves around trade and commodities, so if you plan on negotiating for the *Shakti* and her crew's release, it needs to be an irresistible deal.]

[It is,] I said confidently. [I'm going to offer them something they've wanted for years now.]

Fenrir knew exactly what I was proposing. [Absolutely not!] he exclaimed.

[Do you know what they would do to you?] Nevis added, catching on quickly.

[Yes, I have some idea,] I said gravely. Enslavement of one sort or another. [But I'd be kept alive, which is more than I can presume for the crew of the *Shakti*.]

Chapter 5: The Puppeteer of Ghanis

The few days spanning the time Nevis and I left Harbor to when I arrived in the Overlord's court in Ghanis, passed in a blur. Fenrir and Nevis had made contact with Mandri, and the three of them conspired on a scheme for getting the *Shakti* and her crew freed.

I wasn't allowed to hear very much of it, except for where my participation was pivotal.

[It's not that we don't trust you,] Mandri had said, [but Ghanis is overrun with politics and corruption, and you, my friend, need to be remain guileless and trustworthy in order for this plan to have any chance of success.]

I blocked myself from thinking about the planning conversations and my assigned objectives, as I was escorted by an armed guard detail, from the Alliance's Diplomatic Marina to the Overlord's District. The District was where most matters concerning Ghanisi commerce and government were conducted, and it was as opulent and beautiful as the surrounding region looked neglected and oppressed, from what I saw of the area from the plush seat of my climate-controlled air coach.

The half-dozen guards were silent and unsmiling under their darkened visors, so I didn't bother asking where I was being taken, or why. All I knew was that, as soon as Nevis had downloaded *Persephone*'s manifest to Ghanisi port control and opened the hatch for me, she surprised me with a sound kiss, as though she didn't expect to see me again for a while.

[For luck,] she had smiled, stepping back from me. [Just relax, and be yourself.]

[Take care of my things while I'm gone,] I said, with feigned confidence.

By the time I had disembarked and watched *Persephone*'s shining silver form pull out of the slip and disappear back into her own jump gate, the guards had arrived with orders to escort me to the Overlord's District.

As we stopped inside the gates of what I could only assume to be the Overlord's palace, judging by its massive scale and gaudy, ornate architecture, I was reminded of the comparative grace and simplicity of the Realm's Imperial palace. It was smaller and plainer, by design. Nothing in the Imperial palace was frivolous or wasteful; Emperor Jaeris would've never had acres of useless lawn or hundred-meter-high fountains installed while his constituents had to drink from puddles or stagnant wells, as I had watched some of the citizens in Ghanis do.

The guards steered me into an anteroom and ordered me to wait, without any indication of timing, so I remained on my feet. I peered into a mirror that hung over the polished stone fireplace and barely recognized myself. The brick-red, tailored Alliance uniform was unlike anything that I had worn before, and I still wondered how Mandri had gotten one that fit me so well. My hair was dark amber and curling around my ears and collar, but I was at least clean-shaven, for the first time in weeks, since before Nevis's return home to Harbor.

Nevis. The thought of her made me smile. Not in the same way that memories of Sariah made my heart soar, but there was an integrity and nobility to Nevis's character that fostered my friendship with Fenrir and Mandri. If they could help raise an individual like Nevis and earn her love and respect into adulthood, then they were worthy and true friends, and I was glad to help them. *Even if I don't know what I'm supposed to do.*

A courtier, accompanied by two guards, entered the chamber without bothering to knock and bowed stiffly. [The Overlord's Consort demands your presence.] The man gave me a quick, thorough look, to confirm that I wasn't brandishing weapons — or that I wasn't wearing anything too unfashionable, perhaps — and turned on his heel to lead the way out.

More guards were posted on either side of a set of oversized, gilded doors, which they opened at our approach. Beyond the doors — surprise — was another ostentatious, flamboyant chamber, but this one had a central throne, with a slightly smaller throne adjacent to it.

Across the smaller throne lounged a dark-haired, dark-eyed woman, wearing an embroidered, gilded robe that most people I knew wouldn't have worn outside their bedchambers. Certainly not a public figure receiving strangers in an official setting, in any capacity. There were a handful of courtiers scattered about the throneroom, but none of them seemed to find the woman's posture or clothing the least bit out of place.

[Cyrus Ex,] the courtier announced, as I gave my best bow, as I had recalled it from my days visiting Jaeris and Adella in court. [By your request, your Grace,] he said, following with his own bow, which was far more respectful than the one he had given me.

The Overlord's Consort stood from her throne, her dark eyes focused in my direction, but not necessarily on me. She stepped down daintily from her platform and approached our group with a sinuous gait, and her courtier and guards backed away from me once she was closer.

I stood still, letting the Consort circle me at her leisurely pace. She was not subtle with her gaze, as she looked me over from head to toe and back again.

By Ajle, it's not like she's never seen a man before. I found her prolonged interest both amusing and puzzling, but I kept my countenance bland and neutral. As she passed in front of me, I had a chance to study her features up close. It was hard to tell her age, with her skin and features smooth and supple with the benefit of careful maintenance and luxurious pampering, but her eyes were jaded, cold and assessing.

[Has he been scanned?] she asked her courtier.

He bowed his head. [He carries no weapons.]

[Leave us,] she commanded the room, and she waited until she and I were alone in the throneroom before she spoke. [What species are you, 'Cyrus Ex'?]

[Does it matter, your Grace?] I answered.

[No, perhaps not.] She stood in front of me and looked up into my eyes, her dark brown eyes trying to read my blank visage, but her gaze drifted to my mouth. [Your name on your ship's manifest raised a flag, as we don't often receive anonymous-sounding entities in our ports. What is your *real* name?]

[Cyrus E'lan,] I said simply. I wasn't lying, just incomplete in my answer.

[There is a rumor that you are Eladryz. Are you?]

[If I were, then I would be very unwise to show myself in this sector, or to identify myself as such,] I said. [Besides, EladryzZurylan hasn't been a viable world in centuries, so I must be from elsewhere.]

[That is a shame,] the Consort pouted, [I've never been with an Eladryz man, before. You would've been the first.]

I stifled my laugh, doubting very much that I would've been her first *anything*. I restored my neutral visage when I noticed her crossness at my reaction, but I didn't bother to hide my skepticism. [You lack subtlety, your Grace, but I am flattered by your interest.]

[I made a passing remark,] she said frostily, but she did not back away. [It was not an offer.]

While nothing was spoken, her proximity and hungry stare could not be mistaken for anything but an invitation. Still, I decided to play along with her show of false chastity. [Well, if I've satisfied your curiosity, and you have no other questions, let me waste no more of your time,] I said, [and perhaps I can resume my search for my crew.]

She set her hand on my chest to detain me, and her boldness did prevent me from turning. [I have not dismissed you, nor am I finished with you.] She touched my face and raised herself on her toes to brush her lips against mine. [You will stay, as long as I demand it.]

Oh, great. I was annoyed by her presumptuousness, but felt little else for her. The kiss had barely registered at all, as it was so light as to be nearly imperceptible and void of any genuine emotion. She had done it because she could so with impunity, just as I could indulge in baiting her without worrying about hurting any real feelings.

I couldn't help comparing her to Adella, who was a fraction of the Consort's age and whose dominion on Xon spanned less than a continent, but whose respected authority was engendered and bolstered by her own force of will and charisma. The Consort before me had little of Jaeris's daughter's self-awareness and none of her practiced statesmanship. This woman enjoyed her authority as bestowed by her ties to her privileged husband and possibly as a political convenience to others, but she had little appreciation of what had been gifted to her. I imagined she similarly took most of her extravagances for granted, with barely a thought spared for those who had access to none of them.

[And what else would you have me do for you?] I asked, disinterested and a little bored. I refused to yield a centimeter to her, even as she scratched her gilded nails down the front of my shirt.

[If I commanded you to pleasure me, what would you do?]

I tried to maintain a semblance of interest, but I found her disappointingly easy to read, especially given her exalted status. She was sexually curious about my exotic nature and cryptic manner, but was she attracted to me? Probably not. [I would most likely disappoint you. I have little knowledge about how to please women,] I ventured to discourage her. [I would probably offend you with my coarseness and inexperience.]

My steadfast lack of interest helped me to delivered the lie straight-faced. I could almost imagine Sarc bellowing with laughter at hearing me say such ludicrous things, but I had to try something to dissuade the Consort without disrespecting her outright.

To my dismay, she seemed more enthralled. [Then, perhaps you would benefit from some lessons on how to treat females with respect and tenderness.] I wondered briefly whether she was calling my bluff, then my mind blanked, as she opened her robe to expose herself to me. [Or, in the interest of cultural discourse, you can show me how you treat the women on your world, whatever world that is.]

A part of me — one can easily guess which part — prodded me to set aside my prudishness and just give in to instinct, and I briefly considered the possibility that I was just prolonging the inevitable: if she really wanted me, she'd find a way to have me. Perhaps it would be easier to submit to her demands now, in hopes of being allowed to go free as soon as possible. It was just as likely that she would eventually tire of my continued rebuff and order my prompt execution for my lack of cooperation.

I was spared a decision by the loud rattle of the heavy doors opening. The Consort stepped back and hastily refastened her robe, as the doors yawned wide, and the Overlord marched into the reception hall, with a beautiful, graceful woman next to him. I barely paid attention to the overstuffed robe and porcine head that called himself Overlord of Ghanis, but I was riveted by his courtier.

The woman wore jet-black hair with vivid, electric blue streaks and a tailored, fitted grey suit that was styled like the male courtiers' uniforms, except that hers showed off her hourglass figure and long, shapely legs, ending with spiked-heeled shoes that somehow didn't impede her bold stride. Her cobalt-blue eyes flashed briefly over me but returned quickly to the Overlord and his Consort.

[Your Grace,] the woman greeted her Overlord's Consort with a low, respectful bow.

[How formal you are, dear Nova,] the Consort said, almost smirking. [As the elder sister, you needn't be so proper with me.]

[One must always be respectful to one's betters,] the other woman said, a dangerous edge to her silky voice, like the sound of a knife against a steel.

[We've been notified that Nova has been chosen by the Alliance Nexus to join their tribunal,] the Overlord said, disregarding the verbal sparring between the sisters. [Who is this?] he asked with a dismissive glance at me.

[He was detained at the port. According to his shuttle's manifest, he claims that he is looking for his crew, that was last seen in neutral space near Ghanis,] the Consort said, looking very bored by the details.

[That is hardly a matter that requires the attention of the Overlord,] Nova said stiffly, casting a furtive glance at her sister. She seemed to assess the situation quickly and well enough to know that I was there against my will. [Let him trouble you no further, your Grace,] she said to her sister. [I will deal with this matter personally,] she offered. [He is clearly not Ghanisi, so I should deal with the matter as an Alliance inquiry.]

[Thank you, Nova,] the Overlord nodded, turning his hungry gaze to his much younger Consort. [I trust you'll be able to see to his needs and concerns to his satisfaction.]

[With pleasure, your Grace,] Nova said demurely, with a departing bow. [Come with me, please.]

We departed the throne room in silence, and I noted the Consort's affronted expression as her dark eyes followed us out. Once out of the room, Nova waved aside the awaiting guards and courtiers with a stern glower, establishing her unquestionable authority and command of the situation. Once we were beyond the watch of guards in the hallway, I quickened my step but still struggled to keep pace with Nova's gazelle-like gait.

[My name is Cyrus—]

[I don't care,] she said tersely. [Save it until we can speak more privately.]

[This isn't private?] I asked, looking around futilely for some indication of surveillance.

[This must be your first time to Ghanis,] she said. [My office is just up this way,] she said, turning sharply to the right, almost forcing me to stop short, then breaking almost into a canter for the last several meters to her office. The guards posted by her doors opened them without prompting.

[I am not to be disturbed,] she said brusquely, passing through the doors.

[Understood, Ma'am,] the guards said in unison, and shutting us inside.

In the cocoon-like stillness of her office, Nova crossed her arms and gave me an evaluating perusal. At my lack of response, she remarked: [No doubt my sister has given you a thorough ogling already. Did she just look at you, or was she more hands-on?]

[She didn't have much of a chance to do much more than look,] I said.

[Thank the Overlord's vigilance for your reprieve; he rarely lets her out of his sight for more than a few minutes. Please, have a seat,] she said, more cordially, but she remained on her feet, in order to switch on the surveillance dampening system from a control located behind one of her planters. [I don't normally mind the monitoring devices, for my own security, but this is not my usual course of business. Your name is Cyrus, you said?]

[Yes, Cyrus Ex,] I answered, taking the straight-backed guest chair between her desk and the more comfortable, upholstered seating arranged behind us.

[Unlikely, but deliberately so,] she said. [Your *real* name, if you please.]

[E'lan,] I said shortly, waiting for a change in her expression.

Instead, her face remained inscrutably blank. [E'lan. I met someone a few years ago by that name, and you remind me of him. Pity,] she sighed, [he was all business, too.]

Nova, how do I know the name? Sarc and Slither had mentioned working with someone in the Alliance to free Brahn…was this the same woman? She didn't seem to be feigning her familiarity with his name. [I apologize, you have me at a disadvantage. I've only heard your name briefly, in passing.]

[My name is Eroshim Nova, but you can just call me 'Nova,'] she said, perching on the edge of her desk close to me, crossing one long leg over the other. [I am the ambassador for Ghanis, to the Alliance Nexus, and newly appointed to the tribunal.]

[Congratulations, Nova,] I said, keeping my eyes on her face, instead of wandering to her legs.

[It's an additional time-suck and five more weekly meetings that I don't need on my schedule,] she said bluntly. [But it's visibility, and I would be the first Ghanisi to be on the tribunal in over a hundred years.]

[Congratulations are definitely in order, then, Ambassador Eroshim,] I said with a half-smile.

She looked at me askance. [That grin is unmistakable. You are related to him, aren't you?]

[I'm sorry?]

[You're not from around here,] she commented. [I don't just mean Ghanis. You're not from an Alliance world at all.]

[I'm not sure how you could tell such a thing, Nova,] I said. [There are hundreds of systems and civilizations in the Alliance.]

[Yes, I know. I've met representatives from many of them.] She leaned closer to me. [But none of them has ever said my name like you. There was the *other* E'lan, whose voice is like yours: E'lan Alessarc.] She straightened and smiled knowingly. [I never forget a name or face, no matter how brief the acquaintance. Same uncommon surname, so is he a relative of yours, or not?]

I looked at her evenly. [What does this have to do with my crew?]

She clicked her tongue with disapproval. [You must give something to get something, Cyrus. 'E'lan' is not a subtle name, if you're trying to hide your Eladryz origin, but 'Ex' is almost worse, as a blatant attempt at anonymity. You're lucky that I'm not as mercenary as some of my colleagues and brethren.]

[If I were whom you purport, you wouldn't turn me in for a bounty?] I asked skeptically.

[No, I give you my word, as a daughter of the noble House of Eroshim,] she said humorlessly. [I'd like to help you, but you must demonstrate a little good faith, first.]

What do I have to lose? [Alessarc is my son,] I admitted finally.

[Son, really? I would've guessed brother. No matter,] she said, slipping off the desk to return to her side of it. She pulled up a few displays and did a quick read-through. [Ship registered to one of Ammo Sulimandri's aliases?] she remarked, glancing at me. [Those Ammo boys, always causing trouble. Your crew is held in Building 4, the tall, black cuboid diagonally across the Commons, behind the sentry towers.] She tapped her painted, nimble fingertips across the display, typing a quick message with a skilled, practiced rhythm. [There. I've requested that they be processed for release. There are no charges that I see that should require their detention. A fine for resisting seizure, perhaps, but nothing more significant than that.]

[That's it? There's nothing about any embezzlement plot against the Overlord?] The way Mandri had described it, he had managed to disable a number of the Overlord's private financial accounts and redirect the funds elsewhere.

Nova raised her arched brow. [If such a thing ever *were* to happen, it would be a personal embarrassment for the Overlord, especially if the magnitude of the losses were ever to become public knowledge. His Grace is unlikely to bring charges for such offenses, as it is far easier and quicker to locate and seize the culprit's allies and assets until reparations are made.]

[Won't the Overlord be angry that you've countermanded his order?] I asked.

[He may, but unless he wants to invite scrutiny into why the *Shakti* and her crew are detained without cause, he won't attempt to reprimand me,] she said. [He was trying to intimidate Mandri into surrendering, but no one in the Ammo family gets intimidated easily.]

I got to my feet, feeling a great weight being lifted from my head. [Thank you, Nova. That was very expedient of you.]

She nodded and shut off her display. [I can accompany you there, after we're done here.]

[There's something else?] I asked. *There's always a catch, isn't there?*

She circled back around the desk and stood in front of me. [In most diplomatic negotiations on Ghanis, there is always an exchange of favors. On simple matters, it can be a handshake, and for trickier arrangements,] she said, running her fingertips up my arm, [it can be more involved.]

[I'm guessing that this falls into the latter category,] I said.

[It is simply the way of things on Ghanis,] she said. [Those in positions of power offer their influence, and those who require an authority's intervention,] she said, taking a step closer, [trade other services or desirable goods. Themselves, if there is nothing else to offer.]

[I apologize, this is not of type of bartering that I'm used to,] I said. [I don't think of people like that, like wares for trading.]

Nova twisted her lips with a twinge of disappointment. [Perhaps I should call for a surrogate then, someone who can accommodate both of us? I just assumed, since you have a son, that you preferred women, but...]

[What? No!] I shook my head. [I mean, yes, I do prefer women,] I said quickly. [And you are absolutely stunning, Nova, but I haven't been with anyone since my wife died and ... I don't even know why you'd even want to hear any of that.] I took a deep breath. [There must be something else I can offer you in gratitude, in place of intimacy.]

Nova was considering it. [You have a persuasive voice. That gives away that you're Eladryz, as much as your name does. I could certainly use someone with your innate skills...] Her voice trailed, and a slight wrinkle appeared between her carefully-groomed eyebrows.

[All right, Cyrus E'lan, have it your way,] she said finally. [I imagine my sister has already offered herself to you, so I must seem a poor second choice, by comparison. Consider our debt settled,] she said, touching my hand briefly as final gesture of acceptance. [Your secret, and your son's, are safe with me.]

[That's it?] I asked uncertainly. [You don't want anything else from me?]

[That's it, Cyrus,] she said simply. [Your devotion to your late wife is very sweet and romantic, and forcing you to break your expired marriage vows would inflict more guilt on me than I'd care to entertain.]

[Thank you, Nova,] I said, raising her hand and bowing my head to kiss it softly. [I would never consider you a second choice, by the way, by any measure or comparison.]

Nova tossed her head back in laughter. [You should tell my ex-husband that!] she said, setting her hand playfully on my shoulder. She snatched her hand back instantly, regretting the touch. [I'm sorry, Cyrus. I forget sometimes what's in my perfumes.] She meant the potent chemicals and pheromones that were typical in Ghanisi colognes. [You don't deserve to be manipulated like that. Maybe you should step outside and clear your head.]

I was unaffected by her perfume, but I was impressed by her concern. [I'm fine, Nova. I'm not entirely unaware of Ghanisi practices and ruses,] I smiled. [You're incredible, but I'm also still deeply in love with my wife.]

[How refreshing to meet an honorable man,] she said. [Your loyalty seems a bit extreme, given her passing...]

[It would still feel like betrayal,] I said.

[Even a single kiss?] Nova teased. [Surely, she would've forgiven you for a little stolen peck now and then.]

For Nova's help, I owed her a small token of gratitude. [I think she would allow it, especially for a friend.] I brushed back a strand of Nova's hair, cupped her cheek in my palm and kissed her deeply.

She was surprised that I had followed through with it, and I was surprised at how sweet and lovely the kiss felt. Perhaps I did miss that kind of intimacy more than I admitted to myself, but I was tempted to savor the passion and tenderness of Nova's kiss a little longer. I withdrew after what felt like a minute but was probably only a few seconds.

However long it was, Nova looked a little dazed. I tucked back a loose blue curl from her cheek and brushed my fingers teasingly along the edge of her lips, that were still slack and full with anticipation.

I smiled, secretly glad that I had exceeded her expectations. [How was that?]

[I suppose renegotiating our bargain is no longer an option,] she sighed, composing herself. [What's done is done. Let's go collect your friends.]

I remained on the *Shakti* with the crew until we reached the outpost *Dione*, where we reunited with Mandri and Nevis. I couldn't tell who had been more relieved and surprised to see me: Sistine and the crew when Nova accompanied me to free them, or Mandri and Nevis when we arrived at *Dione* without their assistance or intervention.

[You were faster than our contacts could update us,] Mandri said, impressed. [You went from disembarking at the port to getting everyone released in a day. You were only supposed to be a distraction, and let us take care of the rest.]

Nevis slid a glass of sparkling gold liquid in front of me. [He showed some initiative, Uncle Mandri. I think it's commendable.] She carried a tray of drinks to Sistine, Rosie and the Twins at their corner table and lingered to chat with them.

I sipped the drink that Nevis had served me. It was cool and slightly spicy, with the tiny suspended gold flecks sharp and bracing on the tongue, like ice crystals. [I didn't have to do much at all, once I met the right contact.]

[Eroshim Nova?] Mandri guessed. [She's the only one in the Overlord's District with scruples worth noting, and she navigates the Ghanisi bureaucracy with breathtaking efficiency.]

I nodded. [She's the reason I was able to get the *Shakti* out so quickly.] I looked askance at Mandri. [Did you ask Nova to watch for me?]

Mandri didn't answer, choosing that moment to take a deep drink from his stein. [She and my family go back some years. What did you think of her?]

[She's impressive,] I said. [She's smart and beautiful, and somehow, I think she wields more influence and power than the Overlord himself.]

Mandri grinned. [That's a good and fair observation. She can do quite a bit, because she operates behind the curtain and spends a good portion of her time away from Ghanis. But she's a female in a traditionally male role, so she's learned to exploit the disregard and discount by her peers, to her own advantage.]

[In what way?]

He shook his head. [I don't know all the specifics, but I know she's not one to be underestimated or ignored. She's much better to have as an ally than an enemy.]

I reexamined my interaction with Nova and could not think of a moment when I had cause to antagonize or malign her. [She was perfectly pleasant and charming with me. I can't see why anyone would dismiss or fight with her.]

Mandri snickered into his drink. [That's a question you should ask Kurashi Kilaran, her ex-husband.]

[Kilaran. How do I know that name?]

[Kilaran is my sister's partner, now,] Mandri said. [He was also one of the men that your son helped to free from the Praimos's custody years back. Nova was involved with that part of the endeavor, as well.]

[It sounds like they're getting along fairly well,] I said, [for former spouses.]

He smiled. [They get along better now as acquaintances than they ever did while they were married.]

Nevis slipped back behind the bar and shook her head at our half-empty glasses. [You drink like children. Your beverages are on the house, you know.]

Mandri shook his head. [There's no need for that,] he said. [For what the crew has suffered, I'm happy to cover the bill. I have deeper pockets than you, especially now.]

Nevis chuckled. [Okay, Uncle Mandri. You have a point there.] She left us to pull another round of drinks for the crew.

[Did you really empty the Overlord's accounts?] I asked quietly.

[Not all of them, but the ones hidden from public record,] Mandri admitted readily. [He uses them primarily to manage illicit private transfers, like bribes and contracts.]

I had almost forgotten that Ghanis had a standing contract for the capture of Eladryz like me, then I remembered the Consort's keen and aggressive attention. [What is their fascination with my species, anyway?]

[Who knows?] Mandri shrugged. [He's been obsessed with the mystique of your people for years.]

Nevis picked up her head. [There is that small matter of a prophecy, too.]

Mandri grunted his disdain, as he usually did when anything magical or supernatural was mentioned. [He's a bigger fool that I gave him credit for.] He met my confused stare. [Years ago, the Overlord had his fortune read at a state dinner by some professional charlatan, who told him that his downfall would be 'precipitated by a child of the unbowed.']

[He heard the word 'unbowed' and automatically associated it with the Eladryz?] I had heard my dead homeworld called Eladryz the Vanquished, Eladryz the Desolate ... but "Unbowed" was one of the more popular labels, too. I shook my head, angry that the entire population of my dwindling race was targeted on the basis of some despot's paranoid superstition. [It's like hearing 'lizard people' and immediately thinking 'Laxuyn.']

[Something like that.] Nevis set a glass of fruit nectar in front of me, noticing that I hadn't touched much of my first drink. [That's the Overlord's obsession, anyway. His Consort is purported to be fixated on cuckolding her husband with as many Alliance species as possible, and an Eladryz is still on her wish list.]

Well, that explains the Consort's interest. I sipped my nectar mutely as Mandri frowned his disapproval at Nevis. [You hear entirely too much salacious gossip out here on *Dione.*]

She laughed. [I'm a bartender, Uncle. Trading gossip is part of the job.] She looked at me. [Well, are you ready to head back to my Papa's farmstead, or are you throwing in with Uncle Mandri's crew again?]

That was a dilemma that weighed on me heavily. On the one hand, life was peaceful on Harbor, on Fenrir's farm, but on the other, I could help the people I cared about more readily, if I lived amongst them again. I could also confront and combat those who hunted and stalked my kind, instead of hiding and waiting to be found.

Mandri wiped the stray drops of his ale from his whiskers and beard. [It's a big decision to make, Cyrus.]

[What would you do, if you were in my place?] I said.

[Depends,] Mandri said. [When I was younger and brasher, I rarely stayed anywhere for more than a year or so, because there was so much to do and see. As I became older, I wanted to slow down, but there were too many responsibilities that demanded my regular attention,] he said, avoiding a glance at his crew's table.

[Harbor and the *Shakti* will both always welcome you, but I may have a third option for you to consider,] Mandri said. [I could take you someplace where you can study and train without fear of being hunted, or endangering others with your presence.]

[That sounds intriguing,] I said, drawn by the idea of not having to worry about anyone around me. [What's the catch?]

[It's more isolated than you may find comfortable,] he forewarned. [And I do have to check with the hostess first, on whether she can accommodate you on such short notice.]

Chapter 6: Free-Range Tiamat

Mandri's eyes darted to the comm panel on the console, time and again. It was subtle, like an occasional glance at a rock or a houseplant to make sure that nothing unexpected would happen, except that he *was* expecting something to happen.

I checked my satchel a final time. Not that I had bothered to unpack much since Nevis had returned my belongings that she kept for me, during my brief visit to Ghanis, but I wanted to make sure that my weapons were still safely stowed. "Is this your friend's usual habit, to meet you in the middle of empty space?" I asked at last. "We're parsecs away from any outposts or settlements."

"It's what I prefer, for her sake," Mandri nodded. "She's not the type that blends in."

"Is that why she lives alone?" I was expecting to meet a grizzled crone or some misshapen wretch, but I was keeping my mind open for anything. Mandri had certainly never disappointed me with his variety of acquaintances for me to meet.

"She is singular, in all senses of the word." Mandri turned around in his seat to face me. "Despite Fenrir's assertion, I'm not above asking for help when matters are beyond my ability to handle. You need more than what he or I can provide. The *Oelivan* and *Shakti* can outrun most things, but if you're going to have poachers and hunters consistently on your tail, you need someone faster and more skilled at hiding."

I frowned, thinking immediately of home. "But you still think Xon's going to be safe, that no one will hunt for Sarc?"

"If anyone looks for Sarc, it won't be because he's your son," Mandri said drolly. "Sorry, I shouldn't have joked about that," he amended, noting my trepidation. "Sarc will be fine; Slither and others will keep an eye on him. It is better for both of you, to have some distance."

The proximity sensor triggered, but there was nothing on the displays. A single word flashed on the comm: *Incoming.*

"There she is," Mandri said brightly.

I stared, as the behemoth appeared suddenly on the display grid in front of us. There was no viewscreen in the cockpit of the *Oelivan*, but I imagined that whatever it was, would have filled my entire field of vision. "That's really close," I said, noting its position, practically on top of us.

"Don't worry," Mandri said blandly. "She doesn't hit anyone unless she intends it."

Mandri powered down the engines and took the navigation controls offline. The *Oelivan* shifted just slightly, then drifted forward smoothly, and I realized that we were being towed into the larger vessel.

Mandri stood from his seat and stretched overhead, grazing the bulkhead with his long fingers. "Come on, Cyrus. It's best not to keep her waiting."

Once the *Oelivan* came to a stop, Mandri powered off the remaining ship functions and led me off the skiff. As I stepped off, I gawked at the cavernous, empty and pristine docking bay. Devoid of people or other ships, the bay's dimensions nonetheless suggested that it had been designed to accommodate several vessels at a time.

"This was one of the Laxuyn worldships," Mandri explained, leading me to one of the exits with barely a glance around. "She helped evacuate the population of our planet when it came time to leave."

I considered the timeline. "That was eons ago, but she looks brand new."

Mandri grinned, touching one of the wall panels to open the door to the lift, which was perfectly timed to our arrival. "Self-care is a worthy virtue."

Inside the lift, I noticed that there were no controls to indicate our intended destination. Mandri was nonplussed and announced: "Bridge, please." The ride was brief, and when the doors opened, Mandri gestured for me to step off first.

The bridge itself was also empty, except for autonomous machines that zipped around the circular chamber, and a continuous console that looked as though it had once held displays. "Where is everyone?" I whispered to Mandri.

Mandri threw up his hands, gesturing to the chamber. "This *is* everyone."

‹‹Welcome back, Mandri,›› intoned a warm, soothing woman's voice in Laxuyn. ‹‹I didn't think you'd be back quite so soon.››

I looked around the bridge for a source of the voice, but Mandri shook his head to let me know not to bother. [I'm grateful that you were able to receive us so quickly,] he said. [May I introduce Cyrus

75

E'lan,] he said, glancing at me expectantly.

Uncertain of where to face, I bowed awkwardly. [Hello. Thank you for your hospitality.]

The woman's voice trilled with soft laughter. [You've brought another Xonen, how wonderful! Welcome, Cyrus E'lan.]

"She can tell by your accent. She also knows the Xonen languages, too, so you may speak to her in whatever feels comfortable to you," Mandri advised. "Hold still."

"What?" I started, feeling a pinch behind my knee. I looked down in time to see a small machine scooting away from me, into an open wall panel. "What was that?"

"She does that to everyone who comes aboard," he said. "She needs to know about your biology, your requirements… that sort of thing. It'll just be a moment for her to analyze your bloodwork."

[Eladryz!] the voice said with delight. [It is a pleasure to meet you, Mister E'lan. Your son Sarc recently stayed with me, and he honors and favors you.]

As I processed her warm response, Mandri said, "Cyrus, I'd like you to meet the Laxuyn worldship *Numolo*."

For hours after Mandri left in the *Oelivan*, I lingered in the docking bay, watching the maintenance automatons busy at work, sweeping and scrubbing the floor to return it to its meticulous state. I sat on the floor, with my back against the wall.

"Do you need a guide back to your quarters?" the *Numolo* asked softly. She spoke elfyn with a Red Lake lilt, similar to Sariah's voice.

"No, thank you, *Numolo*," I said. "I remember the way. I'm just trying to get myself acclimated. I've never been on a ship this vast…or a vessel like you, at all."

"I am considered a mid-range worldship," she said. "Some of my sisters were even larger. Would you like a tour of my facilities?"

I appreciated the *Numolo*'s attempts to be welcoming. "Perhaps later, *Numolo*. I am still adjusting to the idea of your company. It is my own limitation," I apologized. "I have lived my entire life in the company of beings like me."

"You and Sarc were the only Eladryz on Xon," she remarked.

"Like me, in the sense of bi-pedal beings with…faces," I clarified. "This feels very eerie to me."

"Would you feel more at ease if I presented a hologram to interact with you?" she offered.

I shook my head. "No, *Numolo*, I think I just have to learn how to keep an open mind about new experiences like this," I said, getting to my feet. "I used to consider myself fairly flexible and intellectually curious, but these past few years away from Xon have shown me that I am woefully inexperienced and unsophisticated when it comes to the workings of the universe."

"It is more likely that your experiences were simply more limited on Xon, as the Eladryz are known for their high adaptability and natural intelligence," she said. "You will have many opportunities to explore and study while you are in my care, if you wish to continue your education. You are, after all, still a young Eladryz adult."

"It would seem that I will have plenty of time, so I'll attempt to make the most of it," I said, amused at the idea of being considered a young adult, as I was already well in my fifties. I traced the gridlines on the floor, following them to the docking bay's outer door. It was one of the few areas on the *Numolo* with clear panels, through which I could see into space; after all, the ship herself had no need of windows.

"Would you like to see something interesting?" she offered.

"Sure. What do you mean by 'interesting'?"

"I've encountered various phenomena during my travels that some of my former passengers have found curious and worthy of study," she explained.

I noted the shifting of the view outside the bay doors, then a change in the view altogether. In terms of movement, I had felt none. "Did we just relocate?"

"I opened a gate and jumped, yes," she said. "I thought you might want to see *that*."

I caught sight of something moving very quickly, across my range of sight. It was like a large comet, except that it shone with a stronger glow and had no tail. Instead, it was accompanied by a much smaller body, a fraction of its size, that somehow stayed in its orbit. "What is that?"

"That is a hypervelocity star, with its planet in tow," the *Numolo* said. "It was thrown by its larger, binary twin thousands of years ago, and moves at great speed, which you would only be able to observe from a sufficient distance."

"That's a star?" I marveled, visually tracking the glowing body as it raced by. "How fast is it traveling?"

"Approximately, a thousand kilometers per second." The *Numolo* pivoted to keep it in view, until the star's light retreated, diminished and faded.

A thousand kilometers per second. That was like traveling from the western edge of the Inearan Peninsula to the *Ajlekyrn*, and back, in the blink of an eye. "It's quite breathtaking. I've never seen such a thing."

"Relatively few creatures have, in person. I positioned us here so that you could view it without instrumentation."

"Thank you, *Numolo*," I said humbly. "That was very thoughtful of you."

"You are very welcome, Cyrus. Your hormone levels suggested restlessness, anxiety and a level of mental uncertainty, so I felt it was best to demonstrate through a visual analogy that you are not alone in your predicament."

"Am I the star, or the planet?" I asked.

"You are both, in turns. Sometimes, you are the star, forced away from your origin against your will or knowledge, with the unknown future ahead of you. However, it can also be argued that you are the planet, pulled along into the wake of a greater destiny, helpless to stop it, yet able to maintain your individuality and not be consumed."

"For an artificial intelligence, you are very poetic," I remarked.

"All intelligence is artificial, by its nature," she replied readily. "Most sentient species develop their self-awareness either through mutation or repeated, gradual evolution against the norms set forth by their natural environments. My intelligence, such as it is, may have been programmed in a laboratory by technicians, but it feels natural and organic to me."

"I meant no offense," I said. "I'm still unused to communicating with a being like you."

"Then I am not offended," she said. "You are young and new to this galaxy, and new even to yourself. You will encounter many firsts over the course of your lifetime, and it pleases me to accompany you for however long you choose to remain with me."

I smoothed my hand down the smooth contours of her corridor wall. "I appreciate your company, Numi."

The *Numolo* giggled. "Jeysen called me that."

"I'd almost forgotten that he and Sarc had spent time with you," I said. It had been years since the boys' stay on the *Numolo*, but for a creature whose life could span millennia, it must have seemed much shorter. Feeling a paternal curiosity, I asked, "Did they behave themselves with you?"

"They were very considerate, given their age," she said. "They were friendly and respectful of my spaces, and I missed their company when they left me. Especially Jeysen."

I grinned, recognizing the swooning tone from others when talking about Sarc and Jeysen. "They were trained to act as gentlemen and perform as guardians, but it is already in their nature is to be attentive and chivalrous. I'm glad they conducted themselves well."

"You miss them, also, don't you," she observed.

"Of course, I do," I admitted. "I've been a father for more than half my life, and I'm not sure what else there is for me."

"You seek a purpose?"

"I thought I had a purpose," I said quietly, sliding down the wall to sit on the floor. "But he's outgrown me."

"That is unfair of you, Cyrus. You son should not bear you as his burden."

I was taken aback by her mild scolding tone. "Excuse me?"

"Children cannot be expected to provide meaning and purpose for their parents, as they look to their elders for their own direction and guidance," she said. "Our Laxuyn creators did not lose themselves after we outgrew our need for them; they continued to create and nurture others. So, you must create and nurture, in your own way."

"I hadn't thought about it that way," I said quietly.

The *Numolo* was silent for a moment. "Why are you here?"

"Because Mandri wanted me to remain someplace safe."

"That is how you came to be aboard, but *why* are you here?"

I didn't quite understand the question, too tired to think too deeply. "Because I trust Mandri to know how to keep me protected?" I ventured.

That apparently wasn't the answer she wanted, as she repeated, more tersely: "*Why* are you here?"

"I don't know what you're asking!" I snapped, annoyed at her stubbornness.

She paused, almost like a sigh, and tried, more gently: "Why are you?"

Her question became clearer, with the unnecessary last word removed. "I understand your question now, but I don't have an answer," I said. "I'm still adjusting to my changes."

"You will be changing throughout your life, so your adjustments will never stop," the *Numolo* said. "You may feel that you are adrift, without a clear path, but all you need is a direction. If only you still had a parent of your own."

Someone to answer my questions and provide guidance, or at the least understand my experiences and help me through them. "Unfortunately, my parents have been gone for years, and there are no other Eladryz on hand."

"Did Mandri tell you so?" Some of the gridlines glowed to form a path leading towards the interior of the ship, and as I followed the path, the door opened for me. "About other Eladryz, I mean."

"Yes, he did. Are you sending me to my room, Numi?" I joked.

"You don't have to retire to your quarters, if you don't want to, but you seem tired."

I couldn't remember the last time I had rested for longer than the span of a short nap. I had stayed awake for most of the ride in the *Oelivan* to rendezvous with the *Numolo*, too busy thinking of where I had been, and where Mandri was leading me.

"I could use some tea," I said. "Something to calm my nerves."

"I can synthesize something stronger for you?" she offered.

"No, thank you, Numi. The tea will be fine for now." I looked around the blank walls. "Do you even have a galley?"

"Not in over two hundred years," she said. "Without a crew, such spaces are redundant. Your tea will be waiting for you in your quarters."

As I approached at my door, it opened readily. My packed satchel was still on the floor next to the bed, and there was a steaming cup of tea set neatly on a saucer atop a small table against the back wall. Above the small table was a window to the outside. "That window wasn't there earlier."

"No, it wasn't," she said. "But given the amount of time you spent in the dock, I presumed that you prefer a view to the outside."

I looked through the window at the star-specked blackness of space outside, as the fragrant steam wafted from the teacup. I could just make out a sliver of the *Numolo's* gleaming silver hull if I pressed my head against the window. "Thank you, Numi. That was very considerate of you."

"You are welcome, Cyrus," she said. "You are my guest, indefinitely, so you deserve to be comfortable."

I gazed at the wispy cirrus clouds drifting across the deep azure sky, as Sariah's honey-brown hair brushed against my chin, catching in my beard. The clover and rye grass felt cool underneath me, and a brightly-hued swallowtail butterfly flitted past our heads. *I miss this.*

I know. Sariah lifted her head from my chest, and she was as beautiful and perfect as on the day we met. Her voice was warm and lyrical—stronger than it had been during the last days of her life. *But you can't stay here.*

I knew it was a dream, as it was one that I had often. Sometimes we were there, in the Dark Lands, and other times we were on the beach in Mione, and the other players changed from one night to the next, but Sariah was always with me. *I know, but I just want to stay a few minutes more.* It was the closest I would ever get to holding her again, until death would reunite us.

I don't mean this here, in the dream, she smiled, sitting up on the grass. *I mean here, in the past. I am gone, Cyrus, and you need to learn to live without me.*

I know you're gone, I said gruffly. *I remember the day we buried you on the mountain, like it was yesterday.*

Yet, here I am, mi aelore, she said. *You've taught our son to adapt, to grow from his pains, and to forgive himself, and it's time that you did the same. I am no longer suffering, I no longer feel anything.* Before my eyes, she started changing from the vibrant young woman I knew, to the weak, pale figure she was before she died. *I'm just a worm-eaten –*

Stop! I cried, and shut my eyes. I refused to see my Sariah like that. *Why are you doing this?*

Because you cannot continue to use me as a crutch, Cyrus, she said sternly, touching my cheek with a soft, warm hand to signal that it was safe for me to look at her again. *You're still clinging to me, and to your past on Xon, but you must let us go. Xon needs you to be untethered, and so do the people who depend on you.*

Untethered? *I don't understand.*

Let yourself live free of ties, free of fear. Possibly even free of loyalties. You must live apart and outside from what you cherish, so you will know what is required, when the time comes.

I'm afraid to lose you.

I will always be a part of you, my love, she said with an encouraging smile, holding out her hand. *Don't be afraid.*

I awoke before I could take her hand, the verdant, lush meadow of my dream gradually replaced by the cool, smooth surfaces of my quarters aboard the *Numolo*. It had been bittersweet to be with Sariah again, as seeing her churned up old feelings, as always, but I was also a little annoyed to be reminded of my past, when the point of her visit had been to propel me forward. How could I let her go when she still haunted me?

"Good morning, Cyrus."

"Good morning, Numi." I looked out the window at the inky emptiness, now with a chalky, pastel-hued nebula in the distance, as a service bot whirred into my chamber and delivered my morning tea and a small plate of biscuits. It felt like barely a day had passed after my arrival, before the *Numolo* had ascertained my tea temperature and flavor preferences, as well as my favorite snacks. By the end of the week, she had determined my preferred times and portion sizes for meals, too. "Where are we today?"

"I am collecting data on a pulsar near the center of that nebula. Have you decided yet on your plans for today?"

"Nothing nearly as daunting or involved as yours," I said. The *Numolo* routinely pooled the data she gathered with her sister worldships, communicating with one another across galaxies with their own special links, capable of transmitting massive packets of data nearly instantaneously. "I was going to shadow your maintenance bots today."

"Why would you want to do that?"

"I am curious about what's involved with your upkeep," I said, anticipating that at some point in the future, I would need to understand the basics of maintaining a craft of my own, even if it would never be as sophisticated as the *Numolo*. "I won't get in their way or touch anything, I promise."

"Today's maintenance schedule is largely superficial. You may find it banal," she forewarned. "It would be like watching someone applying cosmetics or grooming themselves."

I wondered briefly if she was forming her opinion based on her experience of monitoring her own passengers. "Indulge me, Numi. Personally, I used to love watching Sariah pampering herself and playing with her hair."

By the second month of being aboard the *Numolo*, I had begun to read her silences, similar to how spouses and close partners can sense one another's moods and feelings. I was disadvantaged in our relationship, as I couldn't gauge her mental and physical state through her vital signs, as she was able to do with me, but I tried to deduce her inclinations based on her patterns of interaction, or lack thereof.

I had been watching the bots upgrade her wiring in some of the consoles on the bridge when I saw a three-dimensional, holographic image appear in the center front of me, which I recognized as a star chart, peppered with green lights, with a brighter golden light at its center. As suddenly as it had appeared, it vanished, replaced by a narrower view, with larger and fewer dots appearing within specific systems.

"Something for one of your sisters?" I asked, holding a panel open for the bot as it completed the filament soldering.

"No," she said, belatedly. "Something for you."

"For me?"

"I am autonomous, used to charting my courses and following my own whims. I have no fences and no boundaries, but I have also been alone for most of my life." When I picture the *Numolo* in my head, sometimes I still envision her as a gigantic, awe-inspiring behemoth, fierce and uncaged, swimming free in the openness of space. "You, however, are still young and require more structure and guidance."

"Yes, we've discussed this," I said, recalling our first conversations.

"I have been deliberating on whether to override Mandri's directive regarding contact with other Eladryz," she confessed. "There is someone who is available, but Mandri would not approve. This Eladryz is challenging."

Another Eladryz? "Challenging in what sense?"

"He asked to be isolated, because he otherwise is a danger to himself and others."

I was beginning to think that Mandri was correct in not considering this person as a candidate to mentor me, but I also had little cause to doubt the *Numolo's* judgment or intentions. "Would I be safe with him, or would I need to remain on my guard?"

"If you are willing to work with him, I will monitor you closely," she assured.

"What if he doesn't want to work with me?"

"He has no choice in the matter," she said. "It is a requirement of his sentence."

Sentence? "Is this man a criminal?"

"Not anymore," she said. "He hasn't committed a crime in over a hundred fifty years, and he has no opportunity to ever do so again." She paused. "How well do you tolerate the cold?"

Chapter 7: Hellgate

Through the window in my quarters, I watched the flat, featureless landscape zip past my view, and I was reminded both of my memory of my first mission on a barren planetoid with the crew of the *Shakti*, over four years ago, and of the *Numolo*'s insistence earlier that day that there was nothing noteworthy on the planet surface. I really needed to start heeding Numi's advice, as she was usually correct.

My view was so unobstructed, and the permafrost tundra so bare that I could have almost made out the curvature of the horizon, had the planet not been so vast. Within the insulated shields and hull of the *Numolo*, I was unexposed to the outside cold and wind, but with nothing to see but the endless kilometers of ice, I could imagine a quick and horrible death if I were to be out for more than a few minutes without protection.

"How did you find this place?" I asked the *Numolo*.

"I was looking for an uninhabited world where I could remain undisturbed for long periods of time, and I found this place over five hundred years ago," she said. "There are thermal springs and rich mineral veins below the ice, but they are too deep for other species to mine efficiently and cost-effectively, and the planet is too isolated for anyone to find it worth settling, so I have it all to myself."

She spoke of centuries the way I would speak of years. "How often do you come here?"

"As often as needed," she said. "At least once every several years, to recharge and refuel," she said. "I usually come alone, as my Laxuyn keepers find this environment inhospitable, as most reptilian species do."

"I think most species would," I said, "but there's something quite beautiful and peaceful about this stillness. With all the chatter and comm feeds that you monitor constantly, this must be a welcome change."

"I must always remain vigilant for anyone approaching," she said, "but yes, my systems are less taxed and less active, when I am here. I feel more...restful."

As I heard the distant low hum of her main engines powering down, and the higher-pitch of her secondary engines kicking in, the landscape outside changed, as we were descending rapidly.

"We're not landing?"

"Not here," she said. "There is a trench below the surface that I consider my refuge. I do not like to stay up here, either, longer than I have to. I am more vulnerable when I am resting, and I have no intention of ever becoming enslaved again."

I awoke in a house, in a bed. Not the *Numolo*, or any other ship, cabin or cargo hold.

A real bed, with soft, weathered quilted bedding and a deep-cushioned mattress, in an actual house, complete with rooms, painted walls and a stone fireplace. The fireplace jogged my memory, as I recalled remarking on the novelty of glowing-red rocks in the hearth instead of burning wood or coals...

As I sat up in bed, I recounted the hours before I had arrived. After the *Numolo* found her landing spot at the bottom of the Hellgate Trench—her name for it, not mine—she had assured me that the air was safe to breathe, as she had kept it replenished whenever her sensors noticed a dip in the oxygen levels, so I didn't need an environment suit to go outside.

However, I had still needed to dress warmly, and the *Numolo* provided insulated clothing and boots for me. I didn't ask her how she knew my dimensions so precisely, having long given up the notion of keeping anything secret or hidden from Numi, and just accepted that she knew everything there was to know about me, inside and out.

The *Numolo* had downloaded an avatar to a spherical scout drone, which led me away from the landing strip, into the ice caverns, through a maze of crystalline tunnels, and finally to a metal door set into a wall that resembled the *Numolo*'s own gleaming chrome hull. The drone had opened the door silently and led me inside.

The inside of the space was what had struck me. The walls and ceilings were smooth and painted, the floor was stone-tiled and accented with hooked rugs. There was a doorway leading towards more of the house-like structure, and the glowing rock pile warmed the room from a stone fireplace. There were no pictures on the walls, and the colorful furniture was spare, but artfully crafted, with elegantly-turned legs and flourishes.

"This looks like someone's home," I had remarked to the drone, to the *Numolo*.

[It has become that,] she had replied through the drone. [I am not a cruel warden, so I have allowed him to have some comforts.]

"Where is he? The other Eladryz?" I had asked.

[He is resting, as you should be, also,] she had advised. [You will want to be alert when you meet him.]

The drone had led me to a small bedchamber where I could take a brief nap. Not knowing how long I would be staying indoors, I hadn't bothered to remove my heavy, bulky garments, but I still managed to fall asleep quickly and deeply.

And now, I was awake again, thanks to an alarm or trigger from the *Numolo*'s drone, no doubt. It stood near the foot of the bed, its sentry light blinking slowly and steadily, as if anticipating my waking.

[Did you sleep well?] her voice greeted.

"I did, thank you," I said, rubbing my eyes. I looked around the room and noticed its configuration had changed. A section of the wall had been replaced by an open doorway. "I didn't imagine that as a solid wall before, did I?"

The drone spun to follow my gaze, then completed its rotation. [No. This structure is modular, much like my own interior, and I can choose to erect and remove pieces as needed. If you are ready, it is time to meet the Proctor now.]

The Proctor. It sounded so formal, and I wondered if it was the other man's name or his honorific, but before I could ask, my attention was drawn by an oddly mechanical, rhythmic shuffling.

[Hello, who's there?] called a raspy man's voice from another part of the house.

[Good evening,] the *Numolo* replied. [I have brought someone with me.] I recognized the rhythm as footsteps, but I couldn't place the accompanying metallic clink. In the meanwhile, a light switched on over the *Numolo*'s drone to project a holographic image of a pretty, dark-haired girl who stood with her hands demurely knitted, waiting for someone to greet us.

['Someone,'] the voice echoed, sounding stronger as the footsteps came closer. [Odd word. Does it mean some part of a collective *One*, or an individual one?] he mused, more to himself than to us. He was no hologram, as his sparse white hair and grizzled beard and vellum-like skin looked much too solid to be a projection but he, too, moved with the use of devices. His gait was fluid and natural, but his legs were crafted of metals and plastics, as was most of his left arm.

[Just one,] the *Numolo* said.

I tried not to stare, but it was difficult not to gawk at the intricate, graceful lines of his artificial limbs, with their gears and fittings exposed, and I had to finally shut my eyes when he wriggled his articulated metal toes with an amused grin.

[Look all you want,] he said. [There's only the two of us here.] He glanced at the *Numolo*. [Three, almost. Two and a half?] He raised his right hand casually and flicked a couple of fingers, and a few lights in the room turned on. [You have questions, clearly. I have some of my own.]

[How are you feeling, Proctor?] the *Numolo* asked.

[I am fine, Lady *Numolo*,] he replied with mock formality. [Everything here is working fine, as always,] he added, seeming bored.

[Is 'Proctor' your name, or your title?] I asked, taking Numi's cue to stay with Alliance-speak.

[Yes,] he said, scratching his silver beard. [At this point in my life, it makes little difference.]

[How long have you been here?] I asked, trying to infer his state of mind from his erratic behavior. [Or, if it's easier, how old are you?]

[How old am I!] he exclaimed, then turned to the *Numolo*. [How old *am* I?] he asked sincerely.

[Three hundred standard years, Proctor,] she answered readily.

[Three hundred,] he stated confidently, then glanced at the *Numolo* again. [Three hundred? Really?]

[Yes,] she nodded. [This is the Proctor's third cycle here,] she said to me.

Three fifty-year cycles meant a hundred-fifty years. He had been here for half his life?

[I've been here for a hundred fifty years already?] he asked, flabbergasted. [Has anyone missed me? No one's come to look for me, at all, not even the Praimos,] he said, almost disappointed.

[That was by your design. You said you wanted to stay hidden, so that you could help oversee the juveniles,] the *Numolo* reminded gently. [Have you reconsidered?]

As the Proctor seemed lost in his thoughts, I noticed a slight shimmer of light around him, and it reminded me that the *Numolo* had brought me here to learn from an older, more experienced Eladryz. I was momentarily dismayed that I would end up like him: alone and forgotten, suffering from some degree of madness.

He raised his brow, suddenly alert. [This must be your first cycle. You look at me as though I'm a hoary, senile wretch. Maybe I am, since I seem to have even lost track of my limbs,] he joked, flexing his mechanical left hand and rocking back and forth on his artificial heels.

[You're the first other Eladryz I've met,] I confessed. [I guess you could say that I've lived a sheltered life.]

[We are a rare lot,] he nodded. [Where were you raised?]

[Xon, in the Pavo system,] I said, preparing to expound, given the obscurity of the planet.

To my surprise, he nodded. [With some of the Laxuyn ex-pats, no doubt. The planet is lousy with them. Still, in the time that you've spent away from home, your beacon must have attracted attention...] He looked askance at the *Numolo*'s avatar. [Oh, I see. That must be how you were entrusted to our sweet, bewitching *Numolo*.]

The *Numolo* seemed unaffected by his off-hand, semi-sarcastic compliment. [He was hunted more than he was sought by other Eladryz, so it was safer to dampen his beacon as much as possible.]

[Of course, of course,] he said, returning to his distracted manner. [Are you hungry, Xonen Eladryz?]

[He has not eaten for over twelve hours, and only had coffee in the six hours before then.]

[Dehydrated and hungry,] the Proctor said. [Coffee... courtesy of Ammo Sulimandri, I'm guessing. Ammo Ulini doesn't involve himself with Eladryz much.]

[Ammo Ulini?] I asked.

[Third of the Ammo siblings: Sulimandri, Fenrir, Ulini, Silithis and Brahn,] he recited easily. [Their grandfather and I spent some time together. Anyway,] he said, tapping his chin, [what do you eat on Xon nowadays?]

I tried to remember what I used to make for Sariah and the children, as well as consider what I was craving. [Fresh fruits, vegetables, breads, biscuits...]

[Cheeses?] he ventured. [Eggs and meats?]

[Yes, in moderation,] I said.

[Noodles,] he tried. [Pasta?]

Neither sounded familiar to me. Maybe I had seen them mentioned somewhere in one of the learning modules? [No, sorry.]

[You poor, deprived young man,] the Proctor said, looking at me sympathetically. [Spaghetti alla carbonara, it is, then.]

Over the next several days, the Proctor served me an assortment of dishes from various Alliance cultures and regions. He observed my reactions, as I gamely tried everything he put in front of me, and I realized that he was gauging my physical tolerance and overall tractability regarding new experiences, but I couldn't determine whether he was pleased or not by my reactions.

The *Numolo*'s drone arrived one morning for her regular visit just as I was finishing my breakfast of salted egg and fish rice porridge. She gave me a friendlier greeting than she bestowed on the Proctor, despite their longer acquaintance. He seemed slighted and peeved by her preference for me, but he seemed more hurt than angry, and he never spoke rudely to her.

The *Numolo*, for her part, did not seem to care. She had chosen a holographic image of a small red-headed boy that morning, and the Proctor seemed both discomfited and drawn to the avatar she had selected.

[Do your Laxuyn keepers know that you are here, I wonder?] the Proctor asked the *Numolo*, clearing our dishes with a wave of his hand. [Or that I am here? Or him?]

[They trust me to do what is necessary,] she replied, folding her dimpled, freckled hands in front of her, as her blue eyes watched him without warmth or humor.

[I will leave you to your business, then,] he said, giving a slight bow as he left to give us some privacy.

"How are your upgrades and renovations going?" I asked, returning to my elfyn-speak.

"Well, thank you," she nodded. "How is the Proctor treating you?"

"He's very generous about food," I said. "He prefers to ask about me, and shares little about himself."

Her avatar's blue eyes widened. "What does he ask you?"

"About my background. About Xon, my family and children. I told him I've been gone for almost five years. Why?"

"It is unwise to share too much with anyone," she cautioned, "but especially the Proctor."

"Why is he here?" I asked her in a whisper. I noticed a smudge left by a fallen grain of rice on the sphere's gleaming surface and buffed it clean with the tail of my shirt. "And if you don't really trust him, why did you bring me here?"

"You need the guidance and model of an older Eladryz, even a flawed one, to understand your potential," she said. "The Proctor has overseen the transition and tutelage of many young Eladryz like you, as an attempt at penance for his past cruelties."

The *Numolo* was selective with her words, speaking neither in hyperbole nor in euphemisms, so her disclosure was a deliberate one.

"About his crimes," I said, returning to my seat. I remembered his unsavory interest in the *Numolo*'s juvenile guises, and my jaw tightened. "Were they crimes against children?"

Her holograph nodded. "His memory is selective and weakened, so he does not remember the harm he caused. His crimes occurred centuries ago, and even the families of his victims no longer recall the events," the *Numolo* said. "My memory, however, is intact and uncompromised, so I remember for all of them. He is my prisoner, and

I am his warden." She flashed a different child's image as her avatar, followed by another, then another, and I realized that she had been deliberately taking the guises of his victims.

"How many?" I swallowed.

"He confessed to thirty, but he also admits to not recalling all of them, or even the extent of what he had done to some," she said. "By his own admission, he is unfit to rejoin society."

"So you keep this place as his prison," I said. "For the rest of his life? Is there a point to even keeping him alive, if what he did was so heinous?"

"My keepers have taught me that all people have value, but not all are suited to live amongst others," she said. "I will not end his life while he remains useful and compliant."

I recalled his careful restraint around her presence. "Has he ever tried to hurt you?" I whispered. "Could he, if he wanted to?"

"He could try," she said, "but it would gain him nothing to harm me. This device has self-defensive measures, but this is only my drone. He cannot reach me directly unless I allow it."

I had doubts about that. I had seen the Proctor move and manipulate things with his mind, similar to how the mages on Xon had used the powers bestowed on them by their magestones, their augments. The *Numolo* was observant and cautious, but I worried about her limitations, if the Proctor were to try to move against her.

"Do you worry for me, Cyrus?" she asked quietly. "You shouldn't. In the contingency that I am compromised or destroyed, you would still be able to access any of the ships in my storage bay to leave without my aid."

I ignored the hologram of the child and looked directly at the drone. "I'm not worried about being able to leave," I said. "You're my friend, and I don't want to see you damaged."

"That is your nature," she said. "It is rare that you wish to see anyone hurt. Does your mercy extend to the Proctor, knowing what you know about him?"

"I don't know," I said honestly. I didn't know the details of his crimes, and I wasn't sure that I wanted to, but given what Numi had said, did I want to hurt him, personally? "As long as the Proctor is respectful and honest with you, I see no reason to be anything but kind to him." I reserved the right to change my mind, if his conduct altered, as well.

"That is fair and reasonable," she answered. "Your open mind serves you well. Just be careful not to become too open and let down your guard. Remember that the Proctor is a prisoner here, and he is unlikely to ever be rehabilitated. Just as it is in your nature to defend, it is in *his* nature to prey on others, whether he knows it or not."

At the *Numolo*'s recommendation, I began recording brief journal entries into her drone during her visits, as a way of keeping track of my progress under the *Proctor*'s tutelage, and to keep myself grounded. She engaged me in daily conversation, to gauge my mental state and to give me an alternative to speaking with the Proctor. Given his distracted and mercurial behavior, Numi did not want me to pick up his quirks or odd patterns inadvertently.

The first journal entry started awkwardly, as I stared at the blinking light of the drone without knowing how to start. Sensing my frustration, she advised: "Pretend that you are sending a message to Sarc, to let him know how you are."

With my son in mind, the words came more easily. I told him about what I had learned in the few days since my arrival, and how much I was looking forward to seeing him and the others soon. "How is that?" I asked Numi.

"It is a personal message, and I did not listen," she replied. "Do you feel better, for having voiced your thoughts?"

"I do," I said. Some of the restless energy I had felt from not having a confidant like Mandri or Sarc around, had dissipated. "That was very helpful. Thank you."

We continued the ritual with a weekly regularity, sometimes more often if I had additional thoughts that I wanted to express. Sometimes, I rambled, working aloud through a problem or puzzle that the Proctor had assigned to challenge me, and the drone recorded everything faithfully, taking my recorded words back to the *Numolo* at the end of our visits, for safekeeping.

On one visit, after what felt like months of working with the Proctor, the *Numolo*'s drone rolled into my room and sealed the wall for privacy, as per its usual pattern. Instead of her usual morning greeting, however, she began: "I have a confession to make."

I had never heard her say those words, and contrition sounded very odd and unnatural in her voice. "Did you do something in error, Numi?"

"I have lied by omission," she said. "Today seems to be an appropriate time to tell you: you have been here longer than you think."

I wasn't entirely surprised by her disclosure. Without real windows to see the passage of days from the depths of the Hellgate Trench, and no calendars to mark, the days flowed easily from one to the next. "How much longer? A few months, give or take?" I asked casually.

"Today marks your son's thirtieth birthday," she said.

What? I sank onto the edge of my bed, dumbfounded. I had been away from Xon for ten years already? That meant that I had been with the Proctor for years, not months. "How is that possible? It doesn't feel anything close to that."

"Time is dilated on this world and moves at a different pace," she said, "so this seemed the optimal place to keep you hidden and out of harm's way, until you no longer exhibited signs of your cycle, and until the Praimos's latest bounty on Eladryz had expired."

Sarc is thirty years old. "I've missed so many of his birthdays," I said. "I've missed so much of everything."

"Not entirely," Numi said. "I have sent your recordings to Slither, to pass onto your son, so that he is aware that you are still alive and doing well. He is aware that time is passing differently for you," she explained. "The day is just beginning for him, so if you would like to speak with him directly, I can open a connection for you."

"I thought that wasn't possible from inside the Trench," I said. "Or, did you just tell me that so that I wouldn't ask to speak to him more often?"

"I refrain from connecting from here in order to minimize our exposure," she said with clipped precision, "as any outgoing signals, even temporary ones, can potentially draw attention to this planet." She added, more gently, "However, today is a special occasion that warrants an exception."

"I would very much like to speak with him," I said. "Thank you for the offer." I wasn't upset with Numi for her concealment of the truth, as she never acted out of malice or selfishness. Whatever secrets she kept, she did so in the interest of those under her care.

As I waited, she cautioned: "It will need to be brief. Any connection longer than a few minutes can expose our location."

"I understand," I said, carefully choosing and planning the words I would say to Sarc, after not speaking to him for years—

"Hello?"

Any glib or eloquent statements I had plotted vanished from my head at the sound of my son's voice. He sounded just as I remembered him. *Except that he's older now.* "Happy birthday, Sarc. I'm sorry I've been out of touch."

"Dad!" The one word was enough to fill me with joy, relief and anticipation. *"It's good to hear your voice."*

"I only found out this morning how long I've been gone," I said. "I had hoped that I would be home by now."

"That doesn't matter," Sarc said, but there was a tinge of

melancholy in his voice that betrayed that it did, in fact, matter a great deal to him. *"From your messages, it sounds like the years have been well-spent. You sound well, and happy."*

"I was happy until I realized how much I've missed," I said.

"You haven't missed much here, and it appears that you're learning much more, there. From what you've said, it sounds as though Eladryz are basically mages without the magestones," he said, trying to distract me from my guilt. *"The Laxuyn engineered the Char'she as augments for other species to help keep the Eladryz from becoming too powerful?"*

"That's what the Proctor had told me," I said, trying to recall when I had recorded that for the journal.

"But you don't believe him?" Sarc asked, and I could almost picture his thoughtful scowl.

"It's more a matter of trust than belief," I said. "The *Numolo* doesn't tell me everything, but I trust her to act for the greater good, while the Proctor has his own motives for teaching and training me, that he keeps to himself. He may be factual, but…"

"Sounds a little like Junus," Sarc said, recalling his old master and trainer.

"A little," I said, thinking more of their physical similarities than their moral directives. Whereas Junus used his position in service of the Emperor and his Realm, the Proctor used his power and knowledge for his own advantage. It was better, by far, for Sarc to have trained under Junus than under the Proctor.

The light on the drone blinked faster, signaling that time was running out. "Quickly, son, catch me up. How is everyone?"

"No pressure," Sarc said drolly. *"Adella has a daughter, who is five now, and a son, who was born in late summer. Leode was lost to us in mid-autumn, swept overboard in a freak storm, as he was sailing back home from Petarus."*

I grieved for the Empress, raising two young children alone while she mourned her husband, but if there was anyone who could manage it with grace and prudence, it would be the stalwart Empress Adeliaraine of the Realm. "And Jeysen, Clyara and Jaeris?"

"Jaeris is feeling his age," Sarc said tactfully. *"Clyara defies hers, as always. And Jeysen … well, he's Jeysen."* I imagined Sarc's helpless shrug.

The drone's light was blinking frenetically now, and I made sure to squeeze in: "I love you, son."

"I love you, too," he replied quickly. *"Be careful – "*

I continued to stare at the drone for a moment after we disconnected. The *Numolo* reset the lights on the drone, as if to remind me that the connection had ended.

"The Proctor is waiting for you for your morning lessons," she said.

"Thank you, Numi," I said.

"I felt it best to give you a verbal reminder, as you seemed lost in reverie."

I smiled. "Yes, thank you for the reminder, too, but I'm more grateful that I was able to speak with Sarc. It means a great deal to me, that you coordinated this for me...for us."

She didn't respond immediately, as though she was analyzing my statement in detail. "You are welcome, Cyrus," she said at last, and opened the wall panel. The Proctor was waiting in the common area outside my rooms, with a patient, anticipatory smile, as always.

I toweled my face and arms dry after stepping from the shower stall and sensed voices from the common hall, through the walls like vibrations. The *Numolo* had already left earlier in the day, before I had started my morning exercises, so who could be speaking with the Proctor? Instead of rushing out to the meet the newcomer, I took my time dressing and focused on the tones of voice, the emotions and the overall mood of the conversation through the energy I was feeling.

By the time I entered the hall, I had already assessed enough of the situation to know to be on my guard. The Proctor and the other man, a little younger than me, rose from their seats to greet me.

The Proctor made the introductions. "Cyrus, this is Lynier from the Io System, another Eladryz from your generation. Lynier, this is Cyrus, from the Pavo System."

Lynier was a few centimeters taller than me, with bold, chiseled features. He looked large and imposing with the thick insulating layers covering him, but from the broadness of his shoulders straining against the sleeves and the sliver of his taut, muscular torso peeking through his open coat, it was clear that he didn't need the bulk of heavy clothes to look impressive. His hair was sleek and dark like tar, and his smooth complexion was evenly tan. A perfect specimen in every way, and still pulsing with the magnetic energy of his first fifty-year cycle. It was fascinating to observe it as an outsider, and I wondered briefly if I had looked that way to others. Just the glow, that is, not the jaw-dropping beauty and physical power that Lynier commanded.

[A pleasure to meet a fellow first-cycler,] I said, taking his arm in greeting.

[The same,] he said, in a deep, booming voice. *Of course, his voice would be heroic and grand, too.* [I've heard so much about you, that I feel like I already know you.]

I glanced at the Proctor, who shook his head. [Lynier is here by Ammo Sulimandri's direction,] he explained. [He's spent the past months with the crew of the *Shakti*, who shared their recollections of you with him, and Mandri suggested that Lynier may wish to stay out of sight until his symptoms subside.]

Lynier looked sheepish. [We were approached by Eladryz women on three occasions, who were drawn by my beacon. I told Sistine that she didn't have any cause for jealousy, but you remember her temper.]

I nodded, fitting the pieces together but keeping my thoughts concealed. [It's good to have another presence here. I'm sorry to have missed Mandri.]

Lynier grinned. [He couldn't wait to leave this place, I think. The cold doesn't agree with him, at all.]

[Is he still wearing his fleece-lined fur coat?] I smiled.

[He wouldn't be Mandri without it!] he laughed. [Sometimes, I think it's fused to him.] He looked back and forth between the Proctor and me. [So, it's just the two of you here, I understand. How long have you been here?] he asked me.

[Six years, give or take some months,] I said.

[Six *years*?] Lynier exclaimed. [I think I would go crazy after six months here,] he said, then looked apologetically at the Proctor. [No offense, Proctor Wen.]

The Proctor raised his brow, wearing his ever-patient smile. [None taken. It helps to be a little mad to stay here.] Without further explanation, he left the room.

[Is he coming back?] Lynier asked, staring after him.

[Probably,] I shrugged. [Maybe. He's either gone to prepare an assortment of food, or he's decided to take a nap.]

The *Numolo*'s drone rolled into the common hall from the Proctor's rooms. It was her usual morning routine, to patrol and inspect our private chambers and shared spaces.

[What a clever little contraption,] Lynier said with amusement. [When the Proctor gave me the tour and showed me my quarters, the little drone was following us, like a little dog.]

I smiled mildly, careful not to give away more about Numi than Lynier needed to know. If neither Mandri nor the Proctor had made any mention of the *Numolo* to Lynier up till that point, I resolved not to betray her, either.

[Is it a maintenance drone?] Lynier asked, as it rolled to a stop between us.

[It is,] I said simply. It had been one of the *Numolo*'s several dozen service bots, before she had modified it to be her surveillance drone and avatar, so I wasn't lying. [It checks the environmental conditions to make sure there are no repairs or upgrades needed.] To ensure that the Proctor kept nothing hidden from her, the *Numolo* included all the rooms in the house in her daily inspection, including mine. I stepped aside to allow the drone to roll into my chambers for its daily visit, now that my rooms were vacant.

[What do you do for fun around here?] Lynier asked with a wiggle of his brow. [It must get lonely sometimes.]

[I think of this place as a monastery, of sorts,] I said, unsure of how much Mandri had told Lynier about the Proctor's past. [The lack of distractions doesn't bother me.]

[But six years!] Lynier marveled. [Do you and the Proctor ever...you know?]

It felt like I was speaking with a sex-obsessed teenage boy, not a grown man, and I had to remind myself not to shout out a snide comment to the *Numolo*. [I'm good, really. I got all my boyhood urges out of my system when I was younger, and I was happily married for a number of years.]

[Yeah, but this fifty-year surge is like a constantly heightened state,] he said. [I feel like I have to be with someone, all the time. It's irresistible, isn't it?]

Maybe for you, not for me. [I think it hits everyone a little differently.] I was wasting my breath, as he looked at me blankly, seemingly unable to grasp that I didn't share his hormonally-fueled urges. Then I remembered: *second puberty*. My effects had largely subsided, apart from my glow that I could turn on or off at will, but Lynier was still at his peak.

I excused myself to retire to my rooms, once I saw that the drone was finished with its inspection. *I'm living with a senile pedophile and a teenage boy in a grown man's body. It really does feel like a mad house now.*

The disruption to our routine was minimal, surprisingly. The house was reconfigured to be rectangular, with each of us occupying our own corner suite of rooms, and the common and kitchen areas in the center and the fourth corner. The three of us met each day for meals, and aside from a daily morning session that the Proctor and I spent to go over lessons, we spent our hours alone in our chambers. Thankfully, Lynier didn't question the intelligent design and self-configuration of our residence, and never gave the *Numolo*'s drones a second glance during its daily patrols.

A few months into Lynier's stay with us in the Hellgate Trench, I was interrupted during my morning exercises by a visit from the *Numolo's* drone. I had been lost in a near-trance state with my driving, thrashing music selections crowding out all my unnecessary, distracting thoughts, so drone signaled its arrival by shutting off my music abruptly.

The *Numolo* never sent her drone into my rooms without first requesting entry with a chirp or a blink at my door, so I knew something was different.

"What is it?" I whispered. It merely backed out of my room, towards the common area, and I knew Lynier must be close by, for Numi to not wish to speak. I snatched a towel to wipe myself and emerged from my room, winded and damp with perspiration.

Lynier was dressed to go outside into the cold, the first time I had seen him outfitted like that since his arrival months earlier. Seeing me drained and tired, he chuckled. [You torture yourself like that every day, for hours. Why do you bother?]

Lynier was not alone, as I saw that the Proctor and Mandri were there, also. It was good to see Mandri again, and he smiled slightly in greeting.

[Not everyone is as naturally gifted and blessed as you, Lynier,] Mandri said. [I think Cyrus should be commended for his continual efforts to overcome his many failings and shortcomings.]

Same old Mandri. I had missed his sense of humor, and apparently, the Proctor and Lynier missed it, too, in a different way, in that they weren't sure whether to laugh or berate Mandri for his remark.

I laughed to indicate that I took no offense. [What would I do without you to remind me of my limitations, Mandri?]

[Find someone else to point them out, most likely,] he rejoined jokingly. [You've always been your own worst critic, anyway.]

Lynier clapped and rubbed his hands together expectantly. [We'll let you return to your exercises, then. I'm looking forward to rejoining civilization, to find my exercise in other, more pleasurable ways. Somewhere *far* from here.] He extended his arm to me. [I'm glad we had a chance to meet, Cyrus. Maybe we'll cross paths again.]

I nodded, taking his arm. [Take care of the *Shakti* and her crew,] I said, then turned to Mandri. [It was good to see you again. Give everyone my regards?]

[Of course,] Mandri nodded solemnly, then flashed a quick sideways glance at the Proctor. [Try not to stay too much longer, Cyrus. You're well-loved, and sorely missed.]

Chapter 8: Learning to Let Go

"On Xon, it is the Year of the Emperors 963."

The *Numolo*'s emotionless statement echoed in my head, filling me with despair. How had so many years passed so quickly? My despair had deepened when she informed me that Slither had contacted her earlier that morning, with dire news: Jaeris Thorne's poor health had worsened further, and he was close to death.

"Jaeris would like to speak with you," she relayed.

"Of course, whenever he wishes," I answered automatically, forgetting all thoughts of breakfast or anything else that normally occupied my mornings. "Do you mind opening a connection to Xon for me, please?"

"I will try to open a connection as soon as possible," she promised.

Aside from taking a moment to inform the Proctor that I would be unavailable to work with him that day, I remained in my chambers, fidgeting and pacing restlessly. He offered to prepare some food or drink for me, and I declined; my stomach was in knots, and I was too distracted to think of eating or drinking anything.

A couple of times, the *Numolo* was able to connect to the comm in Jaeris's room, and both times, I spoke briefly to Jeysen, who informed me that his father was resting. I could hear the strain and exhaustion in Jeysen's voice, so I asked him to contact us instead, when the timing was better and Jaeris was awake.

I stayed in my room, too anxious and worried about Jeysen's returning summons to risk leaving. Finally, after what felt like hours, the drone's light stopped its tentative blinking. "A connection has been established."

I waited anxiously for the dead air to clear on the comm, now that the connection was reestablished. I knew Jeysen was on the other end, still tending to his own pressing matters, so I waited patiently. I sat up straight when the comm chirped quietly, signaling Jeysen's return.

"He's awake now," Jeysen said.

"Thank you," I said. "Does he wish to speak privately?"

I waited a beat, and Jaeris's quiet voice replied. *"No, I won't say anything to embarrass you, old friend."* I heard a shuffle and the creak of a bed, and his voice sounded a little closer. *"It was good of you to call earlier. I told Jeysen that he should've woken me."*

"It doesn't matter. You need your rest," I said. "You sound strong."

"I'm not," Jaeris replied plainly. *"I'm unable to breathe comfortably on my own, and I've lost feeling in my legs. My voice may be strong, but my body is breaking down."*

Jeysen hadn't mentioned anything about using spells to slow his father's inevitable decline, but I knew that Jaeris's continued cogency wasn't owed entirely to luck, and I was certain that Jaeris was aware of it, too.

"Won't you reconsider letting your sons heal you?" I had to ask. "Or Sarc, or Junus?"

"It would be a temporary stay," he said. *"I've let my sons numb my discomforts, so that I can rest and sleep better, but I am weary. I want to see my Karina again."*

"I'm sorry that I'm not there in your final days," I said, tears welling at hearing my friend's tired, mournful voice.

"Don't be," Jaeris replied. *"I prefer us to remember each other the way we were when we last saw one another, celebrating your fiftieth birthday, without any sadness or awareness that it would be our last day together."*

I recalled how Jaeris had looked that day: handsome and rosy-cheeked with laughter, with a goblet of wine raised in a toast. "And so, I will always picture you in my mind," I said solemnly. "Are you in pain?"

"Not as much as I should be, thanks to our boys," Jaeris said. *"My father used to say: it is time to let go of life when there are no more occasions to look forward to, but I wouldn't want to wait so long. I wish to leave while there is still hope and brightness ahead, to know that even after I am gone, our children will still know love and meaning in their future."*

"Our children?" I asked.

"Of course, my Empress," Jaeris said quietly. *"I will be with you, soon, now that our work is complete. I am so tired, my love."*

I wiped at my eyes, trying not to envision Jaeris's deterioration. It had to be difficult for Jeysen, keeping vigil at his father's bed, seeing his condition worsen without being able to stop it. The line was silent for a moment, and I waited for Jeysen to tell me that Jaeris had fallen asleep, but it was Jaeris's voice that returned. *"Are you still there, Cyrus?"*

"I am, old friend. I am heartened to hear your contentment, but I hope you don't decide to leave prematurely," I chided gently. "You are surrounded by love and beauty, in your palace and in your family; I can think of no greater comfort."

"That is true," Jaeris said. *"That is the greatest temptation, isn't it: to remain past one's time of utility, out of comfort and convenience, and out of deference to one's own fear of death and change?"*

"You and I stopped fearing death when we lost our loves, once we accepted change as inevitable and intractable," I reminded. "And you made yourself obsolete long ago, when you abdicated to your daughter. You should be at peace."

"Adella is widowed, and my granddaughter is missing... how can I have peace without knowing for certain that my family and my Realm will endure?"

"Your grandson will inherit the throne," I reminded. "Augus is still a child, but if he learns from Adella, he will be fine. You must put faith in your descendants, including those to come, that they will preserve your legacy, as well as their own."

Jaeris made a sound that sounded like either a cough or a chuckle. *"I hadn't considered that there may be others to inherit our name, who are yet to be born. Well, Jeysen, do you have something to tell me?"* There was a pause. *"He's shaking his head 'no.'"*

"Not yet, old friend. He's still young."

"Thank you for your perspective, Cyrus. I will miss these talks."

"Not as much as I will, my Lord," I returned. "Good night, my Emperor."

"Good night, old friend," Jaeris said.

The comm went silent again, but the connection remained active. I waited for the click that signaled the end of the connection, or Jeysen to return with anything that he didn't want to say in his father's presence. After close to a minute, I was about to close the connection, when I heard the signaling chirp.

"Dad?"

I smiled. "Sarc."

"Jeysen asked me to keep an eye on the box out here, while he and his siblings are in Jaeris's chamber. How are you?" he asked gently.

I wiped my eyes. "I think you must be having a harder time of it, watching it happen in person. He has always considered you like another son."

"And you were like a brother to him," Sarc reminded. *"He sometimes mistakes me for you when I come to visit."*

"You don't correct him, I hope," I said. Jaeris had always been proud of his ability to recognize names and faces with uncanny precision.

"No, Dad," he said. "I don't mind being confused for you. He usually realizes his slip soon after we start conversing, anyway, since I'm much more respectful towards him than you are."

"You are that," I laughed. "How are the princes and Adella handling it?"

"They seem to be coping, but I'm not here often," he said. "I try not to make a nuisance of myself with a constant presence. I happened to visit today to tell him something, which I hope brings him peace in his final hours."

"Was it truthful?"

"Does it matter? You and I both know that lying is not the worst of sins, not by far," he said. "But what I told him was true, and he did brighten a little bit at hearing the news, so if he does pass tonight, he will be at peace."

"You are a good man, son," I said.

"If I'm good, it's because of your example," he said easily. "And if I'm not, that's on your conscience, too," he added in jest. "It's nice to hear your voice, Dad, but... I hear them in the other room. I think it's time." There was a slight hitch of emotion in his voice.

"Go, be with your friends. I love you, son."

"I love you, too, Dad."

After our connection ended, I sat in silence, contemplating the inequity of life. Jaeris Thorne, one of the best men that I ever had known, was taking his last breaths after barely reaching his seventy-third birthday, while a base predator like the Proctor was enjoying a safe and secure existence, living centuries longer than any of his young victims.

And here I am, wasting my years with this monster. I regretted not being on Xon, to spend some time with Jaeris, or to steal some last moments with Sarc before he outgrew me forever. I had learned everything of significance that the Proctor would ever be willing to teach me, and I suspected that all the little scraps of information he occasionally fed to me were just to entice me to stay longer.

"Numi," I said, looking at the drone waiting attentively at my feet. "I think I'm ready to leave now."

"As you wish," she said promptly. "Would you like to depart immediately?"

I smiled tightly at the *Numolo*'s continued frigidity towards the Proctor. I didn't like him very much, either, but I wanted to remain cordial. "As a courtesy, I should let the Proctor know my intentions, but perhaps we can leave in the morning."

The Proctor seemed distressed and disappointed about my decision, and as I had expected, he attempted to postpone my departure by promising to expand my knowledge further. [There is still so much to learn! I haven't yet taught you about conjurations and transferences—]

[Then I will have to live without that knowledge,] I said, as patiently as I could. [If you had refrained so long from teaching me, then I must not be ready for them, anyway,] I shrugged, weary of the Proctor's attempts to delay me, and annoyed at my own blindness to his ploy. [After all these years, staying another day or another month more will make no difference, if I've already reached my mental capacity.]

I didn't miss the Proctor's quick glance at the *Numolo*'s drone, avoiding the unblinking gaze of her youthful avatar. [If that is what you want, I don't suppose I can change your mind. Dine with me tonight, one last time, then,] he said. [It will most likely be the last meal that I will share with anyone, for a long time.]

I agreed to a last dinner, more as a kindness to the man who had mentored and trained me for the past several years, than from any personal desire to spend any additional time with the Proctor. I was restless and eager to leave, but I chose to be polite.

The dinner was as eerily silent as I had dreaded, as I had nothing left to say to the Proctor, and he had nothing new to share with me. If he had offered something of himself—a detail of his life, like an old memory or even his full name—I would've been moved enough to consider visiting at some point in the future. However, he was more tight-lipped and colder than usual, as though he was already putting me into his past: one more who no longer served a purpose for him, ready to be discarded.

Retiring to my room the last night was a relief. Of all the lessons the Proctor had taught me, the most important was the one that lingered in my mind as I drifted off to sleep: it was better to be alone, than to be in the company of someone who despised me.

Wake up, my love! Please, Cyrus, please wake up!

I heard Sariah's frantic voice but couldn't see her in the darkness. *Where are you?*

It doesn't matter. You need to wake up now, and fight! Fight!

I awoke, unable to move my legs or arms. No, that wasn't entirely true. I could move my right arm, but my other limbs were unresponsive. *No, no, no!* I opened my eyes to find my legs and left arm encased in metal, resembling the Proctor's, then realized in horror that those metal fittings *were* my limbs! I raised my right hand and recognized the Proctor's lined, calloused skin. *What has he done to me?*

The bed was unfamiliar to me, older and worn. *The Proctor's bed.* [Proctor!] I yelled, forcing myself to sit upright. To my dismay, my voice was no longer my own, either. He had found a way to switch our bodies, and he taken mine and left my consciousness in his own broken form. *Transference.* He had mentioned that transference was one of the skills that he had yet to teach me.

[Proctor, is something the matter?] I heard my own voice cajoling me from the common room. [You seem distraught this morning.] He stood in the doorway to the bed chamber to watch me.

I lurched from the bed, still trying to figure out how to balance myself on my artificial limbs. [Why did you do this?] I cried, watching my own body step back out of my reach. Was my smile always so cruel and contemptuous, or was that the Proctor using me that way?

[Why? Do you really have to ask?] he mocked. [Now that you can see what you've taken for granted for your entire life, surely you can't blame me.] He conjured a mirror and admired the reflection that greeted him. [You must have had your choice of women and men, looking like this,] he grinned, raking his fingers through his hair.

My fingers, my hair! [You're planning to leave me here, aren't you?]

[It is time for Cyrus E'lan to resume his life,] he said, dispelling the mirror. [Thank you for all your help, Proctor. I'll be sure to put all the skills you've taught me to good use. I've missed spending time with the beautiful children, most of all,] he said, with a leering grin.

[Don't you dare!] I cried, half-pleading. The thought of him using my body to harm innocents was more than I could bear, and I forced myself to use what I had for the moment. [Don't do this, please.]

[It was impossible to pass up such an opportunity. If our places were reversed, wouldn't you do the same?] he asked rhetorically. [Oh, that's right. Our places *are* reversed now. Farewell, Proctor.]

[Good morning, gentlemen,] the *Numolo* greeted from the main hall, as the front door opened for the drone.

[Good morning,] the Proctor chirped brightly. *If you say anything to her, I will have to destroy the drone and kill you. Without her eyes to witness us, it will be easy to explain a mishap, and by the time she suspects, we will be gone from here.* He joined the *Numolo*'s drone in the common area, leaving me to consider his warning and struggle with his broken body. [Ready when you are.]

I forced myself to relax. The *Numolo* wouldn't leave without saying good-bye to the Proctor, regardless of her opinion of him. I had a few minutes to figure my way out of this impossible situation, but I had to hurry; the *Numolo* wouldn't wait forever for me, and she was essential to my escape. *For the Proctor's, too, for that matter.*

[Proctor?] she called, and I heard the approaching whirring of her drone's servos.

I refrained from answering, trying different thoughts and techniques to maneuver the limbs of the Proctor's body. His motion was controlled by a mixture of his body's automatic, neural functions and his mental abilities, almost like spells.

[The Proctor hasn't been feeling well this morning,] I heard my own voice betraying me, with its insidious Eladryz sub-tones attempting to sway the *Numolo*. [I wonder if it wouldn't be more merciful to end his suffering soon, if his condition continues to deteriorate.]

I braced myself for the *Numolo*'s child-like appearance, anticipating the same kind of deviant impulse that I watched the Proctor struggle with daily; if it was a physical, chemical deficiency in his brain, then I would feel it now. When the *Numolo* floated into the room, appearing as a young girl in a white dress with long blond hair, I was actually relieved, as I felt none of the depraved, sickening instinct that I had dreaded. In fact, she appeared as I had always pictured Sarc's daughter Glory, which strengthened my resolve to escape; I could not let the Proctor victimize any child again, whether they reminded me of my granddaughter or not. *I would rather die.*

[I am not myself,] I said to her. [I need help.]

[We can return at another time to address your needs,] the Proctor said, the emptiness of his promise clear in his tone. [But you and I should leave now, *Numolo*.]

The *Numolo* looked at me closely. [What kind of help, Proctor?]

[Not now.] I shook my head, fighting the temptation to tell her everything. Instead, I said: [But I would like to shake Cyrus's hand before he leaves with you. I don't know when I shall ever see him again.]

The Proctor glared at me over the *Numolo*'s projection, but he couldn't deny my request without appearing entirely out of my character. *What are you playing at, Cyrus?*

I waved him closer, my arm still moving slowly and stiffly, and I gave him a resigned smile. [Come, young man, what harm is there in a handshake?]

He came forth hesitantly, under the *Numolo*'s watchful gaze. He was overly cautious, even cowardly: my body was younger, faster and whole, and he still had his centuries of knowledge. There was no physical or magical advantage that I had over him, yet he still shied from my offered hand. [Why are you suddenly wary of me?] I taunted. [I've never been anything but kind to you.] I looked at the *Numolo* and said in elfyn: "I swear it, Numi. On my life."

"I understand," she said softly.

Caught off-guard by our coded exchange, the Proctor turned

away from me to try to deactivate the *Numolo*'s drone or defend against its faster attack, and he missed my stumbling approach. I had summoned a serrated knife into my hand and plunged it into the Proctor's side...*my* side.

Whip-like appendages shot out from the middle of the *Numolo*'s drone, as the sphere rolled towards me, but instead of attacking, they supported my limbs and steered me back, out of the Proctor's reach, before he could try to transfer his agonizing, crippling wounds to me.

[What have you done!] he gasped, clutching his torn side.

[I would rather destroy my body than let you steal it!] I shouted, ending my pretend frailty. [This body you've left me may be flawed, but it will survive longer than the one you've taken.]

I saw the animal panic in my golden eyes, as the Proctor weighed his options. He could die in my body, or remain alive in his own. It was difficult and unnerving to watch myself bleed out, but not as excruciating as the Proctor's pain and anguish, feeling his life ebb with every gush of my blood.

The *Numolo* guarded me closely, but the Proctor suddenly laughed, clutching his side. [You win, Cyrus.]

He vanished and reappeared behind me, grasping my shoulders before the *Numolo* could intervene. [You can have your body back now.] Sapping my life energy would've taken longer, but it took less than a second, like a rubber band stretched and snapped back into shape, for him to switch our bodies back. My eyes blurred momentarily, and my body went numb and limp; then my eyes were wide and watering, and my body was torn, in searing agony.

"Numi," I called weakly, as the Proctor backed away, relieved to be back in his original body. I pressed the tail of my tunic against my side to stanch the bleeding, as I knew exactly where I had sliced my abdomen. I had aimed carefully, striking to inflict pain without harming any internal organs, but I was still bleeding profusely. My strategy had bought me extra minutes, but not hours.

She let me lean on her, but her focus was on the Proctor, who was watching and waiting for me to die there or creep away and perish elsewhere. [This will be my last visit, Proctor,] the *Numolo* announced. [You no longer have my trust.]

[What?] he exclaimed in a panic. [No, wait, please!] he begged, knowing that her abandonment of him would mean a desolate, ruinous end for him, whether physical or psychological, or both. [*This* wasn't my fault,] he said, pointing at me. [He tried to kill me! You saw that!]

[What I witnessed was an attempt at self-destruction,] she said calmly. [You stole his body and refused to return it.] The appendages propped me up further, as they felt me weakening. [Cyrus and I must leave now, if he is to have any chance of survival.]

[Wait!] he said. [After the good I've done all these years, don't I deserve another chance?]

[You owe a lifetime of reparations for each of your victims, and you may not remember anymore, but there were many,] she reminded. [It was by your own design to live in exile here. Have you forgotten, or have you reconsidered?]

It was a question that she had asked him on the day I had arrived there, and this time, the Proctor seemed to give the question serious thought. There seemed to be a lucidity and awareness about him that had been missing during the entirety of my stay. [I can never leave here, can I? I will die here, regardless of what I do, or don't.]

[This was your sentence. I will return once more, to reevaluate your fate,] she promised, softening her tone. [But it must be later. Cyrus does not deserve to die for your inability to reform.]

[Another second, please,] the Proctor said, reaching for me with a shaking hand. [You spoke truthfully: you were never anything but kind to me.]

I was unsure of his intention, but I was delirious in my agonized and weakened state, and I took his offered hand. My failing body was too feeble to offer any resistance or any further value to the Proctor, anyway, so there was nothing to lose in the gesture. [I forgive you.]

He smiled sadly, grateful but regretful. [There are too few of us remaining in the universe, and you are one of the good ones.]

The Proctor's grip on my hand tightened and became painful, and his body began to glow: golden and blinding like morning sunlight. I tried to pull free but had no strength left in me. I shut my eyes tightly against the light, trying to feel something of what he was attempting. Was he trying to strip my body for parts while I was still alive, or —

"It's all right, Cyrus," the *Numolo*'s voice soothed. "It is finished."

The Proctor's hand dropped from mine, and his glow was no longer visible through my closed lids. I eased my eyes open, and the *Numolo*'s drone was next to me, allowing me to lean on it. On the floor in front of us was the Proctor's lifeless body, little more than papery skin hanging loosely on a frail skeleton.

My hand went immediately to my side, which no longer stung and bled.

"He had chosen to end his exile, by giving his life to restore yours," the *Numolo* said.

I took a deep, expansive breath to test my body, not quite believing yet that I really was whole again. I felt through the stained

106

tear in my shirt where I had plunged the knife and found only a thin purple scar over my repaired flesh. "I didn't expect him to do that."

"You are not happy?" she noted from my frown.

"I'm happy to still be alive," I said, "but I'm not happy that the Proctor is dead." I crouched down to look at the remains, with the mechanical limbs now seeming outsized and exaggerated against the wasted stumps,

The *Numolo*'s drone rolled back a quarter-turn. "But you were ready to destroy yourself, rather than let him take your body."

"That was different. It was my body, my own property, that he had no right to steal for his own use. That's not the same as wanting him to die."

The drone rolled in front of me, and the *Numolo*'s girlish avatar met my eyes. "Then you must consider that this was the Proctor's decision, as well: he sacrificed himself to save you, because he did not want *you* to die."

"I feel ill." I felt nauseous, but it was more than the guilt of the Proctor's death that affected me. I teetered and slumped heavily against the wall behind me, my head feeling heavy and unbalanced.

The drone scanned me, and I struggled to keep it in focus, as I slid down the wall and landed heavily on the floor. Her voice sounded distant and distorted. "We will not be leaving this morning. Your situation has become complicated."

Chapter 9: Someone Else's Sins

My limbs were heavy, but they were mine. My head was pounding, and my jaw was sore from clenching tightly for hours, but they were my own. *Thank* Ajle *for that.*

I took a breath and recognized the soothing scents of the *Numolo*'s recycled, purified air filling my lungs. There were other scents, some slightly arboreal and verdant, like moss after a rainstorm, and others reminiscent of the warm, tannic bitterness of coffee. I opened my eyes into slits to sneak a peek, making sure that I was actually aboard the *Numolo*.

I was in bed, in my quarters, with a view of the stars outside the window. I had forgotten how beautiful and serene space was, after living under the surface for years. *How did I consider the Hellgate Trench a normal place to live, for so long?* I was distracted from my view by the clink of a teacup against a table.

My head lolled to follow the sound. Lounging silently in my corner armchair was a long, lean figure of a man, sipping coffee quietly. He had a thin, pointed face, shaggy yellow hair and glowing citrine eyes. *Those are strong genes in the Ammo family.*

I ran through the list of siblings mentally: not Sulimandri, not Fenrir, not Slither and presumably, not baby sister Brahn, so that left...

"Ammo Ulini, at your service," he introduced himself in Xonen elfyn, uncrossing his long legs. "The middle child of the Ammo siblings," he said wryly, "in case you're keeping track."

"It's a pleasure to meet you," I said, sitting up in bed. "I guess you already know who I am."

His smiled politely. "Yes, you and your son are very familiar to my siblings, Mister E'lan."

"Call me 'Cyrus,' please."

It was difficult to tell what Ulini's area of expertise was, based on his simple clothing: white shirt with a fitted black jacket and slim trousers. His long fingers were well-groomed, and he carried a pistol, which he currently had on the side table. Likewise, it was hard to tell what kind of impression I had made on him, as he was more reserved and aloof than any of the other brothers I had already met.

"Did the *Numolo* contact you," I asked, "or are you here at your brothers' request?"

Ulini took another sip of his coffee. "The *Numolo* contacted Mandri first, but he's currently unavailable, so he asked me to step in," he said. "That is my role, in case you were wondering: I am the free agent of the family, and I go wherever and do whatever is needed."

I got out of bed slowly, once I saw that I was in a pair of sleep pants. "I'm sorry, did you have to change my clothes?"

His polite smile broadened into a grin. "Thankfully, no. You had moments of consciousness and delirium, when you did things for yourself and just needed someone to keep you from falling over. Do you recall trying to eat scrambled eggs in the shower?"

I remembered a plate of scrambled eggs, and showering, but not concurrently. "How long was I like that?"

Ulini finished his coffee and set the cup aside, next to his pistol. "The *Numolo* knows the whole story and timeline." He tilted his head. ‹‹How about it, Lady *Numolo*?››

"It's good to have you well again, Cyrus," she greeted warmly. "It has been a week since the Proctor died. When you fell unconscious, my drone was unable to outfit you properly for the cold and return you aboard, so I contacted Mandri for his assistance," she said. "Ulini arrived two days afterwards."

"The *Numolo* had cleaned up and disposed of the Proctor's remains by the time I arrived," Ulini said, seeming a little disappointed. "There was nothing left of him except for his metal prostheses. The *Numolo* had even constructed a gurney and an insulated tunnel to facilitate your transfer. There wasn't much for me to do, besides making sure that you were secured and didn't tumble off the side during the move."

"I had a surplus of materials to repurpose, anyway, now that the extra rooms are no longer required, and I had extra time to prepare, while we awaited Ulini's arrival," she said dismissively.

Ulini shot me a knowing smirk. ‹‹You like Cyrus better than us, don't you, *Numolo*?›› he joked. ‹‹I don't remember that you ever created special devices or configurations to make *our* lives easier.››

"None of you have ever had the Proctor force his way into your mind and take over your body," the *Numolo* returned humorlessly. "I think you would agree that Cyrus deserves some accommodation until he feels like himself again."

Ulini nodded. ‹‹Duly noted.›› He got to his feet, and I saw for the first time that he was the same height as Fenrir and Slither and as lean as Mandri. "Now that you're awake and coherent, I can take a quick nap. I'll be in my quarters, if you need anything," he said to me.

He nodded tersely and left, taking his cup and his pistol with him.

I recalled what the Proctor had told me: *Ammo Ulini doesn't involve himself with Eladryz much.* "Numi, does Ulini have an aversion to Eladryz overall, or just to me, in particular?"

"You need to ask him yourself," she said shortly, implying that she knew, but she wasn't going to speak for him.

I felt restless, and my mind felt cluttered, in a way that I hadn't felt since the symptoms of my fifty-year cycle began. I caught flashes of memories — people, places, emotions and voices — that didn't belong to me. I recognized some faces from the *Numolo*'s avatars, except that their expressions were more open, more trusting...

The bastard. "The Proctor gave me his memories."

"He gave you what memories he still retained," the *Numolo* corrected gently. "He lost the memories of his crimes and their aftermath long ago. It will take time to sort through the new information, but you'll find that he gave you his knowledge, too, including everything that he had withheld to keep you with him, as long as he could."

"You knew what he was doing, all along?" I scowled, now finally understanding the tools and techniques of the Proctor's duplicity from his side. "He wanted to keep me there as long as possible, so would you have just let me stay, indefinitely?"

"You attribute more power to me than I actually have," she said. "The decision to leave was always yours to make. All you had to do was tell me when, which you finally did."

"But the Proctor used his influence, his knowledge ... he even added things to the food I ate. You didn't stop him from doing any of it!" I yelled. For once, I was annoyed that the *Numolo* wasn't a real, tangible individual who could see and hear my anger and frustration.

"Didn't I," she refuted quietly. "Search *his* memories about me, Cyrus."

I closed my eyes and shifted my focus to the jumbled mess of memories that the Proctor had gifted to me, like a fistful of shredded paper crushed into a ball. I caught a glimmer of Numi amidst the tangle and followed it to his recollections of her: interventions, warnings and admonishments, cautioning him to maintain his physical and emotional distance from me. His subtle maneuvering hadn't gone unnoticed, and her reprimands had kept him from becoming bolder, but he couldn't help himself from repeatedly trying to outwit her or me.

"The last day was a misstep," I said, catching the memory of his desperation that morning. "He hadn't expected me to leave so abruptly and didn't have enough time to think everything through. He rushed his plan and misjudged how well you understood me." I paused to reconsider my words.

"I'm sorry that I misspoke. You do know me very well, don't you, Numi?" I said. "Did you know that the Proctor would transfer everything to me?"

"I had hoped that he would realize your potential and set aside his egotism long enough to share what he knew, while he had the opportunity," she said. "You were among the most capable of pupils that he had ever mentored, and certainly the most sympathetic towards him, despite your personal feelings about his past life. If anyone could look past his evils to the value of what he offered, it would be you."

"Now, you're giving *me* too much credit," I said smartly. "Now that I can see his perspective of things, I can tell how ingenuous, foolish and unthinking I was. I wasted far too much time in the Trench."

"You are seeing yourself through his distorted interpretation. The time was not wasted at all," she said. "You saw how closely the Proctor guarded his knowledge; he wouldn't have shared any of it with anyone that he didn't trust, and he wouldn't have developed his trust in you had you shortened your stay."

I recalled the moment when I had stabbed him, when our bodies were switched. I had played on the Proctor's confidence in his own abilities to get him to accept my offered hand, but he had also let his guard down, not expecting any real threat from me.

"Your blood pressure and heart rate are decreasing," she said with concern. "Perhaps you should rest a little more."

"No, I'm done resting," I said, grabbing a tunic from the back of my chair. "I need to take a walk." As I slipped it over my head, I realized it wasn't mine, as the sleeves drooped over my fingertips. "Hmm."

"That's Ulini's shirt," the *Numolo* said.

"I figured that," I said, pulling the shirt off, and looked around for a garment of my own. All the panels on the walls looked identical. I had been gone too many years. "Where are my clothes again?"

The *Numolo* popped open one of the lower wall panels for me, and the drawer slid out and bumped gently into my thigh. "You've gained two kilograms since your departure eight years ago, so your clothes may not fit as you expect," she warned.

Two kilograms, I internally cringed. "Was I eating too much, or just not exercising enough?" I asked, pulling a shirt over my head. To my surprise, it was snug in my arms and chest but not the midriff.

"Neither," she said lightly, almost like a laugh. "Gravity is greater in the Trench than here, so your muscle mass increased to compensate for the additional force. You should feel stronger physically."

"Well," I muttered, "at least that's one good thing to come out of this experience."

My first stop after leaving my room was the *Numolo*'s docking bay. Ulini's sleek, two-seater stiletto ship stood with a few others in the *Numolo*'s hangar, occupying only a fraction of the cavernous bay. I enjoyed an unobstructed view of the immaculately clean, open hangar, and the panoramic vista of space beyond it. It felt like standing at the peak of the soaring *Ajlekuun* for the first time, after spending long months huddled indoors; the change in view and venue was liberating and mind-altering, almost a spiritual experience. I parked myself against a wall and sat down to enjoy the scenery, to stare into empty space and let my mind blank.

My attention returned as I sensed Ulini's presence nearby. It was odd, as he wasn't in the bay, yet. He appeared a moment after I had first detected his proximity, and he seemed surprised that my eyes were already on him when he passed through the doors.

"Planning on taking one of the ships for a ride?" Ulini asked jokingly, standing near me. "I wouldn't let the *Numolo* know you're eyeing other vessels."

Still seated with my back against the wall, I admired the graceful arched lines of my hostess's ceiling. "Numi knows that I'll always choose her, over all other ships. I owe her more than I could ever repay in a lifetime." I looked up at him. "I didn't have a chance to tell you earlier: thank you for your help getting me back aboard."

He grunted his acknowledgement. "You're not like other Eladryz."

I laughed harshly, remembering Lynier and the Proctor. "Is that a positive?"

He smiled. "Did you know that my wife was Eladryz?" he asked, joining me on the floor.

"I didn't know you're married," I said, chagrinned at my self-mocking quip. "I definitely didn't know she's Eladryz."

"Was," he corrected quietly. "She died over a hundred years ago, and took my heart with her. She was extraordinarily bright and exquisitely beautiful, even by Eladryz standards."

"I'm sorry for your loss." My condolences to him were a century too late, technically, but there was still a real and raw emotion in Ulini's voice.

He nodded his acknowledgment. "Have you ever been married?"

"Once, and probably never again," I said solemnly.

"Was she Eladryz, also?"

"Sariah? No, she was Xonen elfyn," I smiled, picturing her in my mind. "I've actually never met an Eladryz woman before."

He stared at me. "Never?"

"I've only ever met two other Eladryz. Both were male, and neither of them make me proud to admit that I am of their species," I said. "Or that I'm male."

"You really are atypical," he grinned. "I can at least tolerate you, which is more than I can say for the others I've met. The women remind me of how much I miss my wife, and the men are odious, narcissistic, predatory, or all of the above. It is perhaps a blessing that you were raised on Xon, beyond the influence of other Eladryz men." He was quiet for a moment, as if weighing his words. "Did the *Numolo* tell you: my wife was one of the Proctor's victims?"

I shook my head. "No, she didn't," I said, understanding Ulini's initial distrust of me a little better, given my prolonged association with the Proctor.

"It was because of her that he was caught and sentenced."

Caught and sentenced, but not tried. Scouring the Proctor's memories, there were no traces of any interrogations, accusations or confrontations, no record of the process to bring the Proctor to justice. His strongest, most vivid memories began with his waking in a windowless, empty cell, with the *Numolo*'s drone announcing that he would never be free, for the remainder of his years. Even in his despair at hearing his sentence, he had seemed unaware of what he had done to deserve it.

"Cyrus?" Ulini looked concerned for me.

"I'm sorry, I have no recollection of his crimes, or what led to his imprisonment," I said. I had no doubt of his wrongdoing, between my faith in Numi and my own experience with the Proctor's cunning. "It feels like he dumped everything else from his mind into me, but it's as though he made himself forget that part of his life, so that he wouldn't have to live with his guilt."

"That's good, then," Ulini said. "You shouldn't be haunted by someone else's misdeeds."

"It's not that simple," I said, feeling cold and numb with the Proctor's store of knowledge zippering with my own, without any conscious effort on my part. "In order to access his knowledge," I said, tapping into the mental store to focus on casting a tiny red flare with a snap of my fingers, "I also have to revisit his experiences associated with it."

I recalled, as the Proctor, casting pretty little red lights to distract and lure a little boy into a quiet alleyway; the Proctor had discarded or lost the memory of what he had done to the child in the alley, but having seen the beginning of the incident, I already knew how it would end.

"So, your knowledge comes with strings attached," he said.

I gave Ulini a wilting look. "As a Laxuyn, you already know: *all* knowledge comes with strings attached."

He shook his head with a disapproving click of the tongue. "Sounds like you've been associating with too many Laxuyn."

"It's not really by choice. You're one of the few species not trying to hunt or kill me."

"Fair enough."

We stared silently at the expanse of space for a moment.

"Although," he said, breaking the stillness, "technically, you are now responsible for the death of another Eladryz. What does that make you?"

I thought for a moment, unproductively. "Is that a rhetorical question?"

He looked at me askance. "Why? Do you have an answer?"

"Not today," I said. "Probably not tomorrow, either." I got to my feet, wobbling a little, and Ulini caught my arm. "Maybe Numi was right about my needing to rest more."

"She's usually right about that sort of thing," he said. "Come on, Cyrus. Let's get you back to your room." Ulini released my arm but stayed close, in case I teetered again.

"I was looking forward to tasting coffee again," I said sadly.

"Back to your room first, then we'll have one of the bots bring you a fresh pot," he coaxed. "Just don't try to drink it in the shower."

Sariah's back was to me, as she faced the crowd of children with me. I recalled them as much from *Numolo*'s avatar holograms, as from my fragmented memories inherited from the Proctor. *Why are they here?* she asked.

They have nowhere else to go, my love, I said. *They are lost and forgotten.*

Why are you their keeper, then, if even their own families have forgotten them? The Numolo *already preserves them.*

The children's glowing, smiling faces belied their cruel ends at the Proctor's hands. I owed my newfound knowledge to them, as much as the Proctor. If not for them, he wouldn't have devoted himself to developing and honing his talents. *To forget them would mean discounting their sacrifice.*

Not sacrifice, she said harshly, turning to me. *Don't you dare attribute a purpose or meaning to their deaths! That monster's depravity had no justification or rationale, and whatever associations or links he'd made between his power and his victims, must die with him. Use what he's given to you, and make it your own. No part of him deserves to live in your head.*

Sariah was the embodiment of my own conscience. The image looked and sounded like my wife, but she was never so blunt with me when she was alive. She was telling me how to move past my aversion and revulsion every time I tried to use my new skills, but the effort had to be mine. *I need to make new associations and links, to replace the ones he gave me.*

Separate yourself from his past, she said. *Let yourself live free of ties, free of fear.*

It was something she had said to me once, in an earlier dream and in a different context, but it still resonated. I looked at the crowd of children again, and I focused on their hopeful and innocent visages. There were Laxuyn, Ghanisi, and some were species that I didn't recognize at all. I wondered which child had grown up to be Ulini's wife. *Which of you were Eladryz?*

Only one stepped forward, a slender, angelic girl with dark chestnut hair and wide brown eyes. She couldn't have been more than nine or ten years old. She looked up at me without fear or concern, and I felt an instant connection to her. She had her own golden light, as all Eladryz do.

What was your name?

I was Seraphine Wen, she said. *One of the last generation to be born on EladryzZurylan.*

Wen. How did I know that name?

The Proctor was my father, she said. *He promised that he wouldn't hurt anyone else, if I didn't say anything, but he lied.* Her eyes dimmed with regret. *I should've realized it sooner, but I was too late to stop him.*

I crouched and looked at Seraphine. I knew she was a figment of my thoughts, but she was more solid and substantial than the others. *You were a child, and he used your love and trust against you.* The words were pointless, as Seraphine had been dead for over a century, but I felt as though I needed to lay her ghost to rest.

Wait a second. Seraphine *was* different. The Proctor's memory of his daughter wasn't softened and edited like his recollections of his other victims. He had recalled that she eventually saw through his deception, but he had also held onto her self-blame; in his twisted memory, it was somehow her fault that he continued his abuses unabated.

You were brave, I said. *Because of you, he was stopped before he could hurt anyone else.*

For my father, living for centuries imprisoned was far worse than a quick execution, she said. *But because of me, he was fated to spend his life in a cell. What does that make me?*

You were the catalyst for justice, I said. *You forced him to answer for his crimes.*

She looked at me a little coldly. *Yet, you gave him a way to cut short his sentence, by ending his own life to save yours. Some would say that it was a nobler end than he deserved. What does that make you?*

That wasn't a perspective that I had really considered. *Was I his tool for escape, then?*

Sariah lifted me to my feet. *Some part of you seems to think so, but then again, you always were your own worst critic.* She gestured to Seraphine. *Remember, she's just a facet of your conscience, as I am.*

I opened my eyes and saw the familiar confines of my quarters. "How long was I asleep this time, Numi?" I cast multiple flares in the room, in quick succession, to wake myself up by performing a task that required my focus, and to make the spell my own by practicing it until I didn't have to think about the original source.

"Thirty hours," she answered.

I shook my head in dismay. "Please don't let me sleep for that long again," I said, still struggling to shake my tiredness. "I need to be able to stay awake, and Ulini needs to return to his...whatever he does."

"He has been checking on you and did not seem concerned about your sleep pattern."

"That's very considerate of him, but I would still like to be more self-sufficient than I've been of late. Can you please make some tea for me, Numi?"

"No coffee this morning?" she checked.

"No, thank you. It's better that I not get dependent on it to stay awake." As I changed into fresh clothes, I recounted my last dream. "Did you know Seraphine Wen? Ulini's wife?"

"She was never brought aboard or introduced to me, but I knew of her," the *Numolo* answered.

"Was she really the Proctor's daughter?"

"She was his only offspring, as he was widowed soon after her birth. She was born on EladryzZurylan approximately a hundred sixty-eight years ago."

One of the last generation born on EladryzZurylan. "When you took me to the Trench eight years ago, you had said the Proctor spent his previous hundred fifty years there, so his crimes predated that. Seraphine was... *ten* years old when her father was imprisoned?" It was no wonder that she had believed and trusted him so unconditionally.

A chirp sounded at the door, and a service bot entered, balancing a tray with my tea and some dried fruit. Ulini was also at my door, but he waited for an invitation, so I waved him in.

"Are you feeling better?" he asked.

"Compared to how I was a week ago, absolutely," I said. "Compared to my normal state? Not so much."

"She was two months short of her tenth birthday when he was taken to the Trench," the *Numolo* replied to my question, ignoring that Ulini was now in my quarters.

He stiffened for a moment, realizing immediately whom we had been discussing before his arrival. "You can ask me about her, if you'd like," he offered. "We didn't have the *Numolo* archive very much about Seraphine, since she was so young when it happened. It didn't seem fair to have her past so documented and exposed."

"I didn't intend to pry," I said. "She was in one of my dreams and told me that she was the Proctor's daughter."

"She *told* you?" Ulini frowned.

"It's complicated," I scowled. "I had been tapping into... *his* memories, and realized that he recalled her differently, maybe because of who she was. Because she had blamed herself, he had shifted some of his fault to her." I noticed Ulini eyeing the dried fruit, and I invited him to help himself.

"Their relationship was complex," he said, taking a dried orange morsel between his fingers. "In some way, I think he was trying to protect her by redirecting his urges elsewhere, instead of trying to find a way to suppress them. Seraphine knew that he couldn't fix himself, and that he wouldn't seek help, so she ultimately took it upon herself to stop him."

"But she was nine," I said. "What could she possibly do against him?"

He smiled grimly. "I told you that she was extraordinarily bright. She wired his room with devices and waited until he had fallen asleep, then detonated them. Had he been a weaker man, he would've died that night; instead, he lost his hand and his legs."

I remembered the Proctor's mechanical limbs. "*She* did that to him?"

"That was just the start of it," he said. "Once their house was in ruins, and the rubble revealed some of his 'souvenirs' that he had tried to keep hidden, everything began to unravel for him. Had the geopolitical situation on the planet been more stable, his fate might have been different; apart from Seraphine, he hadn't chosen Eladryz victims, so he enjoyed a certain level of protection on his homeworld that he couldn't find elsewhere."

I remembered from my history lessons how far EladryzZurylan had declined by that point in time, and the Proctor had mentioned an association with the Ammo family's patriarch. "Is that how he came into the *Numolo's* custody?"

He nodded. "Relations between the Laxuyn and the Eladryz were different back then, and our peoples hadn't gone into hiding entirely, yet. The Proctor—he was Elijah Provost Wen, in those days—had worked with our grandfather Oeli from time to time, so he was hoping for a more sympathetic verdict by appealing for Grandpa Oeli's intervention."

"I'm going to guess that a hundred-fifty years in an ice trench is not what he had in mind," I said.

"No, it wasn't." Ulini finally took a nibble from the piece of fruit he had in his hand, didn't hate the taste of it, and tossed the rest of it into his mouth. "Grandpa Oeli was very protective of children, you see, and while he didn't want to see Seraphine orphaned, he also wanted to make sure that she could never be hurt by her father again. So, he made a deal with his old friend: if Wen surrendered to the *Numolo*, then Oeli would ensure that Seraphine had the security of a loving, nurturing family. Our family, specifically."

"And as you grew up together, you fell in love," I concluded, venturing a sip of my cooling tea. I grimaced, finding the tea weak and flavorless.

"Is something wrong?" Ulini asked, glancing at my cup.

"This is usually my favorite tea, but it doesn't have the same kick that I remember," I said. "It's the right blend and strength, but…"

Ulini took the cup from me and took a sniff. "You know you need to replenish yourself after expending your energy, right?" He passed the cup back to me. "You need something more restorative than this; it's no wonder you're exhausted. Sleep is important, but your food intake needs to change, too. *Numolo*," he called, "do you have the extracts and concentrates that the Proctor kept in his pantry?

"I collected the ingredients, but I don't have the recipe data to mix them properly," she said apologetically.

"You may have to tap into the Proctor's memories for those, I'm afraid," he said to me, then sighed. "In the meantime, *Numolo*, please make a cup of tea for Cyrus with one part chicory root, one part silver cherry leaf, and two parts murkbane, steeped for five minutes."

"I feel like I should know more about this kind of thing," I said, chagrinned.

"I only know this recipe because Seraphine used to drink it regularly. By Nafre, I forget how sudden and overwhelming these changes are for Eladryz," he remarked, noting my lost expression. "Every time you use your energy to do anything, you deplete yourself," he reminded patiently. "Little efforts won't drain you much, but some of the Proctor's skills are well beyond what your body is yet ready to support."

"That sounds familiar," I said. "It's similar to how the augments work for the mages on Xon. As I get stronger, the depletion should slow, right?"

"That's how it usually goes," Ulini said, as the door opened for the service bot with my murkbane tea. "Remember, the Proctor was over three hundred years old, and you're barely a fifth of that, so be patient with yourself. In the meanwhile, drink up, build up your energy stores, and sleep a little longer. I'll stay around until I'm confident that you won't hurt yourself."

He gave me a reassuring smile and nodded and left me to my cups of tea and assortment of dried fruit, minus one piece of apricot.

I sipped my murkbane tea, which had a savory, almost mushroom-like flavor, and was more satisfying and fortifying than tea, more like a broth or a soup. I caught my reflection in a mirror and noticed that thickening scruff around my jaw and sideburns. For a brief moment, my unkempt beard reminded me of the Proctor's grizzled face. "Well, that won't do," I muttered, finishing my tea and stepping closer to the mirror.

Focusing on my reflection, I swept my hand across my cheeks and mouth, stripping the bristly hair from my face, down to my skin. "I am EladryzZurylan Tarynova Cyrus of Xon," I proclaimed. "Husband of Sariah of House Soless, Father of Janin Sariana E'lan and Alessarc Nahe E'lan."

As I said the names aloud, I felt my old identity reasserting itself, reaffixing itself to my flesh and driving any doubts and uncertainty from my head, but what the mirror reflected wasn't exactly the version of me that had come from Xon. I had changed irrevocably from what I had been when I left thirteen years earlier, but I was comfortable with that.

"Elijah Provost Wen." I said the name, trying it out in my own voice, and waited. Not that I had expected him to apparate like a ghost, but I had expected some kind of visceral reaction on my own part to the name, like queasiness or repugnance.

Instead, I had recalled how Ulini spoke the name, referencing it as a bit of historical minutiae but refusing to accede any more significance to it. I wanted to do the same, remembering from my dream: *No part of him deserves to live in your head.* The Proctor had affected me enough while he was alive.

Not anymore, I pledged, studying my reflection a moment longer. I did look a little older, but more in experience than years. I had seen more in the prior few years since leaving home, than I had witnessed during the first five decades of my life, and the cynicism showed in my eyes and my face.

"This is your second life, Cyrus," I reminded myself. "Don't waste it. You may not get another."

Chapter 10: Flowers for the Departed

"No, the flanged one!" I said to my assistant bot, as it offered the fitting to me. I was up to my elbows inside the block, trying not to knock any cables loose, but I managed to turn my head enough to point my chin at the small bolt that I needed. I made it wiggle a little on the tray to give the bot a visual and aural indication.

Ulini was snickering at me, as he was reinforcing the dark metal hull of his stiletto ship, *Seraphine's Mercy*. He had just returned from a commission where he had helped with the "removal" of a dictator named Tyrannus Quarvo and was sharing some of the lurid details, as we worked together on our separate projects.

With the *Numolo*'s bay mostly empty, his hearty laughter echoed off the walls. ‹‹If you want some help, just say the word,›› he offered. ‹‹Or, the *Numolo*'s bots could finish the repairs in a fraction of the time.››

[Where's the fun in that?] I shot back.

‹‹It's all fun and games until your air supply runs out,›› he quipped.

"It won't. I may not be as good at fixing these things as you, but I'm not totally incompetent. I think I can keep a roomful of plants alive."

Ulini and I switched back and forth freely between Laxuyn, Xonen elfyn and Alliance-speak, as we were both equally fluent, and having to switch languages on a turn kept us sharp through the long hours. It was one of the things I missed most about Ulini's company, during the extensive periods when he or I, or both of us, were away on personal business.

Over the prior five years since he had accompanied me back to the *Numolo* from the Trench, we had seen each other perhaps two or three times a year. I had learned as much from him in the brief periods that we spent together as I had in the years I had spent with the Proctor, due to Ulini's openness to sharing Seraphine's experiences.

[I don't think the hydroponics sector has been that full in decades,] he remarked, taking off his welding mask. [How did you even find some of those specimens?]

‹‹Desperation,›› I said, fastening the last bolts in place for the portable air generator. ‹‹Some of the samples and extracts that Numi had taken from the Proctor's stash, like the red ironroot and *rijkil*, were so dilute and overcultivated as to be worthless to me, so I went to gather more viable seeds and cuttings from the source.››

[Wait,] he said, pulling off his protective gloves, [you mean you've actually gone back to our homeworld to collect new samples? The surface of Nafre'Numolotal can't even hold breathable air, anymore.]

‹‹No, it can't,›› I affirmed, turning the device around to inspect it from all angles. ‹‹But dormant seeds don't need much to revive.›› I had donned an environment suit to go to the surface of the Laxuyn homeworld, harvesting seeds, stems and roots of certain plants that had originated there. Once back aboard, I had germinated what I could and used my own energy to resurrect what seemed dead and desiccated. As a result, the *Numolo*'s greenhouse now teemed with flowers and herbs that hadn't been seen in decades, if not centuries.

[All right, off you go,] I said, tapping the machine on the side to send it on its way back to the hydroponics lab. [Go with it, and confirm that it works right,] I said to my assistant bot, which flew after the rolling generator out the door. [*Numolo*, please have the bots check the filters and feeds tomorrow morning to make sure the extra pollen isn't clogging up the works.]

[It is scheduled,] she replied, as Ulini and I packed up our tools.

As Ulini opened a cubby under *Seraphine's Mercy*'s wing to stow his equipment, I noticed a small trinket hanging near the door. From a distance, it had looked like a gaming die, but up close, it looked like a clear glass block with something dark suspended within it. "What is that, anyway?"

Ulini followed my line of sight to the dangling trinket. [Here, see for yourself,] he said, taking it off the hook and lobbing it to me.

When I caught it, I almost dropped it, as I recognized a blackened fingertip, complete with its fingernail and whatever dirt had accumulated underneath it when the finger was severed. "Why do you have this?" I asked, tossing it back to Ulini.

‹‹The wretch at the other end of that fingertip was an Alliance stooge named Arastan,›› Ulini said. ‹‹About seventy years ago, that bastard killed our grandfather because Grandpa Oeli wouldn't reveal our locations. Our brother Slither witnessed it but was helpless to stop it, so he pledged to the rest of us that he would see Arastan die in obscurity, and not celebrated as some great Alliance hero. I asked for a memento, and Slither sent me this.››

I hadn't known that dark, morbid aspect of Slither's personality before, but then again, I was learning more about the Ammo family and myself with each passing day.

‹‹It's not like I look at it all the time,›› Ulini assured me, hanging it back inside the compartment. ‹‹I know it's disgusting, but it's like a lucky charm and a reminder that sometimes justice does still prevail, so if I see an opportunity to speed it along, I do so happily.››

The *Numolo* chirped to signal an incoming call. [We have multiple ships hailing to intercept and board us,] she announced. [There are four incoming signatures; would you like to receive them?]

I saw the subtle pivot in our view out the bay opening more than I felt any movement. Ulini and I were both on our guard, but if the *Numolo* had seen the hailing ships as hostile, she would've already jumped away to safety. [Who are they?] I asked on Ulini's behalf.

The *Numolo* announced them in quick succession: [*Persephone*, adder-class. *Oelivan*, light cruiser-class. *Nemesis Runner*, corsair-class shuttle. And *Naehin*, tiburon-class.]

One by one, gates opened off the starboard side of the *Numolo*, as the ships entered our space. While I was always happy to be on hand for the *Oelivan* and *Persephone*'s visits, I was unfamiliar with the other two. The compact shuttle of the *Nemesis* carried Alliance markings and moved with a larger vessel's speed and power. The last ship, the *Naehin*, was bulky and armored but maneuvered as nimbly as the others.

A quick glance at Ulini told me that he felt some trepidation, too. [Do you recognize those?] I asked, pointing to the latter two, the shuttle and the tiburon.

Ulini nodded. ‹‹I do, but I still don't think this will be good news, Cyrus. There are only two reasons that my siblings and I ever all gather like this: life and death.››

Ulini and I moved to the wall as the ships proceeded into the bay, filling it quickly.

Nevis and Fenrir came out of *Persephone* first. Sure enough, their faces were serious, but they managed to smile at us. Fenrir's hair had grown longer and lightened with some more white strands threaded through the yellow. Nevis was dressed in a trim, dark suit, with her dark lilac hair slicked back from her pretty face.

Mandri disembarked from the *Oelivan* next. For the first time in years, I saw him without his fur coat over his shoulders, and he looked lean and stern. A few steps behind him trailed Rosie, a little taller and broader than I remembered it.

Before I could go to greet the arrivals, the ferocious-looking *Naehin* opened its black alloy hatch, and the most welcome faces appeared: Slither, with his usual broad, mischievous grin muted by the solemnity of what was bringing them together, and my son, Sarc, whom I hadn't seen in years.

All else forgotten, I bolted across the bay and embraced my boy before we even exchanged a greeting. Taken by surprise, he took a second before he hugged me back, and he chuckled.

"I'm glad to see you, too, Dad," he said quietly, his voice thick with emotion.

I stepped back but kept my grip on Sarc's shoulder, hesitant to release him. By *Ajle*, he looked so much like his elfyn grandfather and mother sometimes, with his wide-set golden eyes and autumnal colors of gold, auburn and amber. He was a grown man now, the energy and spirit of his earlier years now tempered with serenity and restraint.

The last new arrival emerged from the Alliance shuttle, a slender woman with long yellow hair gathered into a single braid that fell over her shoulder, and dressed in a tailored dark suit like Nevis's that flattered her lean figure.

She bowed her head to Sarc and Slither, then extended her hand to me in introduction, as she was the only one in the bay who was unknown to me. "It's an honor to meet you, finally, Cyrus E'lan," she greeted me in elfyn. "My name is Ammo Brahn."

While the Ammo siblings and their guests were unloading what little luggage they had brought and resting after their journeys—some longer than others—the *Numolo* had been silently realigning and reconfiguring her internal spaces to accommodate the sudden influx of guests. I remained in the bay to oversee the bots unloading the most precious cargo that had arrived with the *Naehin*, the reason that the Ammo children had gathered.

Slither and Sarc had brought with them the remains of the venerable Ammo Nefiri, or Nefiri-tal—Mother Nefiri—the mother of the siblings, and one-time keeper of the *Numolo* before her retirement to a quiet little town in the Realm on Xon. The news, as solemn and unfortunate as it was, had been quietly relayed from one sibling to the next, in order to minimize the possibility of the Alliance and others picking up the chatter. Moreover, Laxuyn always preferred to discuss these matters in person, instead of relying on the impersonal and remote means of a comm. Ulini had been notified by Fenrir to anticipate a gathering, but as the last sibling in the communication chain, he had no other details until the others had arrived.

Sarc was speaking to Slither privately, reassuringly, until Slither nodded his head solemnly and left the bay, leaving only my son and me in the hangar. Sarc's quiet footsteps were the only sound in the vast chamber, apart from the quiet hum of the *Numolo*'s bots and drones around us.

"Slither tells me that life and death are the only two reasons that all five siblings ever reunite," Sarc said, as we watched the bots gingerly set the insulated reinforced crate onto the floor of the cargo bay. "It had been decades since Fenrir and Ulini had even seen their mother."

"When your lifespan is centuries, and your calling takes you across the galaxy, the years tend to slip away more quickly," I said, as a way of explaining their absence, but the statement was just as true for me. "It's not a justification, it's just…"

Sarc put his hand on my shoulder. "You don't need an excuse, Dad." he said. "Neither do any of Nefiri-tal's children. She was proud of all of them and always knew where they were and what they were doing."

"That's great, it's more than I know about what you're up to," I joked to lighten the mood. Sarc and I were lucky, in that Numi kept us connected over the past few years. "One of these days, I expect you to tell me to stop playing out here, get back to Xon and start acting my age."

Sarc laughed. "If I didn't have responsibilities at home, I'd be here with you, if the *Numolo* would have me," he said, addressing his last words to her directly. "When I tell Glory where you are, her face just glows; her own grandfather is exploring the stars, battling villains and saving lives! You're an inspiration to her."

I shook my head. "Glory is twenty-two years old and believing fiction about me."

"I don't lie to Glory," he said. "She'd see through it, if I ever tried. You'll just have to own up to the fact that you're more heroic and accomplished than you think."

Sarc left my side to check the stability and settings of the insulated crate. "They haven't decided the details of the funeral, so we have to keep her remains preserved until they're ready," he said. "She shouldn't stay in the hangar, either way."

Sarc opened the padded protective crate and gingerly lifted the sealed, capsule-like coffin from it, transferring it to the awaiting gurney, with a few deft gestures of his hands.

"She deserves her own quarters," I said.

"I have already prepared one for Nefiri-tal," the *Numolo* said. "I will see to her transport. Traditionally, Laxuyn family members do not need to be present for such transfers."

"Thank you," Sarc said. "I'll accompany the bots. As Slither's second, I should oversee the move."

"I'll go with you," I offered, as the *Numolo*'s bots towed the transport gurney out of the bay, with us following close behind. "Slither must trust you a great deal, to ask you to be his second."

"I was honored that he asked me. It's a role usually limited to Laxuyn friends and family."

I nodded, remembering what little I had learned of Laxuyn funereal rites. "You're expected to stand in support and in place of the family, so that they can focus on paying their respects without having to worry about all the details. I don't think many non-Laxuyn would be up to the task."

The *Numolo* had chosen a room with extra-wide doors to allow easier passage of the gurney, but she had kept the interior spare, uncluttered by the usual bed and dresser. There was a single table situated by the back wall underneath a window, just large enough to accommodate the coffin.

"There should be some space away from the wall, to allow visitors and the ancestral spirits to move around freely." Sarc gestured a beckoning wave to pull the table and the capsule away from the wall a half-meter or so.

The space was too cold and plain, and from what I had heard about Ammo Nefiri from Mandri, Fenrir and Ulini over the years, she was neither cold nor plain.

Sarc watched me pace the room in measured, calculated steps. "What are you thinking, Dad?"

"This should be a room of respite and reflection," I said, conjuring tufted seats and cushions and soft candle-like lights, to impart a sense of tranquility to the space. Some items I had brought from the *Numolo*'s storage, and some I had taken from my own quarters, so nothing had required a great effort to obtain, but Sarc seemed impressed by my casting ability.

"My father, the conjurer," he remarked. "You've been practicing a lot these past years."

"Just trying to catch up to you, son," I returned. "I still have a long way to go."

To accommodate the social needs of her guests, the *Numolo* had adapted one of her unused rooms into a gathering space for meals and group discussions. We agreed as a group to congregate there, to dine together and catch up with one another, before proceeding to more serious conversations. For those of us who saw each other often, it was an easy reunion, but it was still bittersweet, given the solemnity of the occasion. For others, it was made more difficult by the other challenges in their lives.

Mandri, in particular, was distracted and dour, even with Rosie's calm, stable presence nearby.

[He is worried for both Sistine and Lynier, but more for Sistine,] Rosie said. [The Twins have remained on the *Shakti*, in case of Sistine's return, but they have not received any transmissions or picked up any communications about her.]

When Rosie had told me of Sistine and Lynier's sudden decision to leave the *Shakti*, I was disappointed about Sistine's rashness, but I had also recalled Lynier's magnetism and his mention of a relationship with her, so I wasn't entirely surprised. Sistine was already an adult and capable of making her own decisions and living with their consequences, but I understood and sympathized with Mandri's concern.

[I'm glad you're his second, Rosie,] I said. [He needs and relies on your constancy, more than he probably admits.]

Rosie nodded its head. [He doesn't say much to me, which indicates that he feels comfortable not having to fill our silences with sound and words.] Without a word, Rosie bowed to me and returned to the corner of the room where Mandri stood, not immediately next to him, but close enough to see to whatever he would need.

I heard my name in passing and turned to the sideboard spread, where Ulini and Fenrir were noting the varieties of fresh vegetables and fruit prepared for them.

‹‹You propagated all of these in the greenhouse?›› Fenrir asked me, astonished.

‹‹Technically speaking, the *Numolo* did all of the hard work of providing the right growing conditions,›› I said. ‹‹I just found the plant material for her.››

Ulini cleared his throat gently. ‹‹He went to Nafre'Numolotal for the seed and stock. It took a few tries for Cyrus to find viable samples for some of them.››

Fenrir nodded fervently. ‹‹I can imagine the effort, but...›› He pointed to one of the bowls of clustered, emerald-green berries. ‹‹Those only start fruiting on twenty-year-old canes, and you haven't been here that long.››

I bowed my head. ‹‹I might have used my own energy to accelerate the growth of some of the plants,›› I admitted. ‹‹It didn't make sense for the *Numolo* to keep expending her energy to synthesize food, when the plants can yield so much more than they take.››

‹‹Thank you for all this,›› Ulini said, and Fenrir nodded in agreement. ‹‹Some of these plants and foods have been extinct for centuries, and only known through historical record. Just seeing them is a dream come to life.››

I hope they feel that way about their mother's room, I thought to myself, forgetting momentarily that Sarc was in another part of the room, chatting with Mandri and Rosie. I heard Sarc's familiar laughter in my head, which triggered my own uncontainable grin.

With both Sarc and me in his line of sight, Ulini noticed our connection easily ‹‹When Slither told me that his second was half-Eladryz, I had thought he was a fool, but I now I understand his confidence better. You raised your son well.››

‹‹In some ways, it feels like I'm learning more from him,›› I said, shooting a glance over my shoulder at Sarc.

Fenrir nodded, as Nevis entered the room, with Brahn. ‹‹I feel that way every time Nevis comes home to visit, with a new story to share. She was the first one I had considered to be my second.››

As Brahn went to Sarc to give him a kiss on the cheek for some unspoken kindness, Nevis was more demonstrative with me, wrapping her arms around my neck and giving me a more lingering kiss, then looked back at her glowering father.

‹‹Before you say anything, Papa, that was from Grandmother,›› she said, then turned back to me, as she dropped her arms. [Nefiri-tal's room is splendid, Cyrus. The flowers, the boughs… everything is perfect. Thank you.]

I dipped my head humbly. [You're welcome, but I did have an accomplice,] I said, pointing to Sarc, who was showing the same humility to Brahn. [The *Numolo* told us that Nefiri-tal was fond of silver cherry blossoms and twyg flowers, so we were happy to spare some from the greenhouse.] Out of a handful of cuttings, Sarc and I had worked together to clone and duplicate enough of the flowering branches and sunflower-like twyg sprays to drape Nefiri's coffin and decorate her room, filling it with the combination of their peach-like and spicy-sweet fragrances.

Nevis gave my hand a last squeeze and sprinted over to Sarc, to give him the same enthusiastic show of gratitude that she had bestowed on me. Caught by surprise, he nonetheless recovered quickly and replied with a gallant kiss on her hand, the gesture now second nature after his decades spent in the Imperial Court. Nevis giggled and flashed me and her father a coquettish simper.

In the meantime, Slither had made his way to the table and was sampling some of the fresh berries. [We should make you an honorary Laxuyn after all your efforts,] he remarked.

[He's endangered enough with Eladryz on his profile,] Fenrir said. [He doesn't need the stigma of being identified with Laxuyn, too.

Come on, brother. Let's see what the fuss is about with Mother's room.] Slither loaded a plate with food and followed him out, in the direction of Nefiri-tal's room.

I glanced at Ulini questioningly, and he smiled. [I went to her room before I came here,] he said, [and I saw what you and your son did for our mother. I wasn't just talking about the food before,] he clarified. [You've helped to bring part of our homeworld back to life, and for that alone, our family owes you more than we can ever repay.]

I was moved by Ulini's sincere humility. ‹‹I'm only returning the favors and kindnesses that you and your family have shown to me and mine,›› I said, respectfully addressing him in his own language. ‹‹I'm not a fool, I know the odds are against the Eladryz lasting more than a few generations longer, but the Laxuyn still have a chance to recover, so I'd like to help you preserve what you can.››

[I also owe you my personal thanks, for allowing me to share what I recall of Seraphine,] he said. [It had been so long since I had spoken to anyone about her, that I had started to forget how sweet and good our life together had been.]

‹‹Again, in this case, I believe I owe you more than I gave,›› I rejoined. ‹‹If you hadn't been as open and forthcoming with your Eladryz insights, I couldn't have managed to do so much in the few years I've been with Numi.››

He laughed softly. [We are at an impasse, then, as you seem insistent on remaining indebted. Perhaps I can ask a favor of you, to clear our ledger.]

‹‹Of course, Ulini. What can I do for you?››

[I'd like you to be my second,] he said. [You practically are, already, for the family, so it's more of a formality —]

‹‹I'd be honored,›› I interceded gently. ‹‹Whatever you want, that is mine to offer, is yours.››

Ulini smirked and glanced at Nevis, who was watching us from time to time. [You're lucky that my niece doesn't need a second of her own. Otherwise, if she'd asked you first, you'd *really* have your hands full.]

Over dinner, the Ammo siblings decided on a site for their mother's ceremony on an unaffiliated station named *Kaifeng* that was near the Nexus, which was convenient for the mourners, but not for the *Numolo*, who needed to remain undetected and isolated for her own safety. Laxuyn worldships like the *Numolo* and her sisters were highly sought-after for their intelligence and advanced technology — the same traits that helped them to steer clear of traps and avoid enslavement—but her loyalty to her keepers and her friends sometimes skewed the *Numolo*'s assessment of acceptable risk towards imprudence, and the siblings had to plead with her to stay away from Nefiri-tal's funeral.

As the siblings and the other seconds traveled ahead to the site to meet the early arrivals and prepare for the ceremony, Slither accompanied Brahn in her shuttle, while Sarc and I stayed behind with the *Naehin* to transfer Nefiri-tal's remains.

My small bag of clothes and toiletries did not go unnoticed by the *Numolo*, even as she was busy opening jump gates for the smaller ships to speed their journeys. [Are you planning to return, Cyrus?]

[Of course, Numi,] I said, pausing at the *Naehin*'s hatch, [unless your bots have already mastered the greenhouse chores.]

[Are you not returning to Xon with Sarc and Slither?] she ventured.

That had been a notion that Sarc and I had discussed, but we hadn't come to a decision. As much as I missed home, I knew that I was more useful to Xon and to our friends by remaining off-world. [We haven't determined that yet.]

[I look forward to your return, then,] she said, sounding relieved.

Slipping into the co-pilot's seat next to my son, I leaned into the backrest and closed my eyes, savoring the quiet of the cabin.

You're going to miss Numi, aren't you? Sarc asked, preparing the ship for departure.

Somehow, I think she'll miss us more, I returned, opening my eyes and looking at the array of controls and displays in front of us. "I meant to ask: was it your idea to name this big, scary warship the *Naehin*? Was *Cupcake* already taken?"

Sarc laughed. "It means 'delicate beauty' in elfyn, doesn't it? Yes, Slither let me pick the name. I don't know, she looks pretty to me, reminds me of a gentle horseshoe crab. She's one of the first ships we ever captured on Xon."

"She's a tiburon-class," I remembered from when she first arrived at the *Numolo*, then I *remembered*. "*Hilafra*, is this the ship Mandri repossessed from the dead poachers, back in 950?" The poachers had arrived at the start of my transformation, and I still recalled their attack and the ensuing carnage that had followed, when I had first seen my son's full power and lethal vengeance.

"She is," he said, activating the *Naehin*'s jump engine. "We've repurposed her to make her less mercenary and military but decided to keep her defensive measures intact. We still can't take her out in daylight, and risk spooking the locals, but she's useful for off-world trips like these."

It was apparent that Sarc used the *Naehin* often, judging by his ease and comfort with the control panel.

The trip from the *Numolo* to the gathering site was disappointingly quick, as it seemed that I had barely had time to get around to asking Sarc about his potential romantic prospects before we arrived at the station.

Kaifeng was a former Alliance station that had been decommissioned from active military service nearly a century earlier, then reopened for use as an unofficial intermediary site, utilized by those within and outside the Alliance for various purposes: political negotiations, commercial transactions, and even the occasional wedding. With a number of species displaced or too far removed from their homeworlds, *Kaifeng* was often used as a neutral, nonaffiliated safe haven to gather free from persecution.

In keeping with the peaceful intent and theme of *Kaifeng*, we were directed to the section of the station called the Harmony Wing, and an extensive contract was downloaded to our display for our perusal and affirmation of peaceful intent before the *Naehin* was allowed to pull into the slip.

The bay for Harmony Wing was already buzzing with activity by the time we disembarked, and crowded with ships from dozens of worlds and civilizations. It looked like one of *Dione*'s bays, except that all of these ships had carried family members, mourners and acquaintances from across the galaxy, all coming to pay their respects to Ammo Nefiri, the matriarch of one of the last great Laxuyn clans of Nafre'Numolotal.

I took a quick visual inventory of the hundreds of faces in the bay, spotting each of the siblings, plus Rosie and Nevis, and even the Twins, Frey and Grey, as they emerged from the bay of the *Shakti* and made their way over to Mandri. I mentally paired the siblings with their seconds: Mandri with Rosie, Fenrir with Nevis, Ulini with me, and Slither with Sarc…

"Who's Brahn's second?" I asked Sarc. "She didn't come with one."

Sarc shook his head. "She said it was someone from within the Alliance, so she didn't want to expose the *Numolo* by bringing her along, but she would meet her second here."

Sarc and I both looked at an eye-catching new arrival, a pristine Alliance shuttle with executive diplomatic markings on its side. Brahn sprinted towards the ship to meet its passenger, and she greeted the dignitary with a warm, heartfelt embrace.

As the new arrival emerged from behind the shuttle wing, I recognized the bright blue curls and the long, shapely legs of

Ambassador Eroshim Nova of Ghanis. My immediate mental and physical reaction at seeing Nova, as fleeting as it was, prompted Sarc's bubble of laughter.

"*Hilafra,*" I muttered under my breath.

"Oh, that's right," he grinned broadly. "You and Nova already know each other."

Sarc held out a cup of the ceremonial tea, luring me away from the garlands of greenery and flowering twigs. "The decorations look fine, Dad. Stop avoiding her, and just go talk to her."

I took the tea in hand and visually inspected the gathering space for anything out of place. While the ceremonial chamber was protected by a high dome to preserve its sense of alfresco openness and minimize the natural din of crowds, it was still an enclosed room containing hundreds of guests, but it was as close to an outdoor venue as could be found in neutral space.

"I'm not avoiding her," I said, taking a sip of the sweetened tea.

"But you know exactly who I mean," he said.

"Naturally." My eyes were repeatedly riveted on the vivid ultramarine hue of Eroshim Nova's hair. Despite her conservative, plain black mourning dress, she was still poised and elegant, without a single tear to mar her expert makeup. However, her eyes were missing their usual spark of clever vivacity, and she was slower with her retorts and rejoinders.

"You don't have to be celibate," Sarc commented, following my gaze. "Nova's an incredible woman. I don't know that I have the fortitude to ever call her my stepmother, but…"

I gave my son a reprimanding glare. "I don't entirely trust her."

"You don't have to," Sarc said. "It's clear that she doesn't completely trust you, either, but she's drawn to you, nonetheless. You can just talk with her, be her friend, and see where the conversation leads you."

"When did you start giving personal advice?" I quipped.

"Someone had to fill the void you left back home," Sarc said. "It's not as hard as it looks, but you already knew that. It's easier to speak theoretically, to give advice about relationships when you're just an observer and not actually in one of them."

"Nova's nothing like your mother," I said.

"I agree with you, there, but she doesn't have to be," Sarc returned, just as Nova came to our side, playing with the stem of a white daisy that had fallen from one of the garlands. [Can I get you some tea, Nova?]

132

She smiled sweetly at Sarc. [No, but if you can find me something stronger, I would greatly appreciate it,] she said, taking another step towards me.

[I'll see what I can do,] Sarc said with a gracious nod and stepped aside. "This may take a while," he said in elfyn as an aside to me, with a knowing wink.

Nova held the bruised flower to her nose, and she smiled for the first time I had seen that day. It was a brief, melancholy twitch of her ruby-stained lips, and when she noticed that I was watching her, her mask returned.

[Why a daisy, and not one of the showier flowers?] I asked, gesturing to the scattering of blooms that lay strewn all around us.

She twirled the stem between her fingers, as she gazed down at it. [They grow wild where I grew up on Ghanis. Daisies and sunflowers — weeds to some, but they're my favorites.]

I sensed a hesitation. [But?]

[On Ghanis, this would have a splash of blue, almost a dab of turquoise, at its heart.]

I touched the center petals of the daisy and painted them with a whorl of pale blue. [Like that?]

[Cyrus E'lan,] she scolded laughingly, [have you always been able to do that?]

[No, I had to learn how to be Eladryz first.] I eased the flower out of her fingers and tucked it into her hair as I saw on the other female mourners in attendance, and I was careful not to ruin her hairstyle. [There.]

[Thank you,] she said, pressing her fingertips against the bloom to make sure it was staying in place. [You style hair, too. Is that another Eladryz talent?] she joked.

[My daughter was very fond of wearing flowers in her hair.] It still stung to talk about Janin, even so briefly, and my ache was a little deeper than usual, given our somber setting. But for every sad memory I had of Janin, I had several happier ones. I recalled one to Nova: [Sarc learned from an early age to run whenever he saw his sister come at him with flowers.]

She smiled warmly. [Sarc favors you. He looks like a copy of you, lightened and filtered through a honey-gold tint, with softer angles to his face.]

[He inherited some of his mother's traits, and his great-grandmother's sense of mischief,] I replied. It then occurred to me that I had never inquired: [Do you have children?]

[No.] She looked down at her hands. [First, there never seemed to be any time to spare for such a self-serving effort, and then, there never seemed to be enough security to risk that kind of vulnerability.]

[It's a shame,] I said. [You would've been a great mother.]

She laughed self-consciously. [How do you know that?]

[Because, for all your brash and calculating ambition, you go to lengths to protect what you cherish, and what you know is important.] I leaned a little closer to whisper, [You also try to not let others see how much you care, which is a vital skill for parenting, especially adolescents and young adults.]

[I had no idea you watched me so closely or presumed to know me so well,] she said.

[I guessed by the company you keep,] I said. [Brahn seems as private as you are, so if she requested for you to be her second, that is telling.]

Nova tried to feign indifference. [She claims she owes me her life and her freedom, so I'm sure she considers my invitation more an obligation than a show of personal respect or regard.]

[Perhaps, but you didn't have to honor her invitation,] I said, as Sarc returned, with a cut-glass flute of an effervescent, heady golden liqueur.

[This is either from Nevis's or Slither's bar, I'm not sure whose,] he said, presenting it to Nova. [But they only brought their finest, so you won't be disappointed.]

Nova gave a languid, satisfied sigh. [This is divine, like drinking starlight,] she said. [Maybe I haven't had enough to eat, but this feels like it's going directly to my head. I should find something to nibble, before I embarrass myself. And check on my sweet girl Brahn,] she said, with a sympathetic smile. [She's taking it harder than she lets others see.]

Alone with Sarc, I didn't feel alone just yet.

Nevis caught my eye from across the plaza and flashed a sly smile.

Sarc didn't miss it. "What in *Ajle* is going on here?" he murmured.

"Nothing," I said. "She's just a friend, and Fenrir's daughter. We're not involved."

Sarc shook his head. "Even if you were—"

"Which I'm not."

"—it's none of my business, Dad," he finished. "And here I was worried that you were spending your years obsessing over Laxuyn horticulture, with the *Numolo* your only female company."

"Hardly, son," I said with a stern glance, then sensed a slight disturbance nearby, like leaves shuddering in a breeze. "You want to see something curious?"

"I don't know," Sarc grimaced. "That sounds ominous."

"It's nothing a *keeron* like you can't handle," I said, mocking his elfyn "master" mage title. I led him towards the one of the entrances to the hall, which was decorated like the others, with a trellis arch dripping with wisteria-like clusters of flowers. We stood out of sight, and a half-dozen rough-looking individuals approached the entrance, their hands ready on their weapons.

Sarc straightened, ready to cast or do something otherwise to prevent their entry, but I held his arm and just nudged him aside, out of direct sight. *It's all right. Just watch.*

As the brooding figures entered under the broad, extended archway, some of the vines dropped unexpectedly, as though they had come loose from their ties, and brushed against the newcomers' faces and shoulders. Almost immediately, the hard set of their brows and grimness of the expressions dissipated, and they looked almost enamored as they were met by a clowder of six large black cats that appeared from behind the trellis stands.

[What the hell is going on?] said one of the men, recovering his senses. [Be on your guard, in case this is one of those Eladryz mind tactics or something.]

'Eladryz mind tactics'? Who are these idiots? Sarc asked.

Poachers, from the Rim, following a lead on an Eladryz sighting, I said, not particularly concerned. *Kaifeng Control alerted me when they were cleared to land at the other end of the station. Watch the cats, this is where it gets interesting.*

With the poachers still dazed, each of the cats brushed their tails and whiskers against a target, and one by one, the pairings disappeared with a "pop". By the time the last two hunters realized that something was wrong and screamed in their panic, it was too late, and they vanished with their assigned cats.

"What was that!" Sarc asked, his eyes wide in shock.

Now that the poachers were gone, we were free to speak aloud. "Which part? The sentinel vines, or the cats?" As if on cue, all of the cats returned, unaccompanied, with a quickly-dissipating whiff of sulfur in their wake.

"Both, but maybe start with them," Sarc said cautiously, as the cats filed past me and circled him, purring as they paraded with their tails held proudly upright.

"Those are Carbon and Nero, with four of their children," I said, pointing in turn. "They reside with Fenrir on the family farm in Harbor, but they come and go as they please." I stooped, and Carbon brushed her cheek against my proffered hand before tucking herself behind the trellis and blending into its shadows. "Anyway, they act as his exterminators, in repayment for the food and shelter he provides. I spotted them earlier today, as they were blinking in and out, so I think they're here to make sure things go smoothly.

"As for the vines," I said, tucking one of the loose vine tendrils back over the trellis, "they're highly attuned to the energy and moods of sentient beings, and they're cueing the cats when they find someone who clearly has not been invited."

Sarc offered his palm to the cats to sniff, as he looked for anything out of the ordinary about them. "Where did the poachers go, I wonder?" One of the cats flashed its keen blue eyes at him, and he said, "Oh," with a frown. "I see." It turned and slipped into the shadows of the trellis to join the others, and Sarc and I were alone again. Sort of.

"Our Laxuyn friends have capable allies, as do we," I said, presuming that the cat had shown Sarc a glimpse the nightmarish drop-off site where Nero had once taken me, on the first day of our acquaintance. "Where the cats take the poachers is actually more merciful than where the sentinel vines would have them go," I said quietly, imagining how their native forests must have once looked in their halcyon days, strewn with the brilliant, draping clusters of the vines' sugary, grape-scented blossoms.

"We can communicate with the vines, too?" Sarc asked, reaching for the tendrils tentatively.

"Of course, given where I found them." I realized how little I had shared with Sarc over the past years about my travels, to spare him the worry. "Don't be shy," I cajoled. "Let them speak to you, in their way."

Sarc held up his hand and let one of the tendrils wrap itself delicately around his finger. He gasped quietly, connecting with the flood of sensations and images that he received, and the tendril released him. "It's barren and cold, but there's rubble, and entire forests lie burnt and leveled. The air is almost gone, boiled away with the water. This is where they came from? This is where the vines would send the hunters instead?"

I nodded. "It's all that the vines have known for generations. It's the worst hell they can imagine, especially compared to how their world looked before the Praimos razed it." The vines were sensing my darkening mood and dropped a thicker tendril to wrap around my shoulder, like a hug.

"The Praimos," Sarc scowled. "You went to one of the worlds he's destroyed?" Then it dawned on him. "Not just any world. You said we can talk to the vines because of where you had found them, so you actually went…"

"Back to EladryzZurylan," I nodded. "These vines are Eladryz, just like us."

A couple of the vines drooped towards Sarc, and he dodged their subtle approach. "I'm fine," he snipped, even managing a tight smile. "I'm not upset, just a little surprised, that's all."

"The vines can read you as well as I do, and they know you're peeved," I sighed. "Forgive me for not telling you, but I didn't want you to fret, and the work is important. Just because they don't speak or look like us doesn't mean they're not worth saving. Look around us," I said, gesturing to the Laxuyn plants and flowers on magnificent display. "Some of these plants came from roots and seeds that were dormant for centuries, just waiting for a chance to reawaken."

"You realize you're projecting yourself onto plants," Sarc remarked. "You received a second chance to thrive, and you want to give that chance to others by saving them from extinction."

"You make it sound so dramatic, son," I returned. "I'm just taking up gardening as a hobby, now that I've retired and have some leisure time."

Sarc guffawed at my understatement, then stifled it when we drew some disapproving stares from some of the mourners.

Anger comes from the west.

Sarc and I both looked up at the vines' warning and blinked to the western entrance to the hall, which was guarded by another of the sentinel vine trellises. Wall-shaking, lumbering footsteps signaled the approach of a gigantic, armored figure, clutching an energy rifle in its gnarled claws.

It narrowed its pupil-less black eyes at us, furrowed its spiked brow and boomed: [I have come to collect the bounty on Ammo Ulini, the assassin of Tyrannus Quarvo!]

Chapter 11: Unfinished Work

Hey, for once I'm not the bounty, that's refreshing. [And who might you be?] I asked, safe next to Sarc and under the shelter of the trellis.

[I am Hufu of Io, bounty hunter of —]

[Not a relation or close friend, then?] I asked mildly.

[No! Where is Ammo Ulini?] he demanded, powering up its energy weapon.

I shook my head. [You're never going to see him. Take my advice, and walk away from here, while you can. Quarvo was an incompetent, egotistical demagogue, who was responsible for the death of billions,] I said, remembering the name from Ulini's mention. [The bounty for his assassin is insultingly low, and not worth your effort and risk. Hey, are you even listening!]

The brute was bellowing and shaking its head to block the influence of my voice, finally charging with its weapon raised. Sarc snapped his fingers, as if issuing a reprimand, and Hufu came to a dead stop mid-step, immobilized and off-balance, and fell over with a floor-shaking crash. I followed up with a dismissive wave and transformed the hulking bounty hunter into a small goat, blatting its confusion, as its weapon fell out of its hooves. Immediately, Carbon and Nero apparated with their children, setting on the goat together like a pride of lions on a wildebeest, and the whole snarling and bleating tangle vanished with a "pop."

Ulini came to the trellis, with a drink in hand. [Was someone calling for me?] Sarc and I shook our heads in unison, and Ulini shrugged, as he walked away.

Sarc brushed his boot over a couple of splotches of blood on the runner, cleaning them with a quick spell, and I transformed Hufu's dropped weapon into a tasteful flower arrangement, which I moved to the side. [So, this *is* how you're spending your retirement years,] he said. [Exploring the stars, battling villains, saving lives... just like I told Glory.]

[I guess so,] I sighed. [Is there any other way?]

[I suppose not,] he said. [Not for the likes of us.]

Nevis approached us, her bright eyes a little dimmed. [It's time for the final rites. Are you ready?]

We nodded, and I gave her shoulders a reassuring squeeze as we joined the others. As the seconds, we took our positions next to the siblings who had chosen us, walking alongside them as they approached Nefiri-tal's coffin, to see their mother's remains for the last time.

The rites were solemn, but beautiful in their intentions and their ties to the spiritual world. Each of the siblings presented something of personal significance to their mother as an offering to ease her passage into the afterlife: Mandri surrendered his fur-trimmed coat, worn and well-loved; Fenrir gave the quilt from his bed, which she had stitched when he was born; Ulini gave up his macabre lucky charm, Arastan's fingertip in a clear glass block; Slither offered one of three remaining bottles of Laxuyn ale that Nefiri-tal had crafted the year that he was born, two hundred sixty-eight years earlier; lastly, Brahn set inside their mother's coffin a small box of ashes, the remains of her miscarried child, who would've been twenty-four years old.

In return, the siblings each took something that had been placed around the coffin, as a memento of their mother's life. It wasn't a part of the ceremony that I was familiar with, and judging by the puzzled look on the faces of the other seconds, I wasn't alone.

As the eldest, Mandri spoke: ‹‹Our mother, Ammo Nefiri, believed that our lives are meant to be shared, as widely and as generously as it is within our power to do so. People and their objects are ephemeral, but their energy and impact resonate and endure long after we have returned to stardust.

‹‹And so, while it is not Laxuyn tradition to do this—just as it goes against our traditions to include other species in our rituals—my siblings and I have decided to start something new today.›› He looked at each of the seconds, meaningfully. ‹‹As we owe you our lives, in one way or another, Nefiri-tal would want to show her personal gratitude by sharing something with each of you. And in sharing of herself, she continues to live in each of us, and in each of you.››

Mandri joined his siblings to present us with our tokens. ‹‹We're very close siblings, as you're aware, so whatever you've done for one of us, you've in essence done for all of us. You've served as our seconds, collectively, so likewise are our gifts to you.››

Mandri handed the master key of the *Shakti* to Nevis, making her the new captain. She balked, claiming that she already had her own ship, to which Mandri answered: ‹‹I know you're frustrated by situations where you want to do some good but don't have the resources, so let the *Shakti* and her crew help you. Make your grandmother proud.››

Slither gave Rosie a jar of highly purified synthetic royal jelly. ‹‹I'll be honest, Rosanthus. Our mother originally created this for herself, years ago, to keep her skin immaculate. However, she discovered one day when a honeybee got into the ointment, that it has special properties for drones of different species. She continued to refine it over the years, for you, specifically, in gratitude for your unwavering loyalty to her first-born. In the event that you ever decide that you want a hive of your own, this would be enough to trigger a metamorphosis, and turn you into a viable queen. But, even if you use just a little, it will connect you briefly to others of your kind, so that you will not feel so alone, wherever your journey leads you.››

To Eroshim Nova, Ulini gave Nefiri-tal's jeweled wedding brace, that Seraphine had worn during their years of marriage. Nova was astounded and humbled by the sentimentality and extravagance of the gift, uncomfortable with being entrusted with a family heirloom, and she visibly struggled for a tactful way to decline it. ‹‹Our mother kept it safe, waiting for someone else to get married, but none of my siblings are of the marrying kind. Least of all, Brahn, you can tell by her relationships,›› he said, as a not-so-subtle dig at Brahn's partner and Nova's ex-husband Kilaran.

Brahn gave Sarc a communication device that Nefiri-tal had designed herself, which allowed instantaneous contact to any point in the galaxy, that she had used to keep in contact with the *Numolo*, and with her far-wandering children. ‹‹You're old enough to have your own comm device, Sarc,›› she said, ‹‹instead of having borrow one from Slither or Jeysen.››

To me, Fenrir presented a small vial, containing a single white acorn. ‹‹Our great-grandfather saved it from the white cathedral oak tree that grew behind our home on Nafre'Numolotal. Its roots stretched out across a kilometer, and was still growing when our ancestors had to leave. The species has highly invasive tendencies, so our mother didn't want to try planting it on Xon or in Harbor, but maybe you can find a home for it.››

I sat in *Persephone*'s cockpit for a few minutes, in part because I liked the quiet, once the engines had powered down, but also because I was too exhausted to move. After the three-day ceremony had concluded, and the guests had started to disperse, the siblings were left to contemplate their shared loss in private again, with only their seconds to provide some succor and support through the grieving process.

Eventually, the time came for the siblings and their seconds to resume their lives and responsibilities. Nova and Brahn had to return to Alliance business on the Nexus. Sarc and Slither had obligations back on Xon, including the dissolution of Nefiri-tal's assets and belongings, which would be a painful, emotional exercise in itself. Mandri departed alone on the *Oelivan*, to resume his search for Sistine.

Ulini and Fenrir were taking *Seraphine's Mercy* back to Harbor, where Ulini hoped to find some peace and time for reflection amid the pastoral setting of the family farm. Perhaps one day he would resume his solitary life, but for the time being, Ulini wanted to reconnect with his family roots while he still had the chance. Also, he needed to stay out of sight for a while, until the outrage over his assassination of Tyrannus Quarvo died down.

Nevis prepared to take the *Shakti* out for her first flight as her captain, with Rosie and the Twins pledged to support her. At her father's request, Nevis was returning to Harbor briefly, with a cargo of plants and cuttings that Fenrir and Ulini would try to propagate, to bring some of the Laxuyn homeworld to Harbor.

Rosie and the Twins were looking forward to visiting Harbor again, as it reminded them of simpler times, before Sistine's departure disrupted their cohesion aboard the *Shakti*. Additionally, Frey and Grey were relieved to have Nevis in charge, as it was easier to defer to her command, instead of arguing between themselves about how best to run their ship.

[You'll do fine,] I had assured her, sensing her nervousness.

[Uncle Mandri says the *Shakti* always behaves better with a woman at her helm,] Nevis had recalled. [I'll try not to disappoint him, or her.]

[You won't. You couldn't, if you tried,] I had smiled, intending to give her a friendly peck on the cheek, but she turned suddenly and received my kiss against her lips.

Before I could chastise her, she had taken my hand in hers. [Thanks, Cyrus. You're really sweet, and a very good friend.]

And just like that, I knew that Nevis's crush was over. I had been outgrown, finally, much to my relief. I had looked down at my hand, feeling something small and metal pressed into my palm. [What is this?]

[The master key to *Persephone*,] she had said. [I have to take care of the *Shakti*, now, and you need your own ship, something less grandiose. I love the *Numolo* like a great-aunt, but she's a little too conspicuous for most situations.]

[You think?] I had joked, looking at the intricate, scrolled metal design of the key.

[*Kaifeng*'s management has already seized two abandoned bounty hunters' ships in the bay—you wouldn't happen to know about those, would you?] I had shrugged, trying to look innocent and failing dismally. [Anyway, I'd rather have *Persephone* go to someone who will appreciate her charms.]

I opened my eyes in wakefulness, finding myself back in *Persephone*'s cockpit, and hearing a muffled melody outside in the *Numolo*'s bay. I left *Persephone* to follow the music, which I recognized as a fanfare, with bombastic brass and majestic percussion tones bouncing off the bay walls.

"That's quite a grand welcome, Numi!" I shouted over the music. "It feels good to be back."

She lowered the volume but kept the music playing. "Welcome home," she greeted.

Her phrasing was not lost on me. "Thank you."

"You sound tired."

I smiled. "I'm drained. It has been a tiring few days. Between the energy drain and the emotional toll, I don't think I've been this exhausted in years." I headed for the door, towards my quarters, deciding that my luggage could wait till later, as I needed a full period of sleep far more than I needed my comb and wrinkled clothing.

"If you'd like to rest now, I'll have some tea brought to you later," she offered.

"That would be very nice, thank you."

Back in the cool stillness of my room, I felt the centimeter-wide data cube in my pocket as I was taking off my jacket.

"I have something for you," I called to the *Numolo*. "Slither had worked on it with Nefiri-tal and asked me to give it to you."

I pulled it from my pocket and held it out, and a drone entered the room to take it from me, turning it around deftly in its pincers to evaluate it. "There's a program on the data cube that's intended for you."

I left the drone still examining the data cube, as I went to wash my face and get ready for bed. When I returned to my bed chamber, the drone was still in the same position, but the data cube had been inserted and finished its download of Slither's program.

A three-dimensional image of Nefiri-tal appeared above the drone, resplendent in her gold and white robes, with her thin, weathered face open and smiling brightly. I had only seen her still, wax-like figure within the confines of her coffin, and I was glad to be able to see her for once as others had remembered her in life: ever-joyous and ever-hopeful.

"It is a private message," the *Numolo* said softly. "And Nefiri's holograph."

"I know. I don't expect you to share it," I said. "Slither told me that the message was meant for you alone. The holograph is how she wanted you to preserve her in your memory."

The drone retreated from the room, with Ammo Nefiri's holographic image still hovering above it. "Thank you, Cyrus. Good night."

"Good night, Numi." *And good night to you, as well, Nefiri-tal.*

My routine was this: wake; wash; eat, maybe; dress, sometimes; work in the labs or the greenhouse or on the surface of one planet or another, until I was unable to focus; sleep; and repeat. Sometimes, the routine lasted an actual day, from start to finish, but more often than not, the cycle ran much longer.

Occasionally, I remembered to record a journal entry or open a connection to Sarc directly to talk or leave a message, but I was sure to never miss his birthday. The times I was able to speak to Sarc were the most valuable to me for restoring my focus and perspective. No matter where I found myself, his voice reminded me of why I continued to work.

This was my routine for nearly ten years, over which time, Fenrir and I began to play with the idea of perhaps one day restoring Nafre'Numolotal, EladryzZurylan and other worlds to a habitable state. I was especially interested in EladryzZurylan, not only because it was the home of my species, but because of the Praimos's deep-seated resolve to destroy it. Whatever his reasons, I would not allow him to have the last say on the fate of my native planet.

I increased my time away the *Numolo*, to wean myself off the comforts she provided, and Fenrir agreed to move some of the specimens from the *Numolo*'s greenhouse to the farmstead in Harbor, where the plants could reacclimate to life in a less sterile and artificial environment, and hopefully one day return to a natural habitat.

I was more comfortable in my skin, in every sense, as I could completely obscure my Eladryz traits and blend into the population of the Alliance as easily as any other humanoid species. The freedom allowed me to explore the Alliance territories more confidently, without fear of being hunted and poached. I even partnered with Ulini, Mandri or Nevis, from time to time, when they needed an extra set of eyes or hands.

[You've come a long way since I picked you up on Xon,] Mandri noted after one of our partnerships on the Nexus. [Your aim has improved, but you're still a little slow on the draw.]

[We all have our specialties, old friend,] I said, walking with him back to the bay where our ships were docked. [Weapons will never be one of mine.]

[Suit yourself,] he said. [As long as you have a sure-fire way of protecting yourself.]

[I do.] I stopping at *Persephone*'s hatch. The *Oelivan* stood a short distance away.

[Any rush to go home yet?] he asked. [It's been thirty years since you've been gone.]

[I know, but I think I can do more good here than at home,] I said. [Slither and Sarc have everything in hand and don't need me getting in their way. I already wished my son a happy birthday last week.]

We parted ways and kept our farewells short, as we always did. It was only after I dropped my gun belt and closed *Persephone*'s hatch that I noticed that I had a blinking message light. The glowing, blinking scarlet beacon taunted me while I turned on the systems to prepare for take-off.

As I took my time entering the jump coordinates for my return to the *Numolo*, for our routine maintenance catch-up, I pressed the light to play the message, then I immediately scrambled to change my coordinates, as I heard the four-word message from Slither:

Your son needs you.

I was never as grateful for *Persephone*'s enhanced jump engine as I was then, during my rush home to Xon. After passing through the jump gate, I normally would've had at least another week's worth of travel to get home, but I burned the extra fuel to use the ship's short-range jumps to cut my time.

As I neared the Pavo system, I messaged Slither that I was close, and I received his terse reply: *Your house.*

Given Slither's usual gregariousness, his short responses seemed uncharacteristic, but I confirmed that the messages did originate from his signature, on Xon. I arrived at the hills bordering Mione after dark, and I set *Persephone* down near the same spot where Mandri had landed the *Oelivan* years ago when he first came to my home, I was less nostalgic about the rugged landscape and salt-sprayed breeze than I was concerned about what had happened to Sarc.

The timing was the most obvious clue. Sarc was on the cusp of turning fifty years old, the same age I had been when I went through my Eladryz metamorphosis. There had been some hope that his mother's Xonen genetics would somehow cancel or diminish his symptoms, and I had felt more certain after having spoken to Sarc briefly on his birthday, but that was apparently not to be.

I jogged and clambered over the familiar rocky slopes, more easily than I had when I was there thirty years before, to cut the straightest path to my old house. The cinder-block structure looked well-kept, even recently painted, and the wild roses still adorned the front, joined now by herbs and carved decorative stones.

The front door opened before I was at the threshold, and Slither's relieved smile greeted me. "*Mon Dieu*, Cyrus, your timing is perfect."

Slither closed the door behind me, and my eyes took a second to adjust to the darkness. The drapes were drawn for privacy, just as they had been when I had gone through my changes. Just as it had been with me, there was no mistaking that something had happened to Sarc.

My son was glowing. His light wasn't as luminous and blinding as mine had been at its peak, but it was bright golden yellow, like a citrine held up to a candle. Sarc lay half-reclining in the old black-upholstered armchair, not sleeping, but not entirely conscious, either. As he seemed to jerk and shudder, I noticed that he was bound with some kind of energy tether.

"I'm sorry, Cyrus," Alene said, sitting on a makeshift seat behind Sarc, holding the other end of the tether. "I'd rather not bind him at all, but this is the only way to keep him from blinking away. It took us hours to track him down last time."

With my focus on Sarc's condition, I hadn't seen Alene at all until she spoke. Like Sarc, she hadn't changed much since I had last seen her thirty years ago: a few years older and wiser, but still strong and beautiful. She was one of Sarc's oldest friends, and a fellow mage, and her calm presence was reassuring. She had been unmoving in her seat, with her braided black hair and clothes blending into the darkness, but still... I was usually more observant than that. "Thank you for keeping watch," I said, setting my hand briefly on her shoulder.

She covered it with her gloved hand and peered up at me with her green eyes. "It's the least I can do. He seems more cooperative with me than with Jeysen or Slither."

I remembered that phase well. "Hormonal overreactions," I said. "All his instincts and drives are heightened, almost to an irrational level. I wouldn't recommend letting your guard down, for even a moment, until..." I looked at Slither. "How long has he been like this?"

"He came to see me a few days ago after his morning sessions at the Altaier barracks, saying that he didn't feel well. I messaged you as soon as I saw him." Slither cleared off a chair to allow me to sit next to

Sarc. "I'm sorry I couldn't get into details. I didn't want to chance any poachers camping onto the signal to track him."

"No need to apologize," I said, appreciating and agreeing with his concern.

I set my hand on Sarc's head, and his spasms stopped. He opened his eyes and looked around, confused, finally settling his eyes on me. "Dad?"

"My *aelore* boy," I said, pained by his lost and troubled expression. Although I was aware of his physical age, that by all measures he was a grown man, he was still my child and would always be mine to protect. Recalling how disorienting and unsettling the changes had been when I went through them, I also remembered Mandri's techniques to help alleviate them for me.

I went to the kitchen and set the pouch of roasted, ground coffee on the counter. "I'm going to start a pot of coffee." Slither raised his finger eagerly to signal an order for himself. "I don't suppose we can get an ice bath going," I said, looking around my quaint, simple kitchen. I had gotten spoiled over the years by technological luxuries, like flame-less stoves and refrigeration, and I snapped my fingers to start a flame on the burner rather than hunt for matches. I set the kettle to boil and measured out some coffee; thankfully, the organization of the dishes and spoons had not changed over the years.

"I can provide ice," Alene said. "But someone needs to make sure Sarc doesn't leave."

"I'm lucid," Sarc said. "You can take the bindings off. I won't go anywhere, I promise."

I looked at him worriedly. "How long has he been glowing, Slither?"

"Since the night before last," he said.

"Keep him bound," I advised Alene. "If you were truly clear-headed," I said to Sarc, "you'd ask for your bonds to be tightened, not released. Remember that I love you, son." Before he could respond, I touched his cheek and whispered: *Sleep.* The suggestion took immediate effect, and I caught him easily against me. "I don't know how quickly he'll recover, so keep the bindings on. He'll be easier to examine and get in the bath, while he's unconscious and bound."

Alene nodded, looking at me in surprise. "When did you learn to do that?"

"It's a long story," I said. I went to the stove as the kettle started to simmer, and poured the water over the prepared pot of coffee.

Slither joined me in the kitchen to pull some cups. "He can't drink while he's unconscious."

I poured out three servings. "The coffee is for us. It's going to be a long night."

Chapter 12: Second Fatherhood

"You're here. I thought I'd dreamt your arrival."

I cracked my eyes open and met Sarc's clear-eyed gaze across the bedroom. He sat up in the bed that had once been mine, and I sat up in my desk chair, where I had fallen asleep during my overnight vigil.

His clothes were a wrinkled mess, and his hair was tussled and stringy from his fevered, restless sleep, but he still looked far better than he had hours earlier. His vibrant, glaring light had diminished to a softer glow, and his eyes had shed their manic brightness. "How long have I been asleep?"

"About nine hours," I said. "There's a glass of water on the nightstand."

"Thank you." Sarc drained the glass quickly and cradled the empty glass in his palm. "I recall snippets of the evening. I said some unkind things to you."

"It's all right," I said. Sarc's words had stung when I first heard them, but I had had hours afterwards to reconsider them in the proper context. Sarc had been emotional and distressed, but he wouldn't have spoken to me that way if there wasn't some element of truth in his vitriol.

"It isn't, not to me," Sarc said, finally setting down the glass. "I accused you unfairly—"

"You don't need to repeat what you said," I interrupted. He had said that I had abandoned him to play the hero for others. He still felt resentment for how I had kept him from his mother's bedside as she lay dying, not knowing that it was Sariah who had asked me to keep him away.

"You remember what you used to say to me, before you would leave on one of your missions for Junus, or with Slither? When I would ask you why it had to be you, risking your life?"

It had been a while since we had had one of those conversations, so he looked at me blankly at first, then remembered. "I used to tell you that it had to be me, because there was no one else who could do it."

"I didn't want to believe it, because it would mean that you could be called away at any time, and I would be helpless to protect you," I recalled. "It was both selfish and arrogant of me to think that way: your talents were meant to serve others, not to be hoarded, and you could protect yourself better than I could ever manage."

"I felt a similar way when you left, Dad," he admitted. "It hadn't occurred to me that you weren't meant to stay here. Then, when I saw you on the *Numolo*, and on *Kaifeng*, I finally understood the scope of your purpose. This place," he said, looking around the room, "is too small for you. You've grown beyond what Xon can provide."

"I wish that weren't so," I said regretfully. "If I had lived my entire life here, with raising you as my sole life's achievement, I still would have been satisfied. A smaller, simpler life is sometimes the happiest."

"But we're not made for happy, are we?" he asked, resigned.

I gave him a dubious look. "You've lived long enough to know the answer to that. No, our lives will never be simply 'happy' because that's not our lot. We've both adapted and evolved to do what no one else can do; you can throw Jeysen and Alene into that category with us, too. It's not a curse or a burden, it simply *is*. I wish I could stay and resume a simple life, more than you can possibly know, but I don't see that happening in the foreseeable future."

"But for now, what will you do?" he asked.

"You mean after you and I are done here?" I returned. "Go back to hunting poachers chasing outstanding Eladryz bounties for a while, then help Fenrir in Harbor when planting season comes around. He's going to try cultivating a grain that hasn't been tasted in five hundred years."

"I don't know which part sounds more daunting," he remarked.

I shrugged. "After raising you, nothing scares me," I deadpanned.

Sarc laughed, then shuddered as a ripple of light coursed over him. "How long did you say this goes on? This transition?"

"For me, it was ten years before the last of it subsided," I said, checking his temperature and pulse. "But your experience is going to be different, possibly unprecedented. You're part Eladryz, *and* you have an augment."

I conjured water to refill Sarc's glass and materialized a plate of fruit and bread for him. "You'll dehydrate and weaken quickly, unless you keep up your intake," I advised. "I'll brew some murkbane for you later, too."

"Murkbane," he said, sipping his water. "That sounds scrumptious."

"It's like a creamy, mushroom-flavored broth," I said. "You'll like it, I promise."

Sarc tore off a chunk of bread, his brow slightly furrowed in deep thought, and I waited for him to tell me what he was thinking. "She's arrived," he said.

"Who?" Then I realized the date on Xon: Year of the Emperors 980. Fifty years had elapsed since Clyara's foretelling of her apprentice's arrival. "Your special girl, your *Keeronae*." To Sarc, the prophesied girl had meant something much more than a future ally or fellow mage, and judging by his expression, she still did.

"It feels strange to discuss it, but I just wanted you to know," Sarc said, shaking his head abashedly. "It's weird, knowing that she's actually alive now. I try not to think about it, or about her, any more than I absolutely need to."

"Maybe take up a hobby, something that doesn't involve magic," I said. "Take a walkabout, and leave the Realm altogether. You're welcome to come with me, whenever you want. But do something to distract yourself."

"Maybe." Sarc smiled indulgently at my advice.

"You're humoring me, aren't you?"

His smile broadened. "A little, Dad, but I miss hearing your voice, so you can keep going."

I chuckled. "You used to roll your eyes at me when I kept going on with unsolicited advice."

"But I never forgot anything you said," he rejoined. "That's why you were such a good teacher and tutor, and your students enjoyed their time with you." At my doubtful frown, he said, "Adolescents generally don't admit to liking anything, especially not to adults, but I heard my share of comments, and I knew how lucky I was to have you as a father."

That was heartening to hear. "You really think I should spend more time with children?"

"Not when you put it that way, Dad," Sarc said, recoiling. "But maybe there's someone whom you could mentor or foster." He looked at me, noticing my momentary distraction. "You're thinking of a particular situation?"

I was reminiscing about my time with the Proctor, for the first time in years, and what I had experienced to gain the knowledge that I had. The *Numolo* had placed me with him at a fortuitous time, either by design or by chance, in order for me to receive his legacy. "I wonder if she had always meant for me to take up the Proctor's role, to help others after me."

"'She'?" Sarc teased, raising his brow. "There's yet *another* woman in your life?"

"The *Numolo*," I clarified. "She and I had many long conversations while she was harboring me. If she were a compatible species, I could almost see myself falling in love with her."

"I'd be more comfortable calling Numi my stepmother than Nova," Sarc joked. "But as I recall, the *Numolo* was most enamored with Jeysen."

"Just my luck," I said lightly. What else was new? Neither Jeysen nor Sarc could ever help the effect they had on others, and if my experience was any indication, my son was only going to have more difficulties as he got older. "Since your *Keeronae*'s still an infant, she'll have some time to consider her options, but hopefully, your special girl doesn't fall in love with Jeysen, too."

Sarc's golden eyes widened in horror and revulsion. "No, that can't be allowed to happen!"

"That she falls for your best friend?" I asked. "I know you have your heart set on her now, but if she feels differently — "

"No, that's not it," Sarc pressed. "She can't because they're related."

"Related? How?" Then I remembered Adella's daughter, Aelora, whom Clyara had taken from the Realm and hidden in the Dark Lands for the young princess's own safety. Sarc had relayed the secret to me over the course of our years of discussion, and even shared with Jaeris that his granddaughter Aelora was alive, to comfort our friend in his final hours.

"The baby was just born this year, so... this is Aelora's daughter," I said. "Adella's granddaughter."

Sarc frowned. "Clyara kept it to herself, to make sure it remained a secret. I only found out myself a few months ago. The whole situation's a mess, and I can't tell Jeysen about any of it. Not yet."

I was sorry that I couldn't help my son sort matters out back home, especially since he couldn't confide as completely in Jeysen as he normally would have. "This is what I get for leaving you boys alone for thirty years," I sighed. "Well, unload your secrets on me now, if you want. Once we're done here, I'm not likely to return to Xon anytime soon, to be able to tell anyone else."

During my transformation and the years that followed, I had benefited from the wisdom from Mandri, Fenrir, the *Numolo*, the Proctor, and finally Seraphine, through Ulini. Now, thirty years later, I had all that information stored in my head, ready to help my son through the same process, only to find that his augment, his magestone, was doing its part to take care of him, as well.

Sarc was already awake and alert when I went to check his vitals on the third morning after my arrival. "Good morning, Dad."

"Good morning, son." His pulsing, golden glow had dimmed to a subtle sheen, undetectable to most without enhanced vision. I knew before I touched his head and wrist that his temperature and blood pressure had normalized, and he tolerated my examination without comment. "You're an easy patient this morning."

"There isn't much point to struggling," he said. "I feel perfectly fine."

"You seem so," I said, conjuring some tea and biscuits for him, and dispelling the energy coils that Alene had cast to confine him to bed overnight. "How long have you been up?"

"A while," he said, stretching his freed limbs. "I can feel my magestone processing what's new about me, like it's doing another adjustment, recalibrating and reorganizing a little before it resets me back to normalcy."

He certainly seemed more stable and coherent than he had been when I had first arrived. "You should've said something sooner," I said. "You didn't have to stay in bed all morning."

He shrugged. "I might not have been here to get the *Numolo*'s call, then."

"She called? Here?"

"She knew I had Nefiri-tal's comm." Sarc gestured to the device on his dresser top, secured inside a lacquered jewelry box pieced together from slices of rainbow-grained wood. "It didn't take long for her to guess that you'd be here."

Sarc looked preoccupied, as though he was still thinking about what she had told him. "What is it?" I asked. "What did she say?"

"You're needed more elsewhere," Sarc said. "She didn't say that, of course. The *Numolo* doesn't presume, but..." He smiled reassuringly. "Between what my magestone has learned and what you've taught me, I think I'll be fine here, Dad. Not to kick you out or anything, but I think your skills would be better utilized to help others who have a greater need."

I sat at the edge of the bed, puzzling about who would have a greater need. "What did Numi tell you, exactly?"

"She said to tell you to reach out to the *Shakti*," Sarc said. "Nevis is requesting your help on a matter involving Sistine?"

"Sistine," I repeated, recalling her pale blue eyes and dark coffee skin. "I haven't heard anything about her in years, since before Nefiri-tal's funeral. Does Mandri—"

"Mandri is aware, but Nevis knows you're closer, and the matter is urgent," Sarc said. "The *Numolo* said you may also be better suited to handle the situation, as it involves an Eladryz."

I shook my head. "But Sistine wasn't Eladryz." Then I remembered her involvement with Lynier. *The son of a bitch.*

"It's not Sistine that needs help, not anymore," Sarc said somberly. "It's her son."

I waited at my usual seat at the bar at Nevis's establishment at *Dione*, waiting for my contact to join me. The bar was newly refurbished and expanded, and Nevis herself rarely worked the bar anymore, but she still made the occasional appearance, and the bar still bore her name.

[Well, well, Cyrus Ex,] greeted Nevis's silky voice.

I turned around on my stool and gave her a wide grin. Her purple hair was longer and her lilac skin was a shade or two darker from time spent in sunlight, away from *Dione*, but her fire opal eyes still shone as brightly as when I had first seen them thirty years earlier.

[Ammo Nevis,] I greeted. [How's business?]

[Uncle Mandri never told me smuggling and humanitarian efforts were so lucrative,] she said lightly. [I should've taken over for him years ago.]

I laughed, hearing the irony in her voice. [Lucrative, yes, but much more stressful than serving drinks.]

[Depends on the night, and the business in question,] she said, gesturing subtly to one of the corner tables.

Frey and Grey were seated with a red-haired woman in a black suit positioned between them. They seemed to be guarding her, both for her own safety, as well as the safety of the other patrons in Nevis's bar.

I recognized the woman from the first time I had visited *Dione*, with Mandri all those years ago. She looked older, as was expected, and she gave me a nervous, polite smile, as I joined them at the table. *Arkanist prison supply run, delivered to Tartarus Arkanis, as agreed.*

[Thank you for coming,] the woman said, her voice low and quiet. [Your associates had recommended that you should hear this for yourself,] she said, sliding a small data cube towards me, [but perhaps I should provide some context first. My name is Vesper, and my brother and I engaged the crew of the *Shakti* for a delivery to Tartarus Arkanis, about thirty years ago.]

I nodded. [I remember the job.] I remembered the destruction of the transport from the pickup site; with our suits on, we hadn't been able to tell which of Mandri's contacts had met us at the site, but now it was painfully clear. [My condolences on the loss of your brother.]

[Thank you,] she said, bowing her head. [Our family owes the *Shakti* more than your crew was aware. You see, when we made our arrangement with Mandri, it was with the understanding that the balance of your fee would be paid prior to the delivery to the prison colony. However, when my brother didn't return to his Alliance post after his scheduled leave, an investigation was opened into his disappearance, and the family's assets were frozen and inaccessible.]

[It turns out,] Frey said, [that Mandri paid the rest of us out of his own account, rather than cancel the deal.]

[He never told us,] Grey added, [until we asked him, after Vesper contacted Nevis this last time. There was even more to the mission that Mandri didn't share with us,] he said pointedly.

[The delivery was primarily intended to get one of the serums to our father,] Vesper explained. [He would've died in Tartarus without the treatment, so we owe you for his life. The other supplies saved countless others, as well, so our family is not alone in our debt to your crew. Even some of the prison administrators and their families benefited from your mercy.]

[One of these administrators contacted Vesper, after her father died recently,] Frey said. [And she contacted Nevis, when she came across the data cube in his belongings. It's a message that Sistine had recorded for Mandri and given to Vesper's father for safekeeping.]

Tartarus Arkanis. I picked up the small crystalline cube. [What was Sistine doing there?]

[She and her teammates were captured,] Grey said, [after they had liberated a stockyard in Arkanis-controlled territory. They managed to free and transfer thousands.]

[Unfortunately,] Frey said, [it wasn't her first incident of 'supply line sabotage,' as they called it, so she was sent to Tartarus as an example to discourage other would-be activists. Her time there was mercifully brief...]

[And the rest of her team?] I asked, thinking mainly of Lynier's fate.

[They died at Tartarus soon after their incarceration,] Grey said quietly. [Just listen,] he suggested, setting a player in front of me.

I loaded the data cube and braced myself, as I put on the headset, but the sound of Sistine's strained and weakened voice was heartbreaking.

[I hope this message reaches you, Mandri, but it's a long shot. I know what I did was stupid, but I wasn't thinking straight...but you had told me that from the start, didn't you? Anyway, I don't have much time, so I'll just cut to it.] Sistine's voice became stronger, but more brittle. *[Lynier is*

dead. He was killed trying to protect me, but he didn't just do it for me. I have a son... I – we had a son.] Her voice started to break. [Stonespire didn't realize that I was pregnant when he sent me to his harem, so he thinks the child is his. He had the baby taken from me, and now, I await my execution. Apparently, my son doesn't meet his standards of beauty, so I don't know what's going to happen to him. If you receive this message, please find him and take care of him for me. I'm sorry, Mandri. I'm always causing trouble for you, up to the very end, aren't I?] she said, with a quiet, cynical snicker. [Thank you, everyone, for everything.]

That was the end of the message. The final recording of Sistine's last moments. Date-stamped from ten years ago, long after she had left Mandri's crew.

[Sistine had a child, with Lynier,] I said dully, still not quite over the fact that she was gone.

[Listen, Cyrus,] Frey said. [We tracked him down. Sistine's son.]

[That's what I understand from...] I refrained from naming the *Numolo*, given Vesper's presence. [The message I received.]

[Mandri thought that you would be able to get to him less conspicuously,] Grey said.

[In other words, you pass more convincingly as standard Alliance than the rest of us do,] Frey said more bluntly.

[It's a valid point,] Vesper admitted. [Given their features and notoriety, your associates are more recognizable to authorities than you are. It's much easier to forge false documents for you than for the rest of your crew.]

There was shared disconcertment in the Twins' matching expressions, and it dawned on me why documents would need to be forged. "To help others who have a greater need," Sarc had said. [You'd like me to take custody of him?] I guessed.

[At least until you get him back here,] Frey said. [We can determine who's best suited to be his guardian, once he's safe in our care.]

[Isn't this risky for you?] I asked Vesper. [To go to these lengths to help us get Sistine's son?]

[As I said, our family owes you my father's life,] Vesper said, [so it is only proper that I do what I can to help. I only wish I had known about your colleague's situation or received her message earlier; I might have been able to get the information to you quickly enough to save her.]

[We appreciate your efforts,] Frey said.

[It saddens us that Sistine is gone,] Grey continued, [but we are grateful for the chance to honor her final wishes.]

I nodded in agreement. [It's what we do for family.]

155

Chapter 13: Malfait

I knew from the look of the boy that he would be a handful. He joined the administrator and me in the sparse interview room and slumped into the open seat, clearly unimpressed with the candy-colored room and the two of us adults sitting across from him.

From Sistine's message, and the confirming intelligence from Vesper, I knew that the boy was just around ten years old, but he was already tall. He was bigger and broader than most of the other children at the facility, as well as some of the adults, regardless of species.

He seemed as self-conscious of his size as he was of his dark, mottled complexion and unruly black hair, so he slouched to try to make himself as inconspicuous as possible and tugged his long sleeves over his wrists. His indigo-flecked blue eyes, however, were hard to ignore or hide. Especially against his dark skin and hair, they were startling and beautiful, and they reminded me of Sistine.

Based on the boy's facility records, I knew that the cold-eyed, rodent-like administrator was well-acquainted with him, from various disciplinary and wellness meetings over the past few months. The administrator and the boy seemed to have an accord, to ignore each other's presence as much as they could in the brightly-painted but sterile space.

That only left me, and the boy looked at me with suspicion. He could see that I was well-dressed and groomed, but he seemed to know not to place trust in others based solely on their appearance. There was no trust in his gaze, but no outright hostility, either. I could work with that.

The administrator opened the file in front of him with a sigh. [Stonewall, Malfait,] he said, glancing at the boy, as if to verify his identity. [Male. No living next of kin, no standing instructions on care and guardianship. Age…ten. Species…uncategorized. Planet of birth…data unavailable?] He looked across the table.

Malfait looked irked by the pat, rudimentary recitation of his file remarks, as though all of his brief life's experiences were encapsulated in those few phrases. Based on my own brief review of his official file, I knew just some scant details of his life so far, documented during his time in the foster system. His file contained a short list of foster families and the dates of his stays and invariably, the foster situations grew shorter, as the time between arrangements lengthened.

[Well, there doesn't seem to be anything in the file to prevent the arrangement,] the administrator said to me. [Are you sure you want to take on the responsibility? You've read his case file.]

I didn't bother looking at the administrator, focusing instead on Malfait. [I wouldn't have made the offer, if I had doubts,] I said, seeing some of the traces that I was looking for. It wasn't a particular physical trait that I sought, but something less tangible, like an energy or aura.

[Okay, then,] the administrator said haltingly. [Mister Stonewall,] he addressed Malfait, [what Mister Ulryc here has offered is to assume your full guardianship. He would have full custody of you, to include your guaranteed shelter, wellness and education. The arrangement is pending your affidavit of cooperation, and will be conditional on your acceptable conduct.]

Malfait seemed distrustful, and I couldn't blame him, given the administrator's accusatory tone. Of course, it was usually the burden of the child to prove his obedience and cooperation, and Malfait did not have the look of a docile, passive little boy. [What if I don't want to?] Malfait challenged. [What if I don't like his face?]

[You've been returned by four families in the two months since you came to us,] the administrator reminded sternly. [I would strongly recommend that you make a concerted effort for any opportunities you have remaining, while you still receive them. You age out of the system in two years.]

In other words, he didn't see that Malfait would get foster offers for much longer, and he would be ejected from the program upon his twelfth birthday. If this arrangement fell through, there was a strong likelihood that Malfait would eventually be forced into autonomy, to live on his own with few prospects.

[Can I ask a question?] Malfait ventured.

The administrator started to interject, but I responded first: [You may. What is it?]

[Why did you pick me?] Malfait asked. [There are other kids who are younger, nicer and more obedient.]

[You remind me of myself, when I was your age,] I said. Not in appearance, of course, as his dark, sullen features were very different from my own at his age, but in his overall rebellious attitude and his keen, impatient kind of intelligence. I didn't suffer stupidity much when I was his age, either.

Malfait looked me over and tried to scoff at my remark. I could almost read his thoughts, just by watching the changes in his expression. *What do I have to lose? It'll be a break from this place, if nothing else, and I may learn something useful.* He hadn't realized until his overgrown hair fell in his eyes that he had nodded, and he looked up with surprise in his blue eyes.

[Is that consent, Mister Stonewall?] the administrator asked.

[Yes,] Malfait said, his voice sounding more certain than he felt. [I'll sign.]

[Splendid,] the administrator said, a relieved smile on his face. [Mister Ulryc, if you'll come with me, we'll finish the transfer paperwork in my office. Mister Stonewall can return to his bunk and collect his things, and he'll be brought out to you.]

The paperwork and record-keeping was alarmingly shoddy and rushed, considering that the facility was entrusting the life of a young child to me. Aside from what Vesper and Mandri's Alliance contacts had fabricated for me in terms of personal and financial history, there was little actual documentation regarding the existence of my cover alias, Cyril Ulryc. If the facility had bothered with a more thorough background check on "Mister Ulryc," they would have started to notice cracks in the façade, but my generous donations to the facility and the administrator's modest salary ensured that such scrutiny could be avoided.

Then, there was the boy Malfait, himself. Even the name "Malfait" — an ancient term meaning "malformed" or "badly-made" — was intended to disparage and devalue the child from a young age, and the surname "Stonewall" was something arbitrary that had been assigned and forced upon him, for the sake of expeditious processing. The boy had arrived in the Alliance foster system when he was little more than a toddler, based on his dentition and intake physical forms.

As I waited outside of the administrator's office, I rifled through the scant contents of Malfait's complete file. I had received assurances from the administrator that no other copies of Malfait's file existed, after I made an additional contribution to the administrator's personal pension account. To further help with the scheme, I was careful not to invite closer scrutiny by over-improvising on my "Mister Ulryc" performance, and I erred on the side of cold aloofness.

I skimmed the statements from Malfait's prior sponsors and focused more on the intake and medical history of my new ward. *Surrendered as property seized from the owners of a stripped and shuttered mineral mine. Estimated age: three years old; height: approximately one meter*. His owners indicated on the affidavit that he had been sold to them when he was weaned and hygiene-trained, about one-and-a-half years old, but had no details about his birth parents or origin planet. The boy slave had been provided with basic medical care, to help preserve his owners' investment, but his personal history was considered unnecessary and superfluous…

I looked up at the sound of shoes lightly squeaking against the tiled floors. Malfait approached with a black sack slung over his shoulder — a garbage bag that held all his belongings. I stole a peek at the boy's serious, dour expression and sympathized with the insecurity and helplessness that he must have been feeling, but I kept my own visage neutral. This was not a kid who wanted or trusted pity.

Despite his gauntness and awful posture, Malfait was a handsome boy, with sculpted, strong features. I imagined that the boy's dark and light patched skin and coarse black hair looked peculiar to some, especially with the contrast of his icy, pale-blue eyes. Then again, I also recalled the wary looks that my neighbors in the Realm used to give Sariah and the children because their earthy brown and auburn hues marked them as "too elfyn." No, I didn't give a damn how Malfait looked, as long as he was smart and open-minded.

We left the facility and took the network of footbridges towards the marina where I had left my ship docked. At a little over a meter and a half tall, Malfait kept pace with me fairly easily, and in fact, he walked ahead a few times, as though he was eager to leave the facility behind him, as quickly as possible.

Malfait also didn't talk much, which I didn't mind, either. It was better that he spoke with discretion than reckless abandon. I respected that I would have to earn Malfait's confidence, over time, and that perhaps I would have to share something of myself before the boy was willing to open up to me.

I stopped when Malfait started lagging behind. I turned around and saw his ice-blue eyes wide with astonishment, staring at *Persephone*'s glossy, polished lines. She was sleek and stylized, like all Alliance-designed vessels, but once Nevis had signed her over to me, I had treated her to a gleaming, dark grey alloy hull that set her apart from her bright, shiny Alliance sisters.

[Is this your ship?] Malfait asked, his mouth agape.

[Yeah, why?] It was hard to tell from Malfait's face whether he was impressed or appalled.

[It's really pretty,] the boy said, a trace of a smile.

I nodded, secretly relieved. [Yes, she certainly is.] I brushed the controls on *Persephone*'s hull, and the door slid open for us. [Welcome to your new home, Malfait.]

Malfait was so enamored with *Persephone* that one could almost say he was in love. He had ridden in bloated Alliance shuttles and transports a few times, during ferries between child welfare facilities, or to and from foster situations, but this was his first time inside an adder-class ship built for speed and battle. She was as sleek and elegant on the inside as she had looked on the outside, and he was enthralled by everything about her.

The adders were legendary for their design and agility, even compared to non-Alliance fighters and scramblers, but Nevis and I had made our own upgrades to *Persephone* over the years that made her even more powerful. Malfait was captivated by the controls and gauges that hinted at her capabilities and weapons. [She has her own jump engine?] he marveled. [She must be practically half-engine, to fit all that in here,] he gushed, looking at the interior.

[You know about ships?] I asked, glad to find something that caught my new ward's interest. Apart from the two-person cockpit area, there was only a small cargo area visible, so a tour seemed like overkill. I let him wander freely as we prepared for our departure.

[Not as much as I want to,] he said. [There isn't much room in here, is there?]

[It's enough,] I said, moving easily through the narrow spaces to get to the front. [There are some hidden compartments for stowage, so keep these spaces clear. Excuse me for a moment.]

I took a moment to request clearance from the gate control, and started up the engine, which awoke with a low, rumbling purr. I tapped a button on the main console to close the hatch behind Malfait and returned my attention to him.

[First things first, Malfait. *That* is unacceptable,] I said, pointing to the black rubbish sack that he gripped tightly.

He balked, clutching the bag more closely. [This is everything I own,] he frowned.

[That's not what I meant,] I said, softening my tone. I joined him at the back of the ship and tapped a wall panel and to reveal a compartment containing a sturdy black satchel, woven of a tough ballistic material. I held the open, empty satchel out to Malfait. [If it's important to you, keep it safe. This storage cube is yours to use, whenever you need.] I scowled at the rubbish sack. [Don't ever let anyone treat you or your treasures like garbage, got it?]

Malfait nodded with a grateful, relieved smile. The new satchel, as simple as it was, was likely one of his only possessions that wasn't a cast-off or given in disdain, and he seemed surprised by the gesture. *Well, I need to fix that, then,* I noted for myself.

[Secondly, you see that glowing blue outline?] I pointed to a door-sized, blue-edged panel, standing in the corner. [Hygiene closet. I expect you to respect *Persephone*, as you should any girl or woman, so keep her—and yourself—clean. That light stays on all the time, so you'll always be able to find it, even in the dark. If you make a mess, you *will* clean it up.]

I turned back towards the cockpit. [We have to queue up for the jump, so you'll need to strap in. Once our coordinates are laid in, you can unpack, take a nap or get something to eat.] I tried to read Malfait's expression. [Looks like you might want to do all three?]

Malfait just nodded, as he followed me to the cockpit, where he slipped easily into the co-pilot's seat. He sank into the upholstery and ran his fingers up and down the arms of the seat, as though it was the most sumptuous furniture he had ever known. After a moment, he finally relaxed enough to close his eyes most of the way, but I could tell from his stiffness that he was still on his guard.

He was trying to figure me out. Back at the facility, I had to be paternalistic, stiff and stodgy, but in *Persephone*'s familiar surroundings, I was more myself; I was more active and alert and to Malfait, perhaps I seemed a little more formidable than I was before.

[Are you nervous about coming with me, Malfait?] I asked.

He shrugged, then managed, quietly: [A little.]

[Nervous is good,] I said, playing the console controls with a light touch. [It means you learn from your past experiences, and that you think for yourself.]

The jump was so smooth that Malfait barely noticed, and by the time *Persephone* cleared the gate on the other side, he was nodding off, as the hum of the engines and the softness of the chair lulled Malfait towards sleep.

[Before you start your nap,] I stirred him gently, [there are a few things you should know about me and about yourself.]

Malfait rolled his head heavily to face me.

[My name isn't really Cyril Ulryc; it's actually Cyrus E'lan, but you can still call me Mister Ulryc, if you like that better. And your intuition was right; I did pick you because you were different from the other children, but based on your file, I don't think you're aware of the extent or nature of your uniqueness. Are you still following me?]

[My skin and hair are much darker than the other children's,] Malfait said. He had to be blind not to notice something like that.

[It's a little more than the way you look,] I smiled. [Friends of mine—they're your mother's friends, too—asked me to come get you.

You were born on one of the planets ruled by Arkanis, so you were lost to us for a long time, and you're a long way from where you belong.]

At the mention of a mother, Malfait picked up his head. [You know where my parents are? They're looking for me?] he asked excitedly.

I flipped a setting switch to engage *Persephone*'s autopilot, so that I could give my full attention to Malfait. [I'm very sorry, but your parents are both gone. Your father died before you were born, and your mother died soon after.]

Malfait was frustrated and furious, to have his hopes raised, then dashed just as quickly. [Why did you even tell me?] he yelled. He attempted to swing his seat away, but I held it fast.

[Because you deserve to know the truth about who you are. 'Malfait' was a disparaging label that was forced on you by the man who claimed you before you were born, then changed his mind and cruelly discarded you and your mother.]

[I thought you said my father died before I was born,] Malfait said.

[Your *real* father, the man who loved your mother, gave his life trying to save her and you. Stonespire is the family name of the tyrant who gave you your name, and he's very much alive, I'm sorry to say. He couldn't denounce you or revoke your birthright without acknowledging your existence, so he chose to bury you, so to speak. It would certainly be more convenient for him if you vanished or died, so if he knew you were still alive and where you could be found, you would probably be hunted.]

[I knew you didn't really want me,] Malfait said, rubbing his eyes. [I knew this was too good to be true.]

[I never said I didn't want you,] I said. [Your real father and I weren't close or even friends, but we were like brothers, in a way, and your mother's friends all loved and miss her very much. They're very excited to meet you, and we're *all* happy to welcome you to our family.]

[Are there other children, or is everyone old, like you?]

[Right now, you're the only one,] I smiled, recalling that Sistine was a little older than Malfait when I first met her, but her species matured faster. [But age and years are not quite the same thing. Your mother was just shy of six when she joined the crew, and by the time I met her, she was one of the best pilots I had ever known.]

Malfait smiled, proud at hearing something positive about his parentage. [I wonder if I have that same potential.]

[We'll figure out together where your talents lie,] I said. [Does that mean you'll give us a chance?]

[I guess we can try it out, for a while,] he acquiesced, closing his eyes. [So, my full name is Malfait Stonespire,] he said, trying the name out on his tongue. [Could be worse, I guess.]

[You could always change it, if you don't like it,] I said.

Malfait was thinking about it, and he seemed amused. [I was given my name by a tyrant named Stonespire, and he doesn't know I'm still alive?]

[He may suspect it, but he's taking a chance that you won't have the nerve to show yourself,] I said, and I could tell that Malfait was tickled by the idea of angering a despot simply by staying alive and flaunting his name.

[I think I'll stay with my name, until I think of something better.]

[Perfectly reasonable,] I nodded sagely, returning to the controls to hide my grin. [Your father's name was Lynier, and your mother's name was Sistine, if you need any ideas.]

[Thank you,] he said, hearing his parents' names for the first time in his life. [Mister E'lan?]

[Yes?] I was impressed that he had remembered my name.

[Do you have a child of your own? You act like you've been around children before.]

[I have a son,] I said. [He's a little older than you.]

[How much older?] he asked. [And what's his name?]

[His name is Alessarc Nahe E'lan, a descendent of House Soless,] I said proudly. [How old…] I had to think for a moment. [Back on our world, it is the start of the year 981, so he is presently fifty years old.]

Malfait laughed. He wasn't old enough to guess adults' ages yet, but he could tell that I didn't look old enough to be a father to a fifty-year-old man. [That's preposterous!]

[Yes, I suppose it is,] I said, impressed that the boy at least had a decent vocabulary. [That doesn't make it any less true.]

[He looks so much like Sistine!]

[I think he looks more like Lynier.]

[He's much more handsome than Lynier ever was.]

[Give him some space! Look, his eyes get dark when he's anxious, just like Sistine.]

I smiled patiently at Malfait as the Twins, Rosie and Nevis voiced their initial observations about our newest member, as we stood in Fenrir's kitchen in Harbor. During the trip to the homestead, I had warned Malfait to expect a thorough inspection, especially by the Twins, so he was prepared for any comments that they blurted.

Malfait stole little glances at the unfamiliar faces around him, and Nevis went to find Fenrir, to let him know that we had arrived. He was nervous, a little apprehensive, and I had to remember that despite his appearance, Malfait was still ten years old.

Mandri bowed his head to me and sipped his tea. [Well done, Cyrus,] he finally said. [You are officially a proud father, again.] He looked at Malfait again. [Do we seem like a strange family to you, young man?]

Malfait shook his head. [You may all look different, but you're closer and more welcoming than some of the families I stayed with.]

Mandri nodded approvingly. [I don't know how much Mister E'lan had told you, but this is a very open arrangement. Cyrus is your documented guardian, officially, but he has a very busy, and sometimes dangerous, life, and you deserve stability, especially after the childhood you've had.]

[You mean, I'm not going to stay with you?] he scowled at me.

Hilafra, this is not what he deserves to hear. [What Mandri is saying is that you have a choice. You can stay here in Harbor with Fenrir, or with the crew on the *Shakti*... wherever you want to be.]

[You can bunk with me,] Rosie offered readily. [The Twins' room is too noisy.]

[Rosie's room is a sauna,] Frey quipped. [We would sing you lullabies every night.]

Nevis and Fenrir arrived for the tail end of the comments. [Knock it off,] Nevis said. [He's just met us and deserves some time to think about his options.]

[But if I may extoll the virtues of Harbor,] Fenrir said, [we have wide open skies and kilometers of fields and forests for you to explore. You'd never be bored here.]

Malfait noticed my silence. [Do you *not* want me to stay with you?] he asked.

[You've stayed with me these past few days, so you've had a taste of my life,] I said. [If that's what you want, I'm happy to have you along, but as Nevis said, you can think about it. You can sleep on it, if you'd like.]

Mandri was pensive, seeing Malfait's undeniable resemblance to Sistine. [Cyrus is right. There is no rush. You have a home with us, wherever you choose to be. We are your family, and you will never have to be alone again.]

Malfait seemed torn, but gratefully so, to be in a position that he couldn't have imagined a week earlier: to have a choice of loving homes, all ready to receive him. [Do I have to pick one?] he asked uncertainly.

[Of course, not,] Fenrir answered for all of us. [Come with me, young man. I'll show you where you can sleep tonight.]

Malfait gave me a questioning look, and I waved him off. Nevis and the crew of the *Shakti* decided to head down to the lake to visit Jacques du Lac, leaving me and Mandri alone in the kitchen.

‹‹He hasn't seen your full Eladryz side, has he?›› Mandri asked in Laxuyn, just in case Malfait was still listening somewhere.

‹‹No, he hasn't,›› I said, pouring myself a cup of tea and refilling Mandri's. ‹‹It seems premature, given that we don't know how much of the Eladryz side he's inherited.››

‹‹He seems to respect you. If you showed even a tiny flash of *magic*—like telepathy, levitation or even conjuring a piece of candy— he'd follow you anywhere,›› Mandri said drolly. ‹‹You'd feel better if he didn't go with you, I take it. That's perfectly understandable, if you're finally enjoying your independence.››

‹‹That's not fair,›› I frowned. ‹‹You know that I was on Xon, taking care of Sarc, before I was summoned back. My children will never be a burden or an inconvenience to me.››

‹‹Malfait is not one of your children, except on paper,›› Mandri reminded. ‹‹Are you considering the role in earnest?››

Selfishly, it had felt good to be wanted and needed again, when I had been tending to Sarc during his transition. It had been equally gratifying to show Malfait how to navigate *Persephone*'s console, and talk him through the activation of her jump engine.

‹‹If he's half-Eladryz, it would be helpful for him to have an Eladryz guardian to protect and teach him, in case he starts to exhibit traits,›› I rationalized, then paused and met Mandri's broad, knowing grin. ‹‹You knew which way I was leaning, already, you *frejyk* bastard.››

Mandri was unapologetic. ‹‹Yes, but I wanted to hear you say it. You know I have regrets about Sistine,›› he said. ‹‹In hindsight, I should've been more of a parent to her, since she never had a real one, but honestly, Cyrus, I don't think I have it in me,›› he confessed. ‹‹I don't do well around children. Slither will tell you that I had anxiety about letting your son and his friend aboard the *Oelivan* all those years ago, and they were already older.››

‹‹You think the same thing would happen with Malfait, that happened with Sistine?››

‹‹I know it would,›› he said with certainty. ‹‹I can see in his eyes his spirit, his energy…he's very clever, just like Sistine, and if he's even a fraction of the Eladryz that Lynier was, he'll need a firm hand from a strong parent to guide him.››

‹‹I will consider it, for my part, but it has to be his decision,›› I said.

Carbon meandered into the kitchen, with two young black kittens close behind. She meowed a greeting, so they followed her example. When one of them blinked onto the counter and got too close to my scalding teacup, Carbon leapt onto the counter and seized it by the scruff, before jumping down and herding both of them back from us.

[Thank you, Carbon,] I said. [You're a good mother.]

‹‹Like I said,›› Mandri remarked, sipping from his cup, ‹‹spirited children need strong parents to teach them the lessons of life.››

After my latest visit to the *Numolo*, I arrived in Harbor just in time to celebrate Malfait's thirteenth birthday. I had been gone for less than a month, but it had felt like longer, as I had missed Malfait's animated personality and ebullience inside the quiet, serene cocoon of the *Numolo*. My visits to the *Numolo* were always brief, but I felt it was important to protect her secrecy, and Malfait was still too young to be saddled with the concept of keeping "good" secrets or "bad" secrets from friends and acquaintances.

[Dad! You made it!]

I heard Malfait's deepening voice from across the clearing, and I received his bear-hug with a grateful labored breath, feeling my chest compressed. [I wouldn't miss this for anything, son. I see the crew is already here,] I said, noticing the *Shakti* parked nearby in the clearing.

Malfait nodded. [They're up at the house already. Do you know if Uncle Mandri or Uncle Ulini are coming?]

I hesitated in answering. The last time I had heard from them, they were in the Io system, helping to keep Tyrannus Quarvo's equally inept and corrupt younger brother from seizing his throne.

[I know they're trying to come back in time, but their jobs are complicated.] The bloodier and messier aspects of their uncles' lives, I definitely wanted to keep from Malfait as long as possible.

[I hope they make it, Dad. We've gotten great news! Come on!]

I followed him gladly, beaming at hearing him call me "Dad." It had taken Malfait the first six months of staying with me to realize that I wasn't changing my mind, and that I had no intention of returning him to the foster system. After those six months, he had decided to try calling me "Dad" instead of "Mister E'lan" and found it less awkward and more natural.

Now, more than two years into our father-son relationship, I could hardly remember Malfait's voice calling me by anything else.

Approaching the house, I heard laughter and activity, but

166

something felt off. As I began to distinguish the voices, I suspected the nature of Malfait's "great news," and I forced my smile to stay in place. Malfait ran ahead of me, bursting into the house, and I heard an older version of Malfait's voice from inside the house.

Lynier. I sprinted the last few steps to the house, as much as I dreaded what awaited me inside, and I heard my name called, in the room-shaking timbre of Lynier's bass voice. It had been at least twenty years since I had last heard his voice, but it was unmistakable. It was an Eladryz voice, persuasive and powerful, and immediately recognizable to others of our kind, like me.

I took a deep breath and joined the others in the kitchen. Rosie, the Twins, Nevis and Fenrir were all present, too, but their expressions and greetings barely registered in my mind. With Malfait standing next to his seated father, the resemblance in their stature and features was remarkable, and I couldn't see past Malfait's glowing, unwavering grin.

[By the gods! It is good to see you!] Lynier got to his feet, and I braced myself for a crushing bear-hug, like his son's, but he merely extended his arm. [Thank you for taking care of him for me.]

I didn't do it for you, you narcissistic peacock! I wanted to shout. I took care of Malfait because he was a boy in need of a father, and I was a father who had missed that part of my life more than I had realized. I shoved aside all the snide remarks and reprimands that came to mind immediately, took his arm and said mildly: [It's good to see you well, Lynier. This is certainly a surprise.]

Lynier grinned. [I know. Isn't it amazing? Someone told me that he had seen a smaller, younger version of me at Nevis's on *Dione*, and I thought, 'That can't be a coincidence.' So, I caught every jump gate to get there as quickly as possible, and Nevis told me what had happened.]

I looked at Nevis, who feigned a smile, but looked guilt-ridden as she met my eyes. I nodded to her. *It's all right. You did the right thing, telling him the truth.*

My emotions were obviously mixed, as I loved Malfait as my own, but if this turned out to be an opportunity for him to be with his father, how could I stand in the way of that? It was possible that Lynier only wanted to meet his son and had no intention of raising him—I selfishly and secretly hoped for that to be true—but for Malfait's sake, I hoped that Lynier was a better man than that.

I looked back at Lynier. Okay, I looked *up* at him. [I'm happy you were able to make it out for his thirteenth birthday. He's an outstanding and exceptional young man.]

Lynier smiled proudly. [I know from just looking at him. You've done so much for him, for *us*,] he said, his brow furrowed with heartfelt emotion. [Your kindness and charity are greatly appreciated.]

[I wasn't being charitable,] I said. [He's been as much my child as either of my others.] I wanted to say more, but with Malfait watching us, I didn't think it was fair to cloud his emotions with my own. Whatever happened, I wanted it to be Malfait's own decision, based on his own wants.

[I'm glad that he's behaved himself,] Lynier said. [But I think it's time for him to be where he belongs, with me. I've come to take him home.]

Chapter 14: Fool's Gold

[*Thanks for everything, Dad.*] Those were Malfait's parting words to me.

[I thought I might find you here.]

I looked over my shoulder at Nevis, whose lilac skin and hair took on a bluish sheen in the bioluminescent glow of the lake algae. After Mandri and the *Shakti*'s crew left with Lynier and Malfait, to accompany them to *Dione*, I had taken a walk down to the lake to pay my respects to Jacques. After he shared his thoughts on the matter, and sank back under the waves, I remained on my boulder to consider his advice.

[You probably want to be alone,] she said, unslinging a bag from over her shoulder, [but I don't. Move over.]

I waved my hand and extended the boulder out to accommodate her.

[Show off,] she quipped. [You have your tricks, I have mine.] She pulled an uncorked bottle of wine and two chilled glasses from her bag. [I need a drink, but I never drink alone, and Papa never drinks this stuff, so you've been drafted into service.] She poured out the cold contents into the glasses and handed me one.

[I'm happy to serve,] I said, clinking my glass against hers in a silent toast. [They all took it pretty hard, didn't they? Rosie and the Twins would rather Malfait choose to stay with us, instead of going with his father.]

Nevis took a sip of the chilled wine. [We all knew, as soon as Lynier showed up on *Dione*, that it could happen, but we all hoped that Malfait would choose you. I'm sorry, Cyrus! We shouldn't have brought—]

I leaned over and kissed her forehead, like Fenrir sometimes did. [It's okay. We have enough secrets in our extended family that we kept from Malfait, without keeping this from him. He deserved to know that his father was alive, and Lynier deserves a chance to know his son.]

[You're too noble,] Nevis said. [Where was Lynier these last thirteen years? If he really wanted Malfait, he could've found him at any time, more easily than we could. Instead, he swoops in and snatches him up, with nothing more than a promise and a handshake.]

I took a drink of the cool, pear-flavored liqueur, stronger than wine but lighter than ramsblood. Damn, I was missing ramsblood that night. [Lynier's not my favorite person, either, but he deserves a chance to make amends for his past. Whatever his reasons for not coming forward sooner, he took a risk in coming here. There was no guarantee that Malfait was going to leave with him.]

[You really think Lynier would do a better job of raising Malfait than you?]

[It's not a contest!] I chuckled. [I might not be Malfait's biological father, but I still want him to have the best possible life.]

[Malfait already had the best, with you!] Nevis said hotly. [Every child wants to think the best of their parents, but we're adults, and we know when another adult is *merde*. As his *real* family, we should've told Malfait that Lynier is a piece of crap.]

[Hey!] I said sharply. [We don't know what Lynier's been doing these past dozen years, or what schemes he's planning in his perfectly-coifed head, but we *do* know Malfait. He's a smart boy who doesn't take anything at face value, so if we had disparaged his father without evidence, it would have pushed him away.]

I drained the rest of the glass and let Nevis refill it. [He's thirteen, and he's smarter than he lets on.] I nodded to the lake. [Or, so his confidant *Monsieur du Lac* assures me.] A slow ripple shimmered across the top of the lake. [Jacques tells me that Malfait used to come down here quite regularly.]

[That's sweet,] Nevis smiled. [Jacques has a lot to say, when people quiet themselves enough to listen.]

[Malfait liked to come down because Jacques told him stories about his mother,] I said. [Jacques says Sistine used to be a frequent visitor, too, before she left the *Shakti*, and he reminded me of something that Mandri had taught Sistine early on, that stayed with her into her adulthood.]

[And what was that?] Nevis asked, emptying her glass.

[To stop acting like cattle and refuse to live as prey,] I smiled, recalling Sistine's self-reliance and willfulness. [And Jacques made sure that Malfait understands: he may not know everything that he is, yet, but he is definitely not prey.]

[Uh, huh. That's a lot of faith to place in a young boy. How do you know he won't just fall deeper under his father's spell and forget about you? About us?] She held her glass, as I emptied the last of the wine into it.

[He won't,] I said, more confidently than I felt. [Because when he left, he still called me 'Dad.']

Nova sighed with exasperation, [You have any other children I should know about, Cyrus?]

I gave her my most winning smile and nudged a flute of her favorite bubbly closer to her. [Not that I'm aware, sweet Nova.]

It had been years since I had seen Eroshim Nova in person, not since Nefiri-tal's funeral. She hadn't changed at all, as she took painstaking care of herself, for which I was very glad. She was one of the few Alliance bureaucrats that I actually trusted, and I liked the idea of enjoying her friendship for many more years to come.

Despite how little we had in common, she seemed to feel the same about me. It was for that reason that we often did little favors for one another, such as her summons to me to meet her outside the Alliance tribunal hall at the Nexus: *I have something that belongs to you.*

I had waited at the bar outside the tribunal hall, counting the minutes until the morning session ended. I saw her immediately amid the exiting crowd, as she was the only one who boasted ultra-marine blue hair, and she caught sight of me quickly, as well.

After our tart exchange, she took the crystal flute I offered and smiled more warmly. [I think Mandri is on the Nexus, somewhere, too, but I thought you should be contacted first, given your guardianship status.]

[Your discretion is well-appreciated,] I said. [Should I even ask how my wayward treasure came into your possession?]

She raised her perfectly-arched eyebrow at me, as she finished her drink. [I was approached by poachers, looking to claim a generous bounty that I had posted ages ago on my Overlord's behalf. I might not have even been contacted, and the poachers might not have even gone on the hunt, if I had closed the requisition sooner.]

[Or, the poachers could have claimed the bounty from someone else,] I defended. [Whatever the reason, I'm glad they contacted you first.]

Nova set the glass down and touched my arm. [Come along, Cyrus. I want to reclaim my cargo space, and I'm sure you want your valuables returned.]

I followed Nova down to the Nexus's diplomatic marina, where the guards were much more inconspicuous and discreet. She flashed her credentials and led me to her corvette, a showy, shiny wedge of metal alloy that was typical of Ghanisi design. She unlocked her ship's cargo hold and invited me to step inside first.

Secured inside the cargo hold was a large capsule, sound-proof and insulated against heat and cold. Inside the capsule was my prodigal foster son Malfait, slumbering deeply, oblivious to what was happening just centimeters above him.

Nova closed the hatch behind us and stood next to me, looking down through the clear hood at Malfait's sleeping figure, with almost a maternal concern. [The sooner you take him, the better. He doesn't know me, but since he saw me pay off his captors, he wouldn't be happy to see me when he wakes up.]

[He owes you his life,] I said. [He should be made aware of that.]

Nova shook her head sternly. [I disagree. The less he knows about my involvement, the better. The less *anyone* knows, the better.]

I noticed something in the recycled air that smelled like char and scorched plastics and metals. [What did you do, Nova?]

[My father taught me young: never pay for what you can get for free, especially if it's not even what you ordered,] she said primly. [The Overlord requisitioned a young adult Eladryz, which your son clearly is *not*; however, I couldn't in good conscience let those miscreants take him elsewhere, for someone else to exploit or harm.]

"*Hilafra*," I muttered in elfyn. [You killed the poachers, single-handedly?]

[Yes, single-handedly!] she said, as if I were a little slow. [It would've been suspicious if I had brought an armed escort with me to the exchange. It's better this way,] she repeated. [I can only help you in the future, if poachers believe that they can deal with me safely.]

She noticed my eyes scanning the inside of the cargo hold for traces of the dispatched poachers. [It's not the first time I've executed a passel of idiots and destroyed the evidence, and it won't be the last,] she said coolly. [That burnt stench will dissipate in another couple of cycles, but your son over here,] she gestured to the capsule, [needs to be gone.]

[You're not worried that someone will come looking for the poachers?]

[Who seems deadlier with a weapon: someone who looks like me, or a military-trained team of mercenaries who make their living hunting dangerous quarry? As I said, darling, this isn't my first time.]

[You're hunting the hunters,] I smiled. [You really do care.]

[I'm a politician, and a bureaucrat,] she reminded. [I'm not a hero.]

[We're all heroes in different ways, Nova,] I said.

[I do things that are beneficial and expedient to my position,] she said. [The gratitude and allegiance of mind-controlling sorcerers like you and other Eladryz are definitely a benefit.]

She was deliberate about the neutrality of her words. *Gratitude.*

Allegiance. She didn't want the trappings and distraction of a relationship. [Take him home, Cyrus,] she said, pulling the tarpaulin back over the top of the stasis capsule.

[Till the universe leads us back together again,] I said.

She kissed my cheek. ['Together' sounds nice. Not too close, though. I think the universe would implode if we became anything more than friends.] She handed me the transfer papers brandishing the Alliance seal. [That should be enough to get him back to your ship. If anyone gives you trouble, ask to see Commander Aleci.]

Malfait's feet had grown in the year he had been away with his father, and he took up more space in *Persephone*'s co-pilot seat than he used to. His hair was longer and thicker, too, and braided like licorice ropes. Once I looked my fill of how my son had grown and matured in his year apart from me, I kicked Malfait's foot to wake him.

"Hey, handsome." I spoke to him in Xonen elfyn as a joke, just to see how much he actually remembered.

He answered, automatically, "Hey, Dad." He opened one indigo-streaked blue eye, then the other. "I thought I saw a gorgeous redheaded girl in an Alliance uniform," he said groggily.

"That was Commander Aleci," I said. "She had a couple of her security team unload you, no questions asked. You're lucky you have guardian angels watching out for you." *Specifically, one with bright blue hair and killer legs.*

Malfait sat up slowly and looked around, his eyes returning to a serene pale blue as he recognized where he was. "I've never been so happy to see *Persephone*. I didn't think I'd have the chance again."

I passed Malfait a cup of water. "Yes, I'm sure she's glad to see you, too," I said dryly.

He took the water with an embarrassed grimace. "I should've stayed in Harbor. I should've been more careful."

"And maybe I should've said something to convince you to stay, but there's nothing to be done about it now," I said, leaning against the bulkhead. "What's important is that you're alive. You want to tell me what happened?"

Malfait looked angry and frustrated, but mostly disappointed. "We were at one of the outposts near Io, when we were surrounded by poachers hunting for a Ghanisi bounty. I remembered you telling me once about how Ghanisi bounties pay more for younger Eladryz, so I told him that I would surrender to distract them." Scowling, he finished his water. "He said it was a great idea, that he would come back for me..."

I waited for him to continue, but he let the silence linger. "He left you there?"

Malfait hurled the cup against the bulkhead opposite me, chipping the cup and denting the wall. "I never want to see him again," he growled. "I saw him running, like a coward, never looking back for me, not once! And then he cast his little magic trick and vanished. As I watched him, I knew deep down…that was exactly what he had done to my mother: he had pretended to protect her, just to abandon her when he saw the chance to save himself."

I collected the chipped cup and its broken-off shard and fit the two back together. "A little glue, and it'll be fine," I said, returning to my pilot's seat.

"It doesn't fit exactly," he noticed. "I'll find a replacement for you."

"What kind of replacement are we talking about, exactly?" I asked lightly. "I don't want to be replaced. Do you?"

Malfait chuckled, realizing how ambiguous his comment had been. "I meant the cup, but… I'd understand if you didn't want me back—"

I leaned forward and grabbed his hand. "Of course, I want you back! You're my son, and whatever happens, I'll always love you. As for the cup," I said, looking at it in my other hand, "this represents what we are: we break, we heal, we endure. I don't care that it'll never be what it was before. Perfection is untenable, and boring."

Malfait felt the brittleness of the fine ceramic. "Depending on what glue we use, the patched piece may end up being the strongest part."

"That's right," I nodded. "I've always said that you were smart. That doesn't mean that you don't make mistakes; it just means that hopefully you learn from them."

Malfait sneered, "*Hilafra*, I definitely learned from that one. Now, I'm associated with that *frejyk*, forever and officially."

I grinned at Malfait's command of elfyn expletives. "You mean the custody transfer? The forms that I sent over that your fa… he didn't sign?"

Malfait blinked. "He didn't even sign them?"

I shook my head. "I mean, no one can doubt from seeing the two of you, side-by-side, that you are your father's son, but he never claimed you officially. It's how you were tracked to me." I said, careful of how much I disclosed. "My contact found your stasis capsule, checked your Alliance record, and saw that I was listed as your guardian."

"Thank *Ajle* for that," he said. "If my birth father was listed as my

174

contact, who knows where I would've ended up, and for how long."

My heart cracked a little, seeing Malfait's bitter dejection. "I would've found you again, somehow," I swore, brushing back a thick black braid from his forehead. "You're still my son, and you always will be. And I am never giving you up again."

I gave Malfait a choice of staying with Fenrir in Harbor, or with Nevis on the *Shakti*, and he chose the former. Normally, he enjoyed spending time with Nevis, learning to mix drinks that he was too young to legally drink, but after his past year traveling throughout Alliance space with Lynier, he was ready for a break. The bucolic, natural beauty of the farmstead was calling to Malfait, and he had plenty to tell Jacques du Lac about his adventures in space. Moreover, Fenrir always appreciated Malfait's strong hands and back and youthful energy to help with the regular farm chores.

I didn't tell Malfait where I was being summoned, but he knew with certainty that I would return for him. It was important that he have a father figure whom he could trust, and I was happy and honored to fulfill that role.

It was for that reason that I traveled to Ghanis, despite my continued dislike and distrust for that system. Nova had sent me a compelling message while we were traveling to Harbor, and I replied immediately that I would be there as soon as possible.

Persephone was assigned a diplomatic slip upon arrival, per Nova's instructions, which ensured the ship's security and expedited flight clearance. Most importantly, it also exempted *Persephone* from having to provide an arrival manifest, so I was able to clear security anonymously and meet my assigned escort with minimal delay.

By now, I could almost find my own way through the Overlord's District, but I appreciated the expeditious arrangements that Nova had made for me. My escort detail led me to a small transport that moved through some faster side and back roads—not as pretty or flashy as the official and diplomatic avenues, but quicker for it.

I was escorted as far as Nova's office, and was left to enter alone. Nova was just switching on her dampening devices behind her planters as I approached her desk.

[I'm sure you're well aware that Mandri and Ulini are closer to here than I was,] I said, [so I'll have to assume that you just can't stand to be away from me.]

Nova smiled at my jest. [Mandri is still barred from entering Ghanisi space, and Ulini knows more horrible ways to kill a man than I can count, so I think you're Lynier's best hope for a merciful and judicious fate.] She pulled open her desk drawer and handed me a data cube. [That's a copy of everything I have on his whereabouts: surveillance, ship manifests... Yours to use however and whenever you see fit.]

[Thank you,] I said, tucking the cube into my jacket pocket. [Why do you think I would want mercy for Lynier, after what he did to Malfait?]

She perched on the front edge of her desk, crossing her legs and interlacing her fingers on her lap. [Because you are a fair, level-headed man. You've shown me that there are more important qualities to a man than a handsome face and figure.]

[Thanks,] I said, straight-faced. [I think.]

[You know what I mean!] she laughed, slapping her hand on my chest in a playful rebuke.

[Sure.] I kissed her hand to let her know I wasn't offended. [Let me not keep you from your more beautiful admirers, then.]

[Stop,] she said, unsmiling. [You've just arrived. Can't you stay a while?] I looked at her dubiously. [Seriously. I like that I don't have to watch my words with you. I can be myself, and when you're not here, I miss that freedom.]

[You shouldn't have to hold your tongue,] I said. [Your peers are lauded for their candor.]

[The men, you mean. The women are denigrated as shrews if they speak their truths.] She shook her head. [I won't bore you with politics, as I'd prefer to set it aside and think of more enjoyable topics. Are you still celibate?]

I grinned at her brazenness. [If I weren't, you'd be the first to know.]

[Cyrus!] she laughed, shoving me lightly. [What a pair we would make, though.]

[You would use me up within a month, sweet Nova.]

[Perhaps, but it would be a blissful, unforgettable month,] she simpered. [Or, we could both be surprised, and I could be changed for the better.]

I kissed her perfumed cheek. [You don't need to be better. You're exquisite and indomitable, exactly as you are.]

She looked up at me with her cobalt blue eyes, a slight line on her brow deepening for just a moment before it faded. [Why do you say things like that to me, Cyrus?]

[Because it's true, and I think you need to hear it more often.] I perched on the edge of her desk and held her hand briefly. We were both too old and jaded by our lives to flirt like starry-eyed lovers, but we were comfortable enough with one another to be friends, despite our differences.

She leaned into me and kissed me. It was a tender and affectionate caress, her way of expressing her gratitude for my kindness, and she knew that I wouldn't misinterpret it as anything more. From the brightness in her eyes and a fleeting thought, however, it seemed that she hoped that I would reciprocate in some way.

[Would you care to join me for dinner tonight?] I invited.

[Dinner?] She was surprised by the question, as though she was more accustomed to men who propositioned her more directly.

[Yes, the typical evening meal?] I joked. [It occurs to me that we've never shared a meal, in all the years we've known each other, except at Ammo Nefiri's funeral. Isn't dining together something that friends usually do?]

[Hmm,] she said, acknowledging how peculiar our relationship was. [That is odd, isn't it? All right, I accept your invitation,] she said with her chin raised proudly, as though she were accepting a challenge. [Come to my flat, at eight sharp. I'll make the reservations.]

Nova lived on one of the higher floors in the Commons, a privileged, exclusive complex limited to government officials and dignitaries. The grounds were carefully maintained, beautifully landscaped and well-irrigated, despite the scarcity of water in the poorer areas; I didn't linger in the lush gardens, cutting across the lawns to reach Nova's building in time for our dinner.

I went with no expectations, aside from spending time with Nova in a more private and informal setting. I wasn't nervous about going to her flat, as I trusted her, but I was intrigued about what she had planned for our evening. I brought some flowers with me, as an old-fashioned holdover from my Xonen upbringing to never accept an invitation to someone's home without a gift in hand.

As I announced myself at the door to Nova's flat, I prepared to be greeted then critically examined by a surly house servant, much as I had been when I was taken to see the Ghanisi Overlord's Consort. Instead, I was greeted at the door by Nova herself, sheathed in a sleeveless column of shimmering, cloud-grey satin.

Her blue locks, usually coiled and pinned above her slender neck, were loose and curling about her bare shoulders, and her pristine makeup was softer and less mask-like than for her professional image. It took me a moment to realize that she wasn't wearing any makeup at all, and I was being treated to a rare glimpse of her natural beauty.

[You're right on time,] she said, her bare, rosy lips curved into a

177

relaxed smile.

[You look beautiful,] I said, bowing to her.

[Thank you. Please, come in.] She closed the door behind me and received my modest bouquet of wildflowers with a giggle. [I can't remember the last time that I got sunflowers and daisies from anyone.]

[I thought of you when I saw them. I noticed that your office is full of splashier and more exotic flowers, but you once told me that these are native to where you grew up.]

[I told you during Nefiri-tal's funeral. You have a very good memory,] she said quietly, then went to find a vase for the blooms. [I thought perhaps we could dine in tonight,] she called from the small kitchen area. [I've been meeting with so many committees and delegations today, that I was tempted to cancel our dinner tonight, simply because I'm too tired to talk to anyone, anymore.]

She reappeared with the flowers in a simple pitcher-like vase, that she set in the center of a low table. [But then I realized how rare this opportunity is, to steal you away from your busy schedule for a few brief hours.]

[I'm glad you didn't cancel,] I said, admiring the simple elegance of Nova's home, and her own unfussy style. Her sitting area faced a panoramic view of the royal gardens and lakes from our dizzying height, and the pastoral vista was made all the more impressive by the gold and scarlet hues of the setting Ghanisi sun dipping behind the rolling hills. [I wouldn't have been able to enjoy this view.]

I watched Nova, as she passed behind me, her face and hair accented by the golden sunlight. [Or this view, which is even more enchanting.]

[Be careful with what you say, Eladryz,] she warned, pouring drinks for us. [You can bewitch even the cleverest mind, so someone like me would never stand a chance against you.] She held out one of the tiny, citrus-scented glasses to me.

[I've never seen you do shots,] I said, taking the dainty glass from her.

She drained her glass in a single, quick moment. [I've never seen you do them, either,] she said, refilling her glass.

[There's a first time for everything, I suppose.] I gulped down the heady, lemon-flavored liqueur, as she had done. It wasn't as strong as some of the Xonen brandies, but it had a pleasant, lingering aftertaste. She refilled my glass, and I clinked it against hers in an informal toast. [Here's to first times.]

[To first times.] She smiled and sipped from her glass. [First, but hopefully not the last.]

The hours passed more quickly than I had expected them to, as Nova's charming and engaging conversation kept the evening flowing comfortably. Perhaps it was the earlier shots that loosened her tongue, but she was more candid and less guarded with me than usual. She was certainly less formal than when she embodied her frosty, proper ambassadorial persona for the benefit of her Ghanisi superiors.

To reciprocate, and encouraged by our shared drinks, I also shared some details about myself that I rarely divulged. I waved her closer and said, [I'm going to tell you something that few outside of our Laxuyn friends and Sarc know.]

[Oh, really?] she said, intrigued, as she took a seat next to me on her settee. [What is it?]

[Something lost to me for a long time. I didn't even remember it myself until after my wife and daughter were already gone,] I said.

She became serious. [I'm honored, then. Whisper it to me, and I will keep your secret.]

Nova leaned against my shoulder, as I brushed my lips against her ear, and I told her my name in full. She rested her head against me, and I saw her lips move as she repeated it to herself. [I won't even try to pronounce it as you did. Does knowing your name grant me special powers or privileges over you?] she asked slyly.

I laughed. [I think you must have some power over me already, for me to tell you my secrets so readily.]

She leaned back into me, tucking and folding her long legs against herself, like a cat in repose. [Readily? We met each other over thirty years ago, old friend. You're lucky I still have enough of my senses and faculties to remember who you are.]

I admired her smooth, strong legs, bared by her silken gown's shifting hemline. I didn't bother hiding my stare, just as she didn't bother keeping her roving hands to herself. [Even so, I like that you're a private man,] she said. [You understand the importance of discretion and keeping secrets.] She looked up at me. [I like you, Cyrus.]

[I like you, too, Nova.]

[No, I mean I *like* you,] she said, more pointedly. She turned around nimbly, landing on her hands and knees next to me on the couch. [Stay with me tonight.]

My automatic reaction was to refuse, after decades of declining such offers from others. Had Nova asked me on any other night, I would've replied with my usual, polite rejection, but there was a discernible vulnerability in her expression that prevented me from answering right away.

[If you're drunk…] I began.

[From that?] she asked, pointing to half-emptied bottle of liqueur. [I grew up on that, I can finish half a bottle all by myself with no ill effects. No, I'm perfectly clear-headed, and I'm asking you to spend the night with me.]

[Nothing more than that?] There was something else that she wasn't telling me.

[Just one night, with no conditions,] she promised. [I don't want to deal with anything more complicated than that, any more than you do.]

Nova's voice was soft, but it was more pained than provocative. She wanted some kind of physical comfort, and I just happened to be available. We weren't in love with each other, but at least we were in agreement about that. She was my friend, and she needed me to be present for her. For the next few hours, I could set aside my memories of Sariah, and allow myself to focus on what Nova needed from me.

[I'll stay,] I said, kissing her tenderly. [But, it's been a long time, so I may be out of practice.]

[That's all right,] she smiled, relieved that I hadn't spurned her, as she crept closer to me. [I've had enough practice for both of us.]

Chapter 15: Loose Ends

Nova's arm stretched across my chest, but she maintained a distance between us, both emotional and physical, even as she slept. I reached across to her side to tug at the edge of the fallen bedsheet and accidentally brushed against her bare belly, causing her to shrink away from my touch with a gasp. Awakened by my unwitting contact, she calmed herself once she recognized me, but she still pulled the sheet up, covering herself from my view.

I knew what she was hiding, as the puckered, rough scar across her abdomen had felt very different from the soft smoothness of the rest of her body. I lay on my back and closed my eyes, giving her whatever space she needed. If she didn't want to tell me anything at all, that was fine, too.

[Do you want to hear about it?] she asked tentatively.

[Only if you want to tell me,] I said, keeping my eyes closed.

[I was pregnant, once. My son would've been sixty years old this week, if he had survived.] Her words came more easily, once she started. It was easier for her to speak in the darkness, without having to see my reaction. [Kilaran and I were still married, but the child wasn't his. I never even told him about the pregnancy, as everything was over before I even showed.]

[Did you miscarry?] I asked gently.

[No, the fetus was perfectly healthy,] she said. [But my sister discovered that I was carrying her husband's child, the Overlord's son and heir, and that she could not tolerate. I was asked to choose between my child and my position, but when I took too long to decide, even that choice was no longer mine to make.]

She took a deep breath and reached for my hand in the dark, and I gave it readily. [The most powerful influencers in Ghanisi politics are the eunuchs, because they pose no threat to the Overlord's virility. Similarly, if the Overlord hadn't shown any interest in me and hadn't forced himself on me, I might've ascended the ranks, eventually but slowly, but bearing the Overlord's heir would've placed me above even his Consort, without even trying.]

[Your sister couldn't risk that, so she ordered you to terminate,] I concluded. [I'm sorry.] I couldn't think of anything better to say.

[She values her crown more than she does me, so I had expected no less.] She lay her head on my shoulder. [It was a blessing, of sorts. I learned early to give up the notion of motherhood, and I made the choice for myself to eliminate any possibility of it ever happening again. Without that concern, I can focus all my energy into my work, and I can take my pleasure without worrying about the consequences.]

[You don't sound regretful,] I said. In fact, she sounded proud of her pragmatism.

[I don't regret it at all,] she said. [As fate would have it, soon after I had myself sterilized, my sister discovered that she is unable to conceive. I couldn't be her surrogate now, even if the Overlord commanded it.] She took a deep breath and sighed her relief. [Why am I telling you this, Cyrus? I've never told anyone, any of this.]

I turned my head and kissed her forehead. [I'm honored to have your trust.]

She took my hand and set it on her belly, across her scar, to test whether I would flinch or pull away, but I did neither. I was privileged to be in such intimate contact with her and be entrusted with her confidences.

[I do have one more thing to confess,] she said, almost shyly. [When I invited you here, I did have an agenda. I had intended to seduce you into using your gifts to destroy my enemies. With a few careful words from you spoken into the right ears, careers and lives could be unmade in an instant.]

I had entertained the possibility that she could have that in mind. She wouldn't be Nova, if she had no ulterior motives. However, now that she had shared this particular part of her history with me, I suspected that she had a much bigger target in mind for me.

[But I've changed my mind,] she said, nestling against my shoulder. [It would be better if you leave this depraved, corrupt place, while you can. You should go in the morning, at first light, and erase Ghanis from your coordinate maps.]

[What if I want to visit you?] I asked.

[I'd rather meet you on the Nexus,] she said readily. [Believe me, you don't need this place.]

[You could come with me, then,] I invited, but I already knew her answer.

She laughed. [I've sacrificed and bartered too much to leave Ghanis forever, as wretched as it is. Besides, every once in a while, I find something or someone worth saving here, and the thought of leaving such poor lost causes to struggle unassisted, just feels wrong.]

Like Malfait. [So, you haven't lost your soul to Ghanis entirely,] I said lightly.

[No, I guess not,] she said, sounding surprised. [Or, perhaps, in sharing yourself with me, you've managed to change me for the better, after all.]

I started to reiterate, [You don't need to be better —]

She interrupted me with her kiss. [Yes, I remember what you said,] she whispered, positioning herself over me. [I think you're wrong, but we don't have to agree or be a good fit for everything.] She lowered herself, her breath and beautiful features softening. [As long as we're a good fit for this.]

Nova stirred when I slipped out of her bed before dawn, but she didn't try to detain me. There was no point in staying any longer than I already had, as we had both already gotten what we wanted from each other. She watched me dress and gave me a farewell kiss, but I was certain that I would be speaking to her again very soon, anyway, so it was more of casual "until next time" kind of kiss.

[Be careful,] she said drowsily, lying back on her pillows.

[You, too,] I said and slipped out of the flat before first light.

A team of the Overlord's guards intercepted me as I jogged from the Commons to the marina and docks. Rather than tagging me as an anonymous, suspicious-looking pedestrian caught in the exclusive Commons during an abnormally early hour, the guards identified me by name and ordered my cooperation, by the Overlord's command.

I recognized the march to the Overlord's palace from the last time I had visited, decades ago. I had been far less certain then about my skills and ability to take care of myself, and had also been far less cynical and aware about Ghanis's rampant corruption. This time, I was almost looking forward to seeing the Overlord. *This is going to be fun.*

I was led to a private chamber in the Overlord's office suite. As I noted the plush couches and sofas and heavy drapes that decorated the opulent room chamber, and the layered scents of various perfumes lingering in the air, I felt my temper swelling at imagining Nova and the countless other victims of the Overlord's unwanted attention who had stood in my place.

I was still standing and studying the furniture when the chamber opened for the Overlord. Like most bullies, he enjoyed having an audience of lackeys to do his bidding, so he was accompanied by an entourage of guards and advisors, about six in total. The Overlord was still tall and broad-shouldered, physically dominating most of his retinue, and he looked at me with a dismissive smirk. He had no recollection of me from our first brief encounter decades ago.

You don't need your guards for me, I suggested to him. *Take one of their guns, keep me at arm's distance, and you'll have nothing to fear from me.*

[I will have a private word with the agent,] the Overlord declared to his followers. [Give me your weapon,] he ordered one the guards, arming it as he took it in hand. [Wait outside, and I will summon you when I am done with him.]

He waited until we were alone before he spoke. [So, you are Nova's Eladryz, Cyrus Ex. Yes, I am aware of who you are. I have guards watching everyone who visits the Commons.]

[The ambassador and I are old friends,] I explained.

[She has many of those,] he sneered. [Whatever price she's offered you for your assistance, I can give you ten-fold that amount, if you lend your services to me instead.]

That's unexpected. [What kind of service do you think I can provide, exactly?] Years ago, Nevis had mentioned the Overlord's obsession with a prophecy regarding his downfall, "precipitated by a child of the unbowed," but he wasn't showing any antipathy towards me now.

He stepped around me to study me from all angles. [Don't be modest, Eladryz,] he said. [Your people are renowned and feared for their ability to influence with their touch and their voices. That's close enough!] he said sharply, as he noticed the subtle shift of my stance.

There's that irrational paranoia I was waiting for! I wanted to exclaim, just to taunt him.

[Surely, you wouldn't be above using your influence to help Nova. A well-timed suicide or resignation by one or two of her detractors would be such a small, but significant favor for an 'old friend,' wouldn't it?] he suggested.

[Ambassador Eroshim doesn't ask or require such favors, certainly not from me,] I said dismissively. I was on my guard, however, as his words implied some familiarity with what Nova and I had discussed in the privacy of her bed. [We enjoy each other's company, that's all.]

He grinned lasciviously. [She must've enjoyed yours very much, to let you stay the night. She certainly sounded satisfied. She may be the older sister, but Nova is far more energetic and enthusiastic than my Consort.] There was an edge to his voice that sounded like jealousy.

[I wouldn't know,] I said blandly, hiding my disgust that he had, in fact, been listening to us. It hadn't been a matter of luck, then, that his guards had found me so quickly after I had left Nova's flat.

[One of these days, I should summon her here again,] he boasted. [And see if she's become more agreeable and receptive, and more appreciative of what my favor can provide her.]

The thought of the Overlord using Nova again incensed me, more than it probably should have. Nova was a smart, resourceful woman who had long since outgrown the need for a hero; she was her own champion and could find her own way to handle the Overlord...but like she had said, there were others on Ghanis who were less fortunate, who did require protection.

The Overlord was watching me. [You must not be as taken with her, as she had hoped. Or, perhaps, you're just realistic about how limited your power is here. If you threaten me or take a single step towards me, my guards will be in here and kill you without hesitation.]

[Hush, I'm thinking,] I said quietly, staring unblinkingly at his cruel, hard features, as I considered his fate. [For your own sake, you should shut up.]

He reddened at my quiet reprimand and raised his weapon. [No one has ever dared to speak to me with such insolence!] he snarled, becoming even angrier when I didn't balk at the gun pointed at me.

"Just wait, you *frejyk* bastard, I'm not nearly done," I said in elfyn.

He didn't understand the words, but my impertinent tone conveyed my disrespect well enough. [I should order your throat cut out, Eladryz,] he threatened.

I shook my head and took a seat on the arm of one of the plush couches. "No, this is what we're going to do," I said in elfyn. It didn't matter that the Overlord didn't understand my spoken words, as it was really the thought that counted. Likewise, even if his guards were listening in, they would've just heard gibberish. "Have a seat. I don't want you falling over," I said amiably, gesturing to the sofa across from me.

The Overlord did as he was told, his eyes open with bewilderment and confusion about my intentions, as well as his own inability to resist my command.

I sat forward and looked into his eyes. "Now, you're going to point your oversized gun down at your undersized genitalia." He gulped, but he was helpless to fight, and he pressed the muzzle of the gun into his crotch. It would've been so simple to make him pull the trigger, and let him bleed out to death on his very plush, very expensive antique rug, but I wasn't the type to torture and destroy others without purpose, just because I had the power.

Unlike this sorry excuse for a man. He was sniveling now, but his hands were locked around his gun, so he couldn't even wipe his running nose. "Now that I have your attention, you're going to listen *very* carefully," I said, my voice only loud enough for him to hear.

"And if you don't intend to honor my terms, you'll pull the trigger as soon as I leave the room. If you renege after I leave Ghanis, well... you'll just have to kill yourself some other way, the less competently the better. Nod, if you understand." He managed to nod, shakily.

"Good," I said stonily. "Let's begin."

After I had finished my negotiation with the Overlord, I returned to *Persephone* and started looking at the contents of the data cube that Nova had given me. With a better idea of where to start my search for my target, I caught a jump gate to the Io System.

Emerging from the jump gate, with the stars of Io twinkling in the blackness ahead of me, I received a communication request from Ghanis. [Good morning, Ambassador.]

[What did you do, Cyrus?] she asked scoldingly.

[I believe I did exactly what you wanted me to do,] I said. I wasn't even angry about it. It was Nova, after all, and I respected her practicality, regardless of the circumstances.

[I didn't ask you to confront the Overlord,] she said. *[I appreciate what you did, but I didn't expect or want any of it. As I recall, I expressly said that I wanted you to leave Ghanis, as soon as possible.]*

[But you had to know that he was monitoring your flat. And you knew how I would feel about what he and your sister had done to you. That's not something I could let go unanswered.]

[You make too many assumptions about what I know, Cyrus,] she said. *[Yes, I know the Overlord tries to monitor my activities, as much as I try to disable the devices I find. Did I expect you to be angry about my past? I suppose, but not enough to threaten the Overlord. I never asked you to cause an incident that gets you barred from ever coming back to Ghanis.]*

She was right that I had acted on my own. Regardless of whether it had been for her benefit, she had never asked me to intervene. [Technically, he confronted and threatened me first.]

She laughed. *[Oh, by Nafre, you're like children! The Overlord had no more chance against you than a vole has against a fox. You still think of yourself as a simple creature, don't you?]*

[I'm still the man you met over thirty years ago.]

[No, you're most definitely not!] she said laughingly. *[You barely*

understood what you were then, and now you're a fully-armed Eladryz.]

[You make me sound like a weapon, Nova,] I said.

[That is exactly how others think of you,] she said, [and it's true: your abilities are terrifying. Your words can drive people to madness, or murder.]

[They can also heal and inspire. They could even make you fall in love with me, if I find the right words,] I teased, then regretted the remark.

[Promise me you'll never do that, not to anyone,] she said gravely. [Love is akin to insanity, and just as unreasonable and dangerous.]

[I'm sorry, it was a bad joke,] I apologized. [I would never force my words on you.]

[Of course, you wouldn't,] she said. [You're much too honorable for that.]

[You give me too much credit,] I said modestly. [I did just order your Overlord to yield many of his privileges and resources to your authority and oversight. Manage them well, and your power will rival his in a few short years.]

[His downfall is 'precipitated by a child of the unbowed,'] she quoted. [You could've just ended him in his office, so I stand by my claim: you're an honorable man who doesn't give himself enough credit.]

[If you say so,] I said skeptically. [Have you been briefed yet on your new duties?]

[Yes,] she sighed. [My schedule has become much fuller, and my list of responsibilities has lengthened, thanks to you.]

[You know you love the work,] I cajoled. [And it should be easier to get things done now.]

[The work should be more enjoyable and less frustrating now,] she admitted. [But you may still want to avoid Ghanis for a while.]

[That's fine,] I laughed. [You're the only part of Ghanis that I ever miss.]

[Tease. Are you going after Lynier now?]

[Yes, before Ulini has a chance to find him first,] I said. [Thank you for the data.]

[You're welcome. Be careful, Cyrus.]

[You, too, Nova.]

After disconnecting with Nova, I maintained communication silence on the way to Io's largest station, *Memphis,* letting the incoming messages from Mandri and Ulini go unanswered. Fenrir had undoubtedly let them know that I had been headed to Ghanis, and they were eager to hear what information Nova had given me, but I wanted to give Lynier a last chance to explain himself. It was more than the Ammo brothers would bother to grant him.

On *Memphis,* I took my time outfitting myself before leaving

Persephone, ensuring that I had everything before leaving her in a stand-by mode. I messaged my local contacts as a courtesy but emphasized that I wasn't planning to remain on *Memphis* for very long.

With the information from Nova's data cube crammed into my mind, I scanned the faces and crowded corridors until I reached *Memphis*'s Acropol. Staying hidden under my dark cowl, I stood out of the flow of foot traffic and watched the throngs rushing busily through the Acropol, like ants to their hives, looking for one specific glowing pest amid the thousands.

I spotted Lynier easily, in the company of a vivacious young woman who was clinging onto him, in every sense. He seemed unconcerned, happy and prosperous, with his clothes stylish and neatly tailored. He was smart enough to keep his natural glow visibly contained, but the aura of his energy was harder to obscure.

Lynier and his companion ducked into a quiet, romantic establishment, and I waited a moment before I followed them inside, tracking them by the young woman's shrill giggle to a curtained table at the rear of the restaurant.

A haughty dark-suited man approached me, inspecting me as dismissively as the Ghanisi courtiers used to. [May I help you…Sir?]

[No, but there is a dead rat by your foot,] I whispered, [so you may want to dispose of it before word reaches *Memphis* Control.]

It was simple enough to create an illusion of a bloated, dead rodent by his foot, and he struggled to maintain his composure. As he rushed to get something to remove the imaginary rat without having to touch it, I continued on my way to the back.

Lynier was shocked to see me, but not as much as his companion, who had already started to loosen her clothes. She scrambled to refasten her blouse and started to rise, but I waved her back into her seat.

[You can stay, Miss,] I said, closing the curtain behind me. [I'll only be a moment.]

She hesitated, but seeing Lynier's relaxed manner, once he recovered from his surprise, she stayed seated, but now at an arm's length from him.

[I'm surprised to see you out here,] Lynier said casually.

[You wouldn't be, if you knew anything about me,] I said in kind. [Your son is fine, by the way, but I don't think he wants to see you anymore.]

The woman's eyes widened at the mention of a son, but Lynier shot her a quelling look. [What did you say to him?] he asked, his good humor dissipating quickly.

[I didn't have to say anything. Watching you vanish from his sight, as he was surrounded by poachers, was all that he needed to know,] I said. [He's done with you.]

[How did he get free—] His eyes narrowed. [That Ghanisi ambassador bitch contacted you, didn't she? No wonder she was so evasive when I asked her about him. See, Cyrus, I did try to find him after he was captured!] he said triumphantly.

Wow, you are truly repugnant, I marveled, wondering if Lynier knew or cared how he sounded. [Did you make the same effort to save Sistine?]

Lynier's jaw tightened, and I continued. [Firstly, the Ghanisi ambassador is the only reason that Malfait is still alive, so I would suggest you choose your words carefully when speaking about her. Secondly, your job as a father was to protect your son, not to let him sacrifice himself so that you can sneak away. Lastly, I read the transcripts of your communications to Nova; you weren't even trying to negotiate his return, you just wanted to know that he was alive, to ease your own conscience.]

He grinned at my mention of Nova. [She's one of your lovers, isn't she? Is she good?]

She's amazing. [I didn't come to compare notes with you,] I said tersely. [I'm here to tell you: don't try to contact Malfait again. You wasted your chance, and he may forgive you, in time, but I won't.]

I recognized the rapacious gleam in his eye, from the times I had seen a similar look in the Proctor's gaze. He wasn't going to give up easily, and I secretly hoped that he wouldn't, but I also felt that he needed to understand his position.

[I didn't have to come at all, but as you and I are endangered creatures, I wanted to give you fair warning,] I said. [Malfait's uncles and aunts are feeling far less charitable towards you than I am, especially now, so it's in your own best interests to steer clear of all of us.]

[That almost sounds like a threat,] Lynier smirked. [I could have you arrested.]

I am so glad Malfait inherited his mother's smarts. [Who do you think is responsible for the execution of the Tyrannus brothers and the installment of their sister to the throne of Io, hmm? That's right: our Laxuyn friends.] As Lynier's smile faded, I bowed my head to his companion and turned to go. [Behave yourself, Lynier. For your sake, I hope you never cross my path again.]

[Dad!]

I had arrived in Harbor late in the evening and was not expecting such an animated greeting, certainly not from Malfait, who should have been asleep. I had barely crossed the threshold of Fenrir's front door when my son greeted me with a hug, and I was reminded that although he was almost as tall as me, he was still a child in most ways. I hugged him back and looked past him, spotting Ulini, Mandri and Fenrir in the kitchen, with the same inquiring look for me.

[We got worried when Uncle Ulini and Uncle Mandri said you didn't answer their calls,] Malfait said. [Did everything go okay?]

I patted his shoulder reassuringly as we joined the others in the kitchen. [Everything went fine. What did you think of what I left on your bed?] I had left the package in Malfait's room before leaving for Ghanis, fully expecting him to peek inside it, but he shook his head resolutely.

[You said it was from my birthday, so I wanted to wait until you got back to open it.]

[It was from your birthday *last* year,] I clarified. [You left before I had a chance to give it to you, that's the only reason it's been in your room. Go, bring it down. You don't look like you're ready to go to sleep anyway.]

As Malfait darted off, I took a seat at the counter next to the three brothers. ‹‹I found him and explained the situation,›› I said quietly in Laxuyn, not bothering with Lynier's name. ‹‹I didn't kill him.››

Fenrir rolled his eyes in exasperation, and Ulini shook his head disappointedly. Mandri knew my forgiving nature and only smiled sardonically.

‹‹If I murdered Lynier, I wouldn't be able to look Malfait in the eye,›› I argued. ‹‹Regardless of my feelings, or Malfait's right now, the man is still his father.››

‹‹He's a pretty poor excuse for a man, and an even worse father,›› Fenrir muttered.

‹‹Agreed,›› said Ulini, sticking out his grasping palm expectantly. ‹‹If you won't do it, give me the data from Nova, and I'll gladly put him down for you.››

‹‹I appreciate the offer, and if he crosses us again, I'll do it myself,›› I said, then straightened when Malfait joined us in the kitchen, clutching the box in his hands. ‹‹For now, the poor excuse stays alive,›› I said shortly, ending our discussion.

Malfait shook the box, listening for a clue of what could be inside, and set it down. Nestled in a blanket inside was a medium-caliber Alliance guard energy pistol with its holster. It was, in fact, the same exact pistol that I had used during my early days of traveling with Mandri, and seeing it again brought back memories of simpler days.

Malfait reached for the pistol directly and was brusquely shouted down by his three uncles.

[Lessons first,] Ulini barked.

Malfait pouted at me, and I smiled. [He's right, and he's the best teacher you could ask for.]

[Take good care of it,] Mandri commented. [I had to search through the *Oelivan*'s storage locker for days before I found it.]

Malfait started to set the box aside when he felt something else at the bottom. He searched around and pulled up a small, scrolled metal key. He recognized the design immediately, as it was similar to my own key, and he seemed more excited about it than the pistol.

[This is *Persephone*'s key!] he said excitedly to his uncles.

[That *a* key to *Persephone*,] I said. [I still hold the master, but if you're going to learn to pilot her, you need your own key.]

Malfait was so excited that he was practically trembling, and his uncles and I exchanged a contented smile, all of us relieved and happy that he was back with our family again. [You know, if you had given all this to me on my birthday last year,] Malfait said tartly, [I might not have left with him in the first place.]

The brothers laughed heartily. [He definitely belongs with us,] Mandri remarked.

[Thanks,] Malfait smiled proudly. [It feels good to be home.]

Chapter 16: Perils of Adulthood

I waited in the darkness, stretching my legs out straight after sitting too long. I watched the perimeter display on *Persephone*'s console for signs of Malfait's return, and I was reminded of how I used to wait up for Sarc to return from his nocturnal hijinks as well, too. By the time Sarc was Malfait's age... *By Ajle, I've never even seen Sarc at Malfait's age*, I realized, to my dismay. Sarc was twenty when I left Xon, and Malfait was out celebrating his twenty-second birthday, somewhere in the Nexus.

Year of the Emperors 992. I still measured the years by Xon's Realm standard, as I still tracked Sarc's birthday, as well as other important dates of my life.

I sat up when I heard the perimeter sensor chirp, and I watched Malfait steal onto *Persephone* silently, if a little unsteadily. Malfait kicked into a case near the door, muttered a curse, then erupted into a snorting guffaw. He turned on the bulkhead lights and yelled in surprise, staggering back.

"Dad! You waited up for me!"

I smiled, amused that Malfait spoke in Xonen elfyn by default, when we were alone. "Are you drunk, son?"

Malfait tossed himself onto one of the storage crates, somehow managing not to knock anything loose in the crowded corner. "On my birthday? I think I should be drunker." He looked at me with an exaggerated frown of disappointment. "You should've come with me."

"I had some calls to make," I said, shaking my head. "You didn't get into too much trouble, I hope."

Malfait waved my concern aside, his long braids falling across his half-closed blue eyes. "I just fooled around with some of the girls in the Zócalo, that's all."

"Some?" I laughed. "Do you recall how many?"

"Three?" Malfait said, shutting his eyes. "Maybe a fourth?"

"Maybe?"

"Maybe a girl," Malfait grinned. "Whatever it was, it smelled great, felt even better." He opened one eye to peer at me. "I might regret some of this in a few hours, I think. I think one of them might have slipped something into my drink... Maybe you should've come with me to keep me out of trouble."

I spun in my seat lazily. "No, you're an adult now, remember?" I said mockingly. "You know everything about everything."

"But you're my father," he bemoaned. "You're supposed to take care of me, aren't you? Give me advice about how to sober up and avoid hangovers?"

I shook my head. "No, sorry, sloppy drunkenness and hangovers are different for everyone, so that's for you to figure out yourself. Consider it an adult rite of passage." I returned my attention to the console and started waking up *Persephone*. "You didn't leave anything behind, did you? We're not coming back to the Nexus for a while."

I took Malfait's lack of response as an affirmation, but I looked back at the storage crates to see him sprawled and passed out asleep.

I sighed. "Let's make sure you didn't pick up or leave behind anything you shouldn't have." I leaned over Malfait and checked his pockets; he still had his money, dagger, identification... Jewelry? From Malfait's inner jacket pocket, I pulled a glistening gold chain with a glowing white stone pendant dangling like a teardrop. "I can't wait to hear the story about this, son," I muttered and returned to my seat at the sound of an incoming hail.

[*Persephone*, this is Nexus security. We have a couple of questions.]

Hilafra. [This is Cyril Ulryc, captain of *Persephone*,] I said, returning to my seat. [May I ask what this is about?] I stalled, finding a welding glove under my seat that I hurled at Malfait's head to wake him, while I fired off a quick inquiry to my local contact on the Nexus. As Malfait's surprised grunt signaled his consciousness, I muted the comm and barked at him: "The necklace: surreptitiously taken or freely given?"

Malfait scowled, squinting at the gold chain dangling from my fist. "Ahh..."

[We received a report of a theft at one of the clubs, and the victim reported seeing the perpetrator going aboard your ship,] the security officer replied to my inquiry. [Do you mind if we come aboard and take a look around?]

Malfait staggered to his feet. "Necklace..."

[Just a moment, please. Let me get some clothes on,] I said, muting the audio feed again and glaring at Malfait.

Malfait's blue eyes widened, and he wagged a finger at the bauble in my hand. "Don't let anyone take that!"

"Did you steal this?" I asked, more surprised than disappointed.

"Not exactly," Malfait said, stumbling towards the front. "More like confiscated it. The twit who was wearing it was clueless about it, and had no appreciation of its value."

"Be that as it may, Malfait, it's not your call..." I stopped when I recognized the size, shape and pearlescent glimmer of the caged magestone. I had first seen its like nearly sixty years ago, back on Xon, and then periodically afterwards, but never this far from home. "You made the right call, but this may get a little messy."

A pounding sounded at the door. [We will be forced to open your door, if you do not comply,] ordered the security officer through the comm.

"How's your head and stomach?" I asked, as Malfait took the co-pilot seat.

"Fine, for now. Not sure about later," he said. "Are we leaving?"

I glanced at a reply that crossed my console and cleared it from the screen. "We're not running," I said, slipping the necklace into my pocket. "Stay right there." I unmuted the comm and said, [My apologies for the delay. Unlocking the door now.]

[Remain where you are, hands where we can see them,] ordered the security team lead, as the door slid open and the trio of officers boarded. [That's the one,] one of the officers said, nodding his head towards Malfait.

[Wait,] snapped a female voice from the door. [You don't have a warrant to search the ship or its occupants.] A lean woman with a sulfur-yellow braid, dressed in a senior Alliance diplomatic uniform, stepped aboard. [Captain.]

[Brahn,] I greeted with a nod. *Perfect timing.* The last time I had seen Ammo Brahn, she had been in the company of Eroshim Nova, at Nefiri-tal's funeral, exchanging a sisterly farewell embrace with her. *The strongest women learn to support one other.* [You look well.]

[As do you, Captain Ulryc,] she smiled with a bow of her head. [We're sorry for the intrusion, but the situation seems to have escalated quickly,] she said, giving the security team a chastising frown. [One of the prominent local families has lost an heirloom pendant; it shouldn't have been entrusted to an absent-minded child, in the first place, but here we are.]

[Whatever we can do to help,] I offered. [You're welcome to search the ship.]

Before the security team could start their inspection, Brahn raised her hand. [Give us a moment, first,] she ordered the officers. [The optics of searching a ship with diplomatic credentials would spark an outrage among the Alliance worlds that we don't need right now,] she said gruffly. [Wait outside.]

She watched them leave and close the door before her expression and stance softened. [I swear, you E'lan boys are always causing trouble.]

[Have to keep up with the Ammo boys,] I shrugged. I turned around to Malfait, who was trying to piece the puzzle together himself. [Be a gentleman, and introduce yourself properly.]

Malfait stood and straightened his shirt and jacket. He bowed, unsteadily, but his voice was clearer: [Malfait Stonespire, at your service, Ma'am.]

Brahn nodded. [Retired Lieutenant Lexi Brahn,] she introduced herself. [It's nice to finally meet you, Malfait. My brothers and their friends are very fond of you.]

[You're the youngest of the Ammo siblings,] he recognized the name at last. [I apologize for being a little slow, I was…]

[You were celebrating your birthday, I get it,] she said gently. [What do you know about this missing necklace?]

Malfait shook his head. [I didn't steal it. I just asked her jokingly if I could have it, and she just handed it to me and said I could have it for a kiss.]

I rolled my eyes, recalling that Sarc had met Alene under similar circumstances, when they were children. [They can't have it back, not as it is.] I pulled it out of my pocket and held it up for Brahn.

[Ah, crap,] Brahn frowned, recognizing the shine of the augment within its setting.

[Just hold this end,] I said, passing the chain to Brahn. With minimal effort, I opened the setting like a locket and levitated the magestone free of its housing. Malfait had seen enough of my little magic tricks in recent years to no longer be awed, but he still watched with interest.

It was a translucent, cloudy white stone, and as I held it in one palm to gauge its heft and its measurements, I created an exact visual duplicate in my other hand, which I replaced into the setting. I resealed the setting, restoring the bauble to its former luster, and held the freed augment out to Brahn. [You know better than I do where both of these things need to go.]

Brahn pocketed the necklace and the magestone and shot Malfait a curious glance. [You're lucky that Cyrus is well-connected. You took a big risk taking off with this.]

Malfait was unapologetic. [I saw the stone inside the pendant, and I knew it was special. I was pulled towards it, and I also knew that the girl had no clue what she had.]

[What do you mean by 'pulled'?] Brahn asked.

[I don't know,] Malfait shrugged, feeling the intense scrutiny of Brahn's amber eyes. [It looked brighter to me, like it had its own light. And I know it doesn't make any sense, but it felt like it was telling me that it wanted to be free.] He frowned worriedly at me. [By *Ajle*, was I imagining all that because I was buzzed?]

[Why don't you wash up and get to sleep?] I suggested. [Brahn and I still have a couple of things to discuss.]

Malfait nodded and bowed to Brahn. [It was a pleasure to meet you, finally, Aunt Brahn. Thanks for keeping me out of trouble,] he said sheepishly, and shuffled off to the wash closet.

[What do you think?] I asked Brahn, once we were alone. [He's done this before, feeling the presence of augments before he even sees them. We passed the ones we recovered to Fenrir for safekeeping in Harbor.]

[We could use someone like him on the *Nemesis*,] she said thoughtfully.

[He's a great pilot, a superb mechanic, and he's picked up some coding and cracking from Ulini and Mandri,] I said. [I'd miss him, but he's got his mother's independent streak and won't stay put much longer.]

Malfait emerged from the wash closet looking a little more alert. [Are you talking about me?]

[Always, son,] I said. [You're my favorite topic.]

Brahn grinned at my jest. [I was telling Cyrus that I could use a good pilot and coder on the *Nemesis*, if you ever feel like striking out on your own.]

[The *Nemesis*,] he mused. [Is that that big, black corsair-class cruiser parked over...] His pale blue eyes widened in a way that reminded me of Sistine. [That's your ship?]

[That's my scary baby,] Brahn said proudly. [The one that looks like *Persephone*'s big sister. What do you say? You've spent time with my elder brothers; you think you can keep up with me for a little while?]

Malfait looked at me, and I shrugged. [You're old enough to make your own decisions, and I trust Brahn as much as I trust her brothers.] While I hadn't had many dealings with her directly, I knew her by her company, and by Sarc and Jeysen's fond recollections of their interactions with her.

[Okay,] he nodded. [If you'll have me, I'll give it my best effort.]

Brahn smiled, turning to the door. [Good to hear it, Malfait. Report to the *Nemesis* at eight, and I'll introduce you to the rest of the crew. Go, get some sleep, and I'll go clear up this mess,] she said, patting the pocket where she had stashed the necklace. [I'll let you know if anyone has questions.]

Once Brahn left us, Malfait settled into the co-pilot's seat, stretching out his long legs to get comfortable. [You really think it was smart to let me decide what to do with my life?]

[It's not your entire life,] I corrected, [it's just a few years, if that long.]

[Still,] he yawned, [my last life decision was pretty disastrous.]

[That was nine years ago, and you were a child,] I reminded. [You've become wiser since, I should hope.]

I looked over at Malfait, and saw him nodding his agreement as he was drifting off. Less than a minute later, he was already sound asleep.

I shook out a blanket and draped it over him, sneaking a final kiss on his speckled brown forehead. He wouldn't have tolerated it, had he still been awake.

"Just a few years," I whispered, smoothing back his curling black locks. I had promised never to let him go again, but that didn't mean he wasn't free to leave *me*. "I'll still be here if and when you're ready to come home."

Malfait met me on the Nexus on his twenty-seventh birthday. His thick braids were past his shoulders now, and he had acquired some tattoos that integrated artistically with the natural patching of his light and dark skin. He was a full-grown man, bearing a striking mixture of Sistine's color and Lynier's stature, except in his soulful blue eyes — that was all Sistine.

He brought his satchel to the restaurant with him, so I knew that his tenure on the *Nemesis* had come to an end.

I gestured him to a seat at the table and signaled to our server that we were ready. [Is everything okay?]

[Fine.] he said dismissively. [Well,] he amended, [most of the crew is fine. I didn't always get along with the Commander, Kurashi Kilaran.]

[Did you leave on your own?] I asked, suppressing my own ambivalence about the man. I had never met him before, so I could only form my opinion based on the observations from the people I trusted. [Or were you dismissed?]

[No, I was never confrontational, so there was no cause for dismissal,] Malfait said quickly. [I told Brahn that I wanted a break from travel, which is true, but I think she knew I was ready to move on. They had an excellent trainer device onboard, and I used it constantly, but I think I had reached the limit of what I could learn as part of the crew.]

That didn't sound entirely true. [Brahn is in her two-seventies; I'm sure there was more that she could teach you, but maybe you had had enough of the Alliance life.] Although Brahn and her crew were technically retired, and the *Nemesis* with them, they were still required to conform to Alliance procedures and protocols.

Malfait took a drink of his water. [Honestly, it was mostly that I had had enough of Kilaran.]

[That bad?] I frowned.

[Not always, but I think he suspected that Brahn and I were more closely associated than we had initially told him, so he didn't entirely trust me. It became stifling and awkward to be around him.]

We sat momentarily in silence as our server brought us our food, and Malfait looked at me. [Did you order for us already?]

[Grain pasta with meat sauce and wilted greens, right?] I said, recalling his favorite birthday meal. [It's not as fresh and vibrant as what comes from Fenrir's farm, but I didn't think you'd want to wait that long to eat.]

[Thanks, Dad,] he said warmly. [Technically, this is breakfast for me, but it's just what I was craving.] He took his first generous bite ravenously. [Speaking of Fenrir, how is he? How are you? I was so caught up in my own issues that I didn't even ask, I'm sorry!]

[Fenrir and the brothers are all fine. Nevis and the *Shakti* are in Harbor now, so you may be able to catch them before they leave again.]

[From here to Harbor,] he said, charting the course in his head. [That would require at least a couple of jumps and a fast ship.]

[Lucky for you, I have the perfect one for you,] I said, sliding a metal key across the table to him. [Happy birthday, son.]

His pale blue eyes practically glowed. [Wait, is this *Persephone*'s master key?]

[I've off-loaded my personal settings and directory data, so she's all yours, now. Take care of her.]

He didn't quite believe it. [What about you? What are you going to fly?]

[I'll figure something out,] I smiled. [One of my contacts here said there's a stiletto ship like Ulini's that could use some refurbishing, so I'll take a look.]

He nodded. [You haven't told me how you are.]

I touched his warm hand briefly. [I'm better, now that you're back.]

After our meal, I accompanied Malfait to *Persephone*'s slip and promised to meet him in Harbor once my business in the Nexus was concluded. I returned to my temporary flat in the Tribunal District and found myself in the company of two extraordinary women: both in beauty and in power.

Brahn was outfitted in her black and maroon Alliance uniform, with its diplomatic insignia, perusing my bookcase selection. Helping herself to my decanter of chilled water was Nova, who was dressed in her usual tailored suit and elevated heels. They shared the space easily, like lionesses of the same pride.

[Must be my lucky day,] I said. [What brings you both by?]

Brahn went first. [I feel bad about Malfait leaving the way he did. Kilaran's a jerk sometimes,] she prefaced, [but he's all Alliance, all the time. Malfait is…not, so they just didn't mesh well. I'm sorry it didn't work out. He's an incredible young man, though. You should be proud of him.]

[I am,] I said. [And there's no need to apologize. Malfait's so independent that I'm surprised that he lasted five years on the *Nemesis*. Thank you for not telling Kilaran about Malfait's lineage and history. I know you don't generally like to keep secrets from Kilaran.] The women exchanged a wry simper. [Not that you don't keep secrets, just that you don't *like* to,] I clarified.

[The less Kilaran knows about certain things, the better,] Brahn said, and Nova nodded in agreement. [I'll see you around.]

Once Brahn left, I could give my undivided attention to Nova. [What can I do for you?]

[Oh, the things that come to mind,] she smiled, biting her lip teasingly. [I have a jump-enabled stiletto sitting under a tarpaulin, awaiting your attention.] She slipped a key into my chest pocket. [Deck Seven. You can't miss it.]

[Should I even ask you how you acquired custody of it?]

[The former owner has been missing for a week now,] she said innocently. [You know those free-lance poacher types, always inserting themselves into business where they don't belong. This one had the audacity to try to blackmail me, threatening to tell others that I was actually an Eladryz liberator. She wasn't wrong, but she was careless, so now I have her ship.]

I cringed at Nova's ruthlessness. [What did you do with the body?]

She stroked my cheek soothingly. [You don't have to concern yourself with such things,] she said sweetly.

[My concern is for you,] I admitted, catching her hand. [You are too important to put yourself at risk.]

[Too important of an ally?] she asked, [or too important as a friend?]

[Both, but I'd miss you more as a friend,] I said, kissing her cheek. I savored the subtle sweetness of her perfume, which didn't affect me as it did others, but it still drew me because it was hers. [Maybe a little more than a friend.]

She straightened and seemed to be listening for something. [I don't hear the universe imploding,] she said. [We should just stay friends and not push our luck, right?]

[You're probably right,] I said, letting her slip past me, to let herself out. [But let me know if you want to renegotiate.]

She tossed her head in laughter at my flirtatious tone. [Don't forget to move the stiletto,] she reminded, opening the door. [And go spend some time with your sons. They're much better company for your soul than I'll ever be.]

[Welcome back, Cyrus,] greeted the *Numolo*'s soothing voice, as I left the confines of my stiletto. Despite the years since I had been aboard last, she still felt like a second home.

[Thank you, gorgeous,] I replied. [It's good to be back. I've missed you.]

She giggled. It was always an eerie sound, especially echoing through the empty corridors, but it was also warm and inviting. [Is this your new ship?] A couple of drones and a few bots circled the stiletto, inspecting it thoroughly. [You've customized it.]

[It took me a couple of years to get her the way I wanted, but your bots are welcome to fine-tune it, if there's room for improvement,] I invited. [As long as they leave her in working order.]

[You've changed her name,] Numi remarked. [Her identification now lists her as *Sariana*. That was your daughter's middle name.]

[Sarc suggested it,] I said. [I spoke to him last week for my birthday, and he asked about you. I said I wasn't sure where you were, but you were probably doing something very important for the galaxy. That's what Mandri had told me, anyway.]

[Not this galaxy, but one where one of my sisters resides,] she said blandly. [I'll return there to assist my sister, if her situation requires it, but your birthday is equally important to me, so I came back.]

I was humbled that she thought that I was as important as an entire galaxy. [It was very thoughtful of you to remember, and to offer accommodation.]

[It has been a while since you have been here,] she said, [and this is the start of your one hundredth year, after all.]

Back on Xon, it was the tenth month of the Year of the Emperors 999. [I never thought I would live this long.]

Hilafra, I'm ninety-nine! I felt the years more in my mind than in my body.

[Are you planning to return to Xon or Harbor?] she asked, her voice following me along the familiar path to my room.

[I don't think so,] I said, feeling the smooth, cool contours of her wall, as I closed the door behind me. [I've been feeling stretched very thin over these past couple of weeks, even these past few years, and I think I need some time alone.]

[You sound fatigued,] she said, dimming the lights in my room.

[I am.] I slid into the buttery-soft chair in my quarters, feeling its warmth like a blanket and a cup of murkbane tea. After a moment of stillness, I noticed that the environmental warmth of the room was somehow not penetrating into me, as I felt odd chills run through my core and into my extremities. [I think maybe I'm catching a cold.]

[I don't think it's a cold,] she said quietly. [You sounded different to me, when we last spoke, which is why I offered to shelter you and grant you accommodation.]

The start of my hundredth year... Oh, hell, no! [Numi, is this what I think it is?] I asked with a shudder of cold dread. Mostly cold, but a healthy dose of dread, too. I levitated a blanket from the bed and curled underneath it, feeling the chills that coincided with my uncontrollable spasms.

[I heard it in your voice, Cyrus,] the *Numolo* said, almost apologetically. [Your fifty-year cycle is starting again, a little prematurely. I've known enough Eladryz to recognize the signs.]

"*Hilafra,*" I muttered, feeling the familiar shivers as my skin began to glow dimly, signaling the advent of my second semi-centennial cycle. "Happy birthday to me. Here we go again."

[You will be fine,] she encouraged. [You're stronger and more experienced now than you were the first time,] Numi said, as one of her bots draped another blanket over me and offered me a pillow, while one of the server drones delivered some hot tea.

I huddled under the blankets, unable to get warm. [Will you let Sarc and the others know what's happened?]

[Of course,] she assured. [They know I will keep you safe. You can stay as long as you need to.]

[What if your sister needs your assistance again?]

[I've just received a notification that she does, so you'll just have to come along,] Numi said lightly. [You're in no condition to travel, otherwise. Have you ever been to another galaxy?]

[You know I haven't,] I replied.

[Then your hundredth year will be full of wonderful surprises,] she said brightly.

The stars outside my window changed configuration, and I knew that the *Numolo* had jumped. It still looked like the galaxy I knew, except that a dozen ships, similar to the *Numolo* in shape and color, hovered close by.

I managed a weak laugh. [A pod of worldships, that's a first.]

[That's nothing, Cyrus,] Numi said, like a laugh. [Once you've recovered, a whole new galaxy awaits you.]

+ + + +

Cyrus will return...

And he'll be busy, along with everyone else in this ever-expanding world.
If you've enjoyed this story, please connect with me, and be among the first to find out what happens next.

Thanks for reading!
Ande Li

About the Author

Ande has lived in Hong Kong, China, and the various boroughs of NYC, and has settled in the NJ suburbs with her husband and occasional co-writer Maurice X. Alvarez, their children, their free-range budgie and incredibly forgiving and patient shelter dog.

Discover other titles by Ande Li

The Xonen Archives
Book One: The Healer's Girl
Book Two: The Children of Xon
Book Four: The Trickster's Game
Book Five: The Souls of Stars *(Upcoming Release)*

The Gideon Files
Book One: Red Lotus
Book Two: White Jade
Book Three: Gold Peony

co-written with Maurice X. Alvarez
The Trouble with Thieves
Book One: Return to Averia
Book Two: Trials of Halgarin
Book Three: Elmar of Tranquility *(Upcoming Release)*

Connect with Me!
Follow me on Twitter: twitter.com/andeliauthor
Follow me on Amazon: amazon.com/author/andeli
Find me on Facebook: facebook.com/Room808Press
Favorite me at Smashwords: smashwords.com/profile/view/andeli